Mack Bolan's combat senses cried out

Killing his flashlight, he hovered in the darkness for a moment and stared at the bend in the tunnel twenty feet ahead of him. Seconds later, he saw white beams of light playing over the surface and heard the roar of air bubbles expelling from regulators coming out of time with his own breathing.

His opponents had to know he was lying in wait for them. If he could hear them, it stood to reason that the reverse was also true.

Fisting his knife, he waited until the men rounded the corner, one after the other. Each was armed with a speargun and wore a light affixed to his forehead. Bolan surged forward, slicing in a downward arc and skimming along the tunnel's bottom. As he descended, a pair of spears fired overhead, cutting through the space he occupied moments before.

Bolan didn't give the men time to reload.

MACK BOLAN ®
The Executioner

The Executioner
Don Pendleton's®

DEATH GAMBLE

A GOLD EAGLE BOOK FROM

WORLDWIDE®

TORONTO • NEW YORK • LONDON
AMSTERDAM • PARIS • SYDNEY • HAMBURG
STOCKHOLM • ATHENS • TOKYO • MILAN
MADRID • WARSAW • BUDAPEST • AUCKLAND

First edition November 2004
ISBN 0-373-64312-8

Special thanks and acknowledgment to
Tim Tresslar for his contribution to this work.

DEATH GAMBLE

Printed in U.S.A.

I cannot be intimidated from doing that which
my judgment and conscience tell me is right by
any earthly power.

—Andrew Jackson 1767-1845

I will show the true meaning of justice and terror
to those who would hurt or kill innocents.

—Mack Bolan

To *Wall Street Journal* reporter Daniel Pearl (1963–2002)
who died at the hands of cowards while upholding
the people's right to know. He was working for us all.

Prologue

Nevada

Some men became killers reluctantly, accidentally. Not Talisman. He loved a good blood bath and had traveled halfway across the world to immerse himself in one. The big African soldier checked his watch and knew that in another twenty minutes he'd be rewarded for the sweet anticipation that had nagged him for days.

He checked the load on his AK-47, then stared at Trevor Dade's campuslike home. The thirty-acre compound rose out of the desert like an ostentatious oasis—bright lights, fountains, palm trees, glittering swimming pools and hot tubs dotted the landscape. Three Mercedes convertibles were parked along the circular driveway fronting the luxurious home.

The compound's big gates rolled open and a convoy of SUVs glided into the night, headlights slicing through the inky blackness. They would follow a series of access roads and ultimately catch Nevada's highways, taking the afternoon shift's guards home for the night.

The third-shift crew was inside, getting its briefing. Talisman checked his watch: 11:02 p.m. In six minutes the anal-retentive crew chief would usher the guards outside, just as he did every evening, and send them to their positions.

Talisman ran his fingers over the control board of the small device sitting on its rocky pedestal next to his right knee. A series of lights and beeps told him the device was ready to go.

The Russian had said the apparatus would knock out communication between the security team members and their home base, the Haven. Suddenly, the guards would find themselves isolated and would fall in short order. Or so the Russian said. And considering how badly he wanted Dade, Talisman was inclined to believe what the man told him.

At the same time, the Insider—Talisman didn't even know the Russian's name—with the help of that crazy bastard William Armstrong, planned to ignite a series of explosions miles away, creating a disturbance sure to draw the helicopter security team's attention.

In twenty-four hours, Talisman would be back in Africa a little richer and his blood lust satiated—at least for a while. Shadows drifted in and settled around him—a group of his best soldiers and former Spetsnaz commandos—and they waited to spill blood on American soil.

It was just a taste of the carnage to come.

"SON OF A BITCH!"

The cool desert air pressed against Ethan Sharpe's face as he stormed from the sprawling home and into the black, starless night. He slammed the oak door behind him, ground his teeth together and bit down on another curse. Hoping for a moment that the other man would let the outburst slide, he sensed a pair of eyes scrutinizing him and knew he wouldn't be so lucky.

"What's eating you?" Danny Bowen asked.

Sharpe jerked a thumb over his shoulder and pointed at the house behind him. The words spilled out before he could censor them.

"In there is what's bothering me," he said. "Dade. He may be a hot-shit scientist, but he's a poor excuse for a man. He sure as hell doesn't deserve the kind of protection we give him."

"Not our job to decide that, Ethan."

Sharpe shot his friend a withering look. He realized the guy was right, and replaced it with a grim smile and a shrug.

"Yeah, I know," he said. "Hell, I shouldn't be griping to you, anyway. I'm the damn team leader."

Bowen punched Sharpe on the shoulder. "But I'm the voice of reason. That's why you keep me around."

Sharpe knew that much was true. The two men had become friends, sweating their way through Ranger school together and serving in the same overseas hot zones, even standing as best man at each other's weddings. Sharpe was the hothead; Bowen was a master of tact and diplomacy. If Bowen thought Sharpe ought to suck it up, then by God Sharpe knew he ought to listen.

He exhaled loud and long. When he spoke, his voice was quieter, but maintained its edge. "It burns me to watch this guy snorting coke, hiring hookers, drinking himself into oblivion—all on the company dime. Every night it's the same thing. It makes me sick."

Bowen nodded. "Yeah, but you'd still lay down your life for him, wouldn't you?"

Sharpe didn't hesitate. "Hell yes."

"Damn straight you would. That's because you're a good man. So don't let him get under your skin. Only things we need to fret about are the UFO freaks and scorpions."

Sharpe let his smile widen and felt his shoulder muscles loosen when he did. "I'm rooting for the scorpions. Now get the hell out of here before I write you up."

Bowen nodded and disappeared into the darkness. Sharpe ran over his statements in his mind, kicking himself for what he'd said. He trusted his friend not to share them with anyone else. But it was so damn unprofessional.

It also was true. Dade had become a liability. His drug habit and whore chasing had landed him in trouble. And word was the main headquarters was ready to cut the man loose.

But first they wanted Dade to finish the Nightwind project. Wanted it so bad that the company was willing to overlook the scientist's troubled ways while he wrapped up the project.

Sharpe wasn't supposed to know any of this, of course, but he'd caught enough gossip and filled in the blanks with his own observations. It didn't take a genius to discern what was going on.

So Sharpe had tried to keep his moral judgments to himself—not something that came naturally. Every now and then, like tonight, his disgust bubbled to the surface. Otherwise, he'd put up and shut up. Be a good soldier. Even if his only reward was a gaping hole in his stomach.

Ten minutes passed, and Sharpe decided to check in with the troops. "Hawk command to team. Check in."

"Hawk One okay."

"Hawk Two okay."

"Hawk Three same traffic."

A pause from Hawk Four, Bowen.

The hair on the back of Sharpe's neck bristled. What the hell, Danny? Check in. "Hawk Four, status check."

"Hawk Four," Bowen replied. "I've picked up a couple of warm spots on the infrared scan. Looks like two bodies on a ridge."

Shit. "I'll back you up, Hawk Four," Sharpe said. "The rest of you hold your positions. Look alive and watch your backsides."

The team members acknowledged the radio traffic with terse replies. Sharpe drew a micro-Uzi from his custom rig and trudged forward, boots smacking first against concrete and then sand. Bowen was patrolling the compound's southern quadrant. It would take Sharpe ninety seconds to get there.

In Sharpe's line of work, ninety seconds was ample time for things to go straight to hell.

"They moving on us, Danny?" he asked.

"Negative. Just two blips on the mountain. Probably a couple teenagers screwing. Or someone watching the sky for little green men. You guys chill. I can handle this myself."

"Negative. I'll be there in a few seconds."

"You're the boss. But don't say I didn't tell you so if it turns out to be some harmless freak squad."

Bowen had a point. During the past month, Sentinel Industries had taken the Nightwind—a laser-equipped jet fighter—on a series of midnight test runs. Inevitably, the sight of a strange aircraft had stoked the curiosity of local UFO buffs and conspiracy theorists. Armed with cameras, sketch pads and binoculars they had descended in droves upon the barren desert surrounding Sentinel's research and development site. The security teams usually rewarded the curious with an armed escort from the property and stern warnings to stay away. But some of them just couldn't resist a return trip.

Maybe it was nothing, but Sharpe's instincts told him otherwise.

Bowen's voice, taut with panic, sounded in Sharpe's headset, jerking him from his thoughts.

"There's more and they're coming over the wall," Bowen said. "They're dressed in black and armed to the teeth. Must be a dozen of them. I think they saw me."

Bowen came into view, backpedaling furiously and raising his M-16 as he tried to find cover against the small army bearing down on him.

Bowen cut loose with his M-16. Jagged yellow muzzleflashes and the chatter of autofire split the night. He swept the weapon across the top of the ten-foot security wall, hosing it down with a swarm of 5.56 mm tumblers. Sharpe heard return fire crackle and saw bullets smack into the ground around Bowen's feet.

"I've got your back, Hawk Four," Sharpe said.

Sharpe squeezed the micro-Uzi's trigger. The weapon spit flame and lead as he fired into a trio of men who'd already hit the ground and begun to fan out. One of the men whirled in Sharpe's direction and brought a weapon to bear on the security chief. Sharpe tapped out a burst that stitched the man from groin to throat. Sharpe ripped an identical weapon from his harness.

More gunshots lanced around him, forcing him to thrust his body behind one of the team's armored SUVs. Bowen was still out there. Sharpe's headset flared to life. "Hawk Leader, what's your status?"

"Taking fire. Hawk Two and Three, get over here and back us up. Hawk One stay put, raise central command and get us reinforcements. Watch our butts. I don't want to get hit from behind."

Gunfire split the air around him. Gravel crunching under boots caught his attention. One of the blacksuited men came around the SUV's front end and drew down on the security chief. Sweeping his weapon low, Sharpe loosed a quick burst and took the man's legs out from under him. The guy screamed, dropped his weapon and jerked as lead chewed through flesh and bone. He stumbled backward and, as Sharpe eased off the trigger, the man fell to the ground.

Bullets crashed into the SUV. Sharpe saw the injured man's right hand scrambling along the ground for his lost weapon. Sharpe planted another burst into the man, killing him instantly.

He hadn't heard any more radio traffic, and a cold splash of fear traveled down his back. "This is Hawk leader. Units, report in."

Silence. He tried twice more and got the same results. His luck was equally bad when he tried to reach central command for help. Somehow his state-of-the-art communications system had been jammed.

And where the hell was Bowen?

Moving in a crouch, Sharpe came around the SUV's back end, crunching brass shell casings underfoot as he did. He caught sight of Bowen, who'd taken refuge behind a brick barbecue pit and was reloading his M-16.

Sharpe watched as twin ribbons of gunfire lanced out of the darkness and converged on Bowen's torso. The impact whipsawed the man, shredded clothing and flesh and launched him into a grotesque death dance. His head jerked violently, and he tumbled to the ground.

Bowen's sightless eyes stared at Sharpe, who felt his body go numb. A scream of rage rumbled forth from deep inside him, and he began firing the Uzis at anything that moved. He downed two gunners in rapid succession before his weapons went dry, one right after the other.

Ejecting the magazines, he moved back behind the armored vehicle. Motion to his right caught his attention. Sharpe turned, looked up and saw a helmeted figure ten yards to the west of him.

A laser sight's red dot rested on Sharpe's forehead, then everything went black.

TREVOR DADE EYED the woman he viewed as his latest acquisition. He decided she'd do as Sentinel Industries' going away present to him.

She was a petite, shapely brunette, decked out in a red minidress. She had exposed shoulders, her arms and legs were lithely muscled, smooth and feminine, but pronounced enough to register with him. She was built more like a tennis player or a gymnast than a call girl. Good, he thought as he appraised her like a used car. A woman ought to keep herself in shape. Especially for the money he was shelling out.

Seated on the couch, legs tucked under her, she'd asked him where he came from, about his job, all the usual small talk. She absorbed his curt answers with the feigned interest Dade had come to expect from the endless parade of hookers that populated his life. When he mentioned he designed laser systems for the military, she'd perked up and asked him questions. Dade brushed them off, figuring she was too stupid to understand.

He splashed some Scotch into his glass over ice, added soda and a cocktail onion. He dropped a crumbled Ecstasy tablet into his drink and stirred. She had requested straight vodka. He poured two fingers of liquor into a glass and spiked the drink with a sedative. Word had come minutes earlier that it was all going down later this night and Dade wanted the woman unconscious, dragged away, dumped elsewhere. Whether she lived mattered little to him; he just didn't want to be associated with her. One dead hooker connected with him was enough. It had been enough to set everything in motion.

Tonight I get to play victim, he thought. Go out in style.

A smile tugged at his mouth.

"What are you thinking?" the woman asked. She also smiled, anticipating a shared joke.

"Nothing," Dade grumbled. She frowned momentarily, recovered and plastered her hundred-dollar-per hour smile back across her face. Taking a long pull from her drink, she eyed him over the rim of her glass.

"Okay," she said. "So, how long are you in town?"

"Leaving tonight. Within the hour. I'm flying out." Dade had been told to expect extraction by helicopter.

The woman set the drink in her lap, feigning disappointment. "Tonight? I'd hoped to spend more time with you."

"I'll pay for the whole night," he snapped. "You'll have to earn a living someplace else tomorrow."

A storm of anger swelled in her eyes but passed just as quickly. She unfolded her legs, set her feet on the floor and shifted across the couch to him. She placed a hand on his thigh.

"I guess we should get started then," she said.

"That's what I'm paying you for. First, finish your drink. I haven't got all damn night."

Shedding her veneer of civility, she gulped the remainder of the spiked vodka and slammed the glass on the coffee table. "No, you don't. Not with me, anyway."

He shrugged, settling into the couch, hoping to get his money's worth before the drugs kicked in and the shooting started.

As she began to unfasten her dress, machine guns rattled outside, startling them both. He pushed the woman away and looked at the wall clock: 11:23. They'd come a half hour before they'd said they would.

He'd drill the Russian for this.

The woman looked at him. Her mouth started to open, to form a question. He put a finger to his lips to silence her.

"Shut up," he said, "and let me check this out."

Draining his drink, he rose from the couch with a grunt, shambled to a window and peered through it. Muzzle-flashes interrupted the darkness, momentarily illuminating the shooters. In the repeated glare, Dade saw members of his security entourage twisting, dying, under repeated bursts of gunfire.

Too bad about most of those guys, Dade thought. Except for Sharpe. Sanctimonious prick constantly looked down his nose at Dade. He'd never snort coke with Dade, or shack up with a hooker for an evening, even when Dade offered to pay. Dade wasn't dying to party with the guy; he just liked to own things. And employees who took drugs on the job or married men who screwed around would sign away their souls to keep from being found out. Dade was only too happy to provide the paperwork.

But Sharpe, with his uptight, superhero morality, hadn't been for sale. Dade had no use for him.

He turned. The woman stood behind him, trying to peer around his bulk to see what was happening outside. Her eyes looked clouded, and she struggled to stand. Dade assumed the drug was kicking in.

"What's happening? Who's shooting?" She slurred her words.

He shoved her hard back into the couch. "Sit down, shut up," he said. "No one's going to hurt us. I have people outside."

"We should call for help," she cried.

"Stay where you are. I'll handle this."

The woman looked like she wanted to stand, but she found herself unable to do so as the drugs raced through her system, claimed her will. She stayed seated, fought to keep her eyes open. Dade ignored her. He returned to the bar, fixed another drink. He heard gunshots and screams outside. What possessed these men to lay down their lives to protect someone? he wondered. Even someone as important as him?

He gulped his drink and prepared another.

Dade looked at the woman. She remained on the couch, eyes closed, head cocked to one side, asleep. He stepped behind the bar, withdrew a leather valise and set it on the bar. Popping the case open, he checked its contents, making sure the disks remained inside.

The disks contained the sum total of Dade's dozen or so years of hard work developing the Nightwind aircraft. The world thought the best America could muster were lumbering jetliners outfitted with massive, sometimes unreliable laser-weapons systems. Sentinel and the U.S. military had been only too happy to perpetuate that belief, even as the Feds secretly funneled billions into the Nightwind program.

Sentinel had given Dade the proverbial blank check. In return, he had created a product expected to generate untold billions in revenue while also providing the military with the ultimate weapon.

Now they planned to repay him with a pink slip.

When the gunfire outside finally stopped, Dade stepped into the foyer and peered through the peephole. An army of strangers surrounded the door. A battering ram hit the oak portal with a dull thud. He considered keying in the security code, letting them in the easy way, but decided against it. Let them work for him.

He was, after all, the prize.

1

Freetown, Sierra Leone

It would be so damn easy.

Mack Bolan settled the crosshairs on the murderer's nose, rested his finger on the Remington 700 sniper rifle's trigger and paused.

He could finish the job in an instant, send a bullet crashing into the skull of the man who called himself Talisman, silencing the dozens of tortured souls crying out for retribution.

He'd come to West Africa looking for a kidnapped American scientist. He needed to figure out how a former Revolutionary United Front commander—and rapist and murderer—was tied into a kidnapping that occurred thousands of miles away in the Nevada desert.

After that, all bets were off.

Decked out in his black combat suit, face smeared in black combat cosmetics, Bolan had positioned himself on a rooftop fifty yards from the kill zone. The vantage point allowed him to get the lay of the land before he raided Talisman's compound. Through the scope's magnification, Bolan watched as Talisman took a pull from a joint, held the smoke for several seconds, exhaled. The killer smiled and passed the joint to one of his subordinates who obediently took a hit and passed it on.

Physically, the man was impressive. Talisman stood four

inches taller than Bolan, and moved with the grace and confidence of a veteran soldier. The dossier provided by Stony Man Farm had indicated that the African, a former army officer, had gone rogue nearly a decade ago, joining sides with those sworn to unseat the government. Since then, he'd been linked with the rape, dismemberment and murder of countless individuals.

Bolan had no trouble believing the man was a coldblooded killer. Talisman carried a long-handled ax in his belt and an AK-47 hung from his shoulder.

Setting down his rifle, Bolan tugged at his collar to release the heat from inside his sweat-soaked shirt, and considered what he had seen so far. Several gunners milled about the compound, swigging beer and smoking. The smoke, coupled with the stench of rotting sewage and perspiration, hung in the humid air and assailed Bolan's senses.

Two of the gunners concentrated on the job at hand, scanning the immediate perimeter for intruders.

The hardsite consisted of a large single-story building constructed of concrete blocks and roofed with rust-tinged corrugated metal. Several smaller buildings ringed the main structure. Fences topped with razor wire held the verdant jungle at bay on three sides of the rectangular property. In the distance, Bolan could see Lumley Beach and the white lights of boats traversing the ocean.

Peeling paint, rusting roofs, sagging walls and roaming livestock contrasted sharply with the signs of prosperity littering the property.

A half-dozen Toyotas, Mercedes and BMWs, caked in dirt, but otherwise brand-new, were parked around the compound. A satellite dish was perched on the roof of the compound's largest building.

Moreover, the weapons carried by Talisman's gunners nagged at Bolan. He had expected to face down AK-47 copies, the Saturday-night Special of developing nations. But of the men carried new Beretta 92-F pistols, M-4 assault rifles with grenade launchers and Remington shotguns. Several of the men, including Talisman, wore headsets for communication.

Talisman had either bought the toys with blood money from the diamonds he sold, or someone was bankrolling him. This begged the question whom? But Bolan dismissed it from his mind as quickly as it had entered. If there was more to this than met the eye—and he was sure there was—he'd unearth it after he grabbed the scientist and returned the man to safety.

If he could get the scientist. A sinking feeling told him the mission had been compromised from the start, that he might be walking straight into a death trap.

Over his protests and those of Hal Brognola, head of the Justice Department's Sensitive Operations Group, a team from the State Department's Diplomatic Security Services had been drafted to participate in the raid. Bolan preferred to work alone. Failing that, he wanted the warriors of Phoenix Force or Able Team covering his back. Unfortunately, both teams had been on missions elsewhere. The President had insisted that Bolan have someone waiting in the wings as a contingency plan, in case he took a bullet and couldn't pull off the rescue.

The State Department team had gone MIA, and so had Bolan's confidence in the mission. But the clock was ticking, and he couldn't wait for a better time to make his play.

Bolan inventoried his weapons. The Beretta 93-R with its attached custom sound suppressor was holstered in his left armpit. A .44 Magnum Desert Eagle rode on his right hip. He cradled a sound-suppressed Heckler & Koch MP-5 SO-3, the lead weapon on this assault. A .357 Colt Python with a 2.5-inch barrel was snug in the small of his back, standing by as a last-chance weapon if everything else went to hell. He carried ammunition for the various weapons, a Ka-Bar fighting knife and an assortment of grenades on his combat harness and in the various pockets of his black combat suit. He unloaded his rifle, pocketed the cartridges and left the empty weapon on the roof. The rifle was great for distance, but its size and mule's kick recoil made it impractical for the up close and personal war he was about to wage.

Descending from his vantage point like a silent wraith, Bolan hit the ground and moved toward the compound, crouching in the shadows of a small shed, twenty-five yards from the knot of hardmen. He watched as Talisman laughed and cuffed one of his men on the temple. The man spun away while the others howled in delight. Talisman turned and disappeared inside the sagging house.

There were two guards outside.

Or so Bolan hoped.

Like a sleek jungle cat, the warrior bore down on his prey with deadly efficiency, using shadows and car bodies to shroud his approach.

Bolan crept up on his target, a man smoking a cigarette and scanning the surrounding vegetation with infrared binoculars. As he closed the gap between himself and the hardman, he heard the guy's headset crackle to life.

Spotters.

In a single fluid motion, the man wheeled toward Bolan and raised his weapon. The M-4's barrel was ablaze as the stubby assault rifle churned out 5.56 mm rounds that flew high and wide to Bolan's right. Without a doubt, the guy was fast; but Bolan was faster and he had the drop.

Bolan loosed a burst that hammered the man's center mass, knocking him off his feet as though he'd just been struck by a thirty-foot tidal wave.

Suddenly gunfire flared toward Bolan from the surrounding jungle, chewing into the ground and kicking up geysers of dirt around his feet. He dropped into a crouch and darted left. He stroked the MP-5's trigger on the run and sprayed the jungle with a torrent of 9 mm rippers. The hail of gunfire bought him a couple of seconds and he started for the house.

Another guard stepped across his path, a Beretta 92-F extended in a two-handed grip, the muzzle locked on Bolan's head. The man hesitated for a moment, giving the big American a chance to squeeze off another burst from his weapon. The slugs slammed into his target, striking the hip and continuing diagonally across the man's abdomen, chest and shoulder. The guard crashed to the ground in a dead heap.

Cracking a fresh clip into the H&K, Bolan continued toward the house. He'd hoped to take out the men with knives and silenced weapons. But that idea was shot to hell, thanks to the army of unseen spotters tracking his movements.

Where the hell had they come from? Bolan wondered. He had scoured the area for backup troops and had found nothing. He'd even made a second sweep when the State Department men had failed to show. Had he missed something?

He didn't have time to second-guess himself.

Several men spilled from the doorway of Talisman's stronghold, firing assault rifles and automatic pistols in Bolan's direction. The warrior plucked a fragmentation grenade from his web gear. Pulling the pin, he lobbed the bomb toward his attackers and threw himself behind a nearby Mercedes. The weapon exploded, causing thunder, orange yellow flames and screams to pierce the compound.

Bolan peered around the Mercedes' front end and surveyed the damage wrought by the grenade. Some hardmen were dead; others, soaked in their own blood, fire chewing through garments and flesh as they screamed, shook or gasped for breath. Bolan plowed through the dead and dying, plugging an occasional mercy round into the wounded as he closed in on the house.

More gunfire streamed out of the jungle, whipping around Bolan, passing just inches from his body. He wheeled and spotted a pair of men simultaneously sprinting from the brush and converging on him from opposite directions. Caressing the H&K's trigger, Bolan laid down a sustained burst and hosed the men down.

A dull thud sounded behind him. Anyone else would have missed the sound amid the sounds of battle, but not Bolan. He

had senses, combat instincts, honed to a keen edge from countless battles. Turning, he saw a grenade in the dirt just a few
yards from where he stood. If lucky, he had three seconds or
so before the numbers dropped to zero and he found himself
in the heart of a deadly firestorm.

A door, Bolan's only hope of refuge, yawned open before
him. A gunner with blood in his eyes folded himself around the
doorframe and drew down on Bolan with an assault rifle.

Caught in a no-win situation, Bolan did the only thing he could.

Legs pumping, heart slamming into overdrive, he closed in
on the house and hurled himself forward into what seemed a
certain death.

RYTOVA WATCHED the big soldier fighting it out with Talisman's
men while also taking fire from behind, and decided she'd seen
enough.

Cradling an Uzi tricked out with a sound suppressor, she
pushed her way through the tangles of trees and vegetation surrounding Talisman's compound and closed in on the fence surrounding the property. Autofire crackled ahead of her, a din
occasionally interrupted by screams or a pistol's lone bark.

Rytova stepped into a morass of mud, a leftover from the
rainy season, and felt her foot sink up to the ankle. She grimaced and cursed under her breath. If indeed there was a hell
on Earth, this African sinkhole qualified. Pulling her leg free,
she continued on. Perspiration slicked her palms, and she worried it might cause the Uzi to slip from her hands at a critical
moment. Moisture-laden air and sweat-soaked clothing clung
to her trim form like a second skin, at times seemingly suffo-
cating her. Her ash-blond hair was pulled back in a ponytail and
hidden under a black baseball cap, but loose wet strands clung
to the back of her neck. What the hell was she doing here?

She pushed the grousing from her mind and instead focused
on the job at hand. She'd come to Africa looking for the man—
the monster—who'd decimated her entire life.

Nikolai Kursk.

The very thought of his name stoked a fiery rage within that scorched her heart and soul and seemed her only companion. The bastard had robbed her of everything—killed the two men who'd meant the most two her, her husband and her father. Normally, Kursk barely would remember either one. However, during the past several months, Rytova had taken steps to insure he'd never forget them.

God knew she wouldn't.

Her friends in the Russian Foreign Intelligence Service— the small number of men and women willing to stand up to the Russian Mafia's murder machine—had said Kursk was in Africa, but didn't know exactly where. To get that information, she needed to talk to someone on the inside of Kursk's organization, specifically his African operations. Talisman, who ran guns and diamonds for the butcher she sought, filled the bill perfectly.

She'd expected to find Talisman and his gunners lounging, drunk or stoned out of their minds, easy pickings. Instead she found them engaged in a full-fledged firefight with a stranger. The hell of it was, the stranger seemed to be winning.

She watched as he wheeled, fired on a pair of gunners who burst from the surrounding brush and unloaded weapons in his direction. Both died in a hail of gunfire as the man fanned a sound-suppressed submachine gun in their direction. The weapon seemed an extension of the man, an appendage wielded with deadly efficiency,

The powerful man dressed in black reminded Rytova of Dmitri, strong and confident in battle. But—and it felt a form of sacrilege to think this—the stranger was even more so; he was like a human cyclone, ripping through his opponents with an ease that seemed almost impossible.

Still, he was outnumbered. And no single person could survive against those odds.

Staying in a crouch, she tunneled through the heavy jungle

foliage surrounding the killing field and closed in on the compound. Tracing the muzzle-flashes emanating from within the jungle, she pinpointed at least two of the gunners. One was positioned fifty yards northeast of her; a second was closer, about twenty yards straight north. She moved in that direction.

Rytova had brought a pair of night-vision goggles with her, but had decided against using them. Outdoor halogen spotlights powered by an unseen generator illuminated Talisman's stronghold, and accidental exposure to intense light while wearing the goggles could have left her temporarily blind.

As it was, the lights threw off enough glare to make trudging through the jungle manageable. And, under the circumstances, manageable was about the best she could hope for.

She wasn't sure if the man tearing up the compound was a law-enforcement officer or a military operative. Perhaps Talisman had run afoul of his handler and Kursk had ordered him hit. She dismissed that thought outright. Odds were the man wasn't carrying out a hit at Kursk's behest—he'd send in an army, not a single man, even someone with this man's fighting prowess.

Subtlety wasn't Kursk's style. She'd learned that painful lesson months ago.

Anger again burned through her body and a coppery taste filled her mouth. She swallowed hard and gripped her Uzi tighter. Let the mystery fighter try his head-on assault. She'd rely on stealth.

She came in behind one of the gunners. He shouldered an assault rifle and stared through a scope, apparently trying to catch the black-suited stranger in the weapon's crosshairs.

She drew down on him with the Uzi, hesitated. She'd killed before, but always in head-on attacks. Could she shoot a man from behind?

Her quarry suddenly stiffened and turned, swiveling at the waist as he sought her out with his rifle muzzle. She hadn't made a sound, so how did he know she was closing in? Was it instinct or had someone warned him of her approach via his headset communicator? Sloppy, she was so blasted sloppy. She was thinking like an intelligence analyst again, ignoring her paramilitary training.

Dmitri never would have been taken this way.

But he also wasn't here which was, after all, the whole point.

She stroked the Uzi's trigger, and the weapon coughed out a short burst that tunneled through the man's face, pulverizing his head and knocking him backward, as though an invisible rug had been pulled from under his feet. His gun hand flew up, and in a final reflexive move he triggered his weapon. A brief flurry of bullets stabbed skyward before the weapon fell silent and dropped to the ground. A fresh fusillade burned the air around Rytova, slugs tearing their way through the foliage and buzzing around her like a swarm of angry bees.

She threw herself headlong to the ground and landed next to the dead gunner. Bullets smacked into the corpse's chest, which was sheathed in a Kevlar vest, causing it to jerk around under the impact.

The indiscriminate pattern of fire told Rytova these men weren't a legitimate security force. Fingers working gingerly as bullets flew overhead, Rytova unhooked the man's portable radio and headset, and slipped them on.

Someone was calling, "Lynch? Lynch?" When no one answered, she assumed Lynch was the fallen man next to her. She rolled away, putting precious distance between herself and the fire zone. The voice on the radio continued. "Cole, if we keep firing in there, Lynch is sure to get hit in the cross fire. He might be injured or unconscious."

Another voice. "I don't give a shit. Guy should have been watching his back instead of leaving it for us to do. If he gets killed, I eliminate two problems at once."

"You're a cold son of a bitch, Cole." The speaker sounded angry.

"That's what Nikki pays me for. You remember that. The Russian doesn't like turncoats. Neither do I."

Rytova had heard all she needed to. She triggered the Uzi,

laid down a heavy barrage into a patch of muzzle-flashes and then moved again. A groan of pain and surprise sounded in her headset, telling her that at least one of her shots had hit home.

A voice erupted in the headset. She recognized it as that of the man named Cole. "Wells. Wells. What the hell, man? You hit?"

Dead silence was the only reply.

Autofire pounded Rytova's former position and moved in a horizontal swath until she found herself again hugging the moist ground, gritting her teeth as bullets burned the air overhead. Plant stalks, leaf fragments and wood splinters showered her as she waited out the onslaught. The odors of gunsmoke and rotting vegetation fouled the air.

As quickly as it began, the shooting stopped and Rytova guessed the man was reloading. A grenade launcher sounded from somewhere, and a cold torrent of fear washed over her. The fired object arced overhead and crashed to earth more than two dozen yards west of her. Boiling orange flame spilled over from the blast site, and razor wire tore through trees and plants. Heat and shock waves hammered Rytova and her surroundings, and she stayed still as the tempest wrenched the jungle.

Pulling herself to her feet, Rytova bolted and closed in on the edge of the surrounding jungle. Autofire resumed and rent the air around her. As bullets whittled away at her cover, she squeezed off short bursts from the Uzi and furiously sought a better position. The nearest and sturdiest barrier—a pile of stones about the size of a car—lay ten yards to her left.

To get there, she'd need to cross open land and expose herself as she sprinted. Under fire that heavy it might as well be two hundred yards.

Hurtling from the underbrush, the Uzi stammering out a thunderous cacophony of death, Rytova crossed the broad expanse of rich, red earth and closed in on safety. Another explosion—this one closer to Talisman's home—sounded in the distance.

Autofire burned the air around her legs and torso and tore into the ground in front of her. Slugs passed inches from her right hip. She cut left, fear constricting her breath. Raising the Uzi, she opened up with the weapon. The chances of hitting her hidden attacker, while trying to dodge gunfire and run, were nearly nonexistent. But if she could get close enough to make the shooter dive for cover, it might buy her the seconds she needed to get behind the pile of stones.

The weapon went silent in her hands.

Empty.

She cursed herself for making another amateur mistake. Adrenaline coursing through her, heart slamming against her rib cage, she surged ahead.

Cover lay just a few feet ahead. She knew it'd take too damn long to reload the Uzi. Switching the machine pistol to her left hand, she began clawing for her side arm with her right hand. Only five feet to go.

The first bullet hit her square in the kidneys, spun her and knocked the breath from her lungs.

She tried to unleather her pistol and figure out why her back suddenly felt as though someone had crashed a truck into it. Two more shots pummeled her abdomen, her chest. She gasped for breath. Pain seemed to sear every cell of her body.

The beautiful Russian staggered forward, surrendering her overloaded body to sweet nothingness.

THRUSTING FORWARD with powerful leg muscles, Bolan vaulted for the door and set himself on a collision course with the guard blocking it. As he sliced through the air, the MP-5 churned through the contents of its magazine. Parabellum rounds pounded into the guard's abdomen like punches from a prize fighter, hurling him back into the building.

Bolan passed through the doorway and hit the floor hard. Breath whooshed from his lungs as he skidded across the rotted wood planks. Splinters lanced into his forearms, shredding his sleeves, opening a dozen trails of wet crimson that dribbled down his skin.

Even as Bolan struck the floor, the grenade outside the house exploded. The warrior pulled himself into a ball, shielded his face with his bloodied forearms and rode out the blast. A mass of flame, debris and smoke forced its way through the door, and thunder threatened to split Bolan's eardrums. Bits of mortar blew from between the concrete blocks making up the building. Outside, dirt and debris rained on the corrugated metal roof. When his breath returned to him, Bolan took in deep pulls of air and found it choked with grit. He hacked a few times, trying to clear the filth from his lungs.

The soldier had dropped the MP-5 during his tumble. As the explosion's reverberations died and his senses returned, Bolan fisted the Desert Eagle and came to his feet. Staring down the pistol's snout, he saw two doors to the right and one to the left. The end of the hallway opened into what appeared to be a large kitchen.

Glass shards from broken beer bottles, spent shell casings and smears of mud and dried blood littered the floor. A gas-powered generator rumbled somewhere in the distance, and the air reeked of stale beer and vomit.

Bolan processed the sounds like a human computer, his mind catching and identifying bits of information, looking for the one that might mean the difference between life and death.

Then it hit.

A grunt of exertion. The whisper of steel slicing through air.

Bolan folded at the knees, plummeting as though a trapdoor had opened beneath him. Metal sparked against concrete as an ax cut through the airspace above Bolan and then collided with a wall.

The Executioner spun and brought up the Desert Eagle. The big-bore pistol unleashed twin peals of thunder and a pair of .44 manglers tunneled at an upward angle into Bolan's opponent, boring through his torso before exploding from his back in a bloody spray. The ax slid from the man's grasp as he crumpled in a heap at Bolan's feet.

Footsteps sounded behind him. Grabbing the ax as he hauled

himself to his feet, the warrior turned and spotted a pair of gunners bearing down on him. Cocking his left arm, he thrust the ax forward in an overhead toss. Spiraling end over end as it flew through air, the weapon buried itself into the chest of one of the gunners. A blast from the Desert Eagle finished off the second attacker.

Retrieving the MP-5, Bolan slung the subgun and kept the Desert Eagle locked in his grip. He cleared the room to his left, found it filled with ragged furniture, plates of half-eaten rice and chicken, pornographic magazines and a few stray rounds of ammunition.

No Trevor Dade.

No Talisman.

He continued toward the kitchen, again encountering no resistance. Clearing another room, he began to wonder whether he'd been duped. As he returned to the hallway, a big shadow crossed his path and drove the butt of an AK-47 against his temple. Bolan jerked his head to the side, rolled with the impact and let the force push him back into the room he'd just exited. A vague impression of Talisman's enraged face registered in Bolan's mind as he found himself out of harm's way.

A direct hit from the rifle butt would have been deadly, but even the glancing blow had caused his head and neck to hurt like hell. He felt as though his brain had been disconnected from his body, and he'd lost all sense of time and place. Gathering his senses, Bolan checked to make sure his assailant had retreated and took a moment to collect himself.

Multiple footsteps sounded in the hallway. With the Desert Eagle leading the way, Bolan moved into the main corridor, starting for the front door. A gunner stepped into the doorway as Bolan beat a path to it. The Desert Eagle exploded, hurling a pair of .44 slugs into the man. The soldier ejected the mostly spent clip and cracked a fresh one home as he ran.

Bolan crossed the killing field outside the house. Weaving his way through the mangled human remains littering the yard, he heard an engine roar to life and found himself bathed in the white glare of headlights. Engine growling, tires chewing through dirt and rocks, the vehicle bore straight down on Bolan.

The Desert Eagle cracked twice as the Executioner snapped off rounds at the charging vehicle's front end. As he'd suspected during his initial recon, the vehicle—a Mercedes sedan—was armored and the shots ricocheted off the hood.

With lightning-fast reflexes, the soldier threw himself from the vehicle's path, rolling and coming back up in a crouch. Staccato bursts of machine-gun fire flared from the passing vehicle's gun ports as it raced past. Bolan watched ruby taillights shrink and eventually fade completely in the darkness.

Looking around, Bolan weighed his options. If Talisman had fled, he likely would have taken Dade with him. Dade was the only bargaining chip that the Sierra Leone tough guy had—if he had Dade at all. Bolan sensed there had been more than one person in the corridor when he'd been struck. But whether the scientist was among them remained to be seen.

Bolan took a quick inventory of the vehicles around him. He tried the doors on two of them and found them locked. On the third try, he hit a red Jeep Cherokee with the driver's door unlocked and a key hanging in the ignition. Climbing in, he turned over the engine, slammed the vehicle into reverse and maneuvered it out from between its neighbors. Cutting the wheel left, he gunned the engine and the Jeep lurched forward.

Flipping on the headlights as he went, Bolan saw a silhouette stumble into view. The slender shadow stopped in the middle of the dirt path leading from the compound and shouted, "Stop."

Walled in by trees and buildings, Bolan had two choices: comply or mow them down.

He had a moment to decide.

If it was one of Talisman's men and he struck them, so be it. Such were the fortunes of war.

But if it was an innocent person…

The decision clear, the Executioner did the only thing he could.

Paris, France

ONE DAY EARLIER Mack Bolan had sat in the den of a Justice Department safehouse in Paris. Hal Brognola had paced the floor and ground an unlit cigar between his teeth with the vigor of a German shepherd gnawing on a rawhide bone.

Worry creased the older man's features and weighed on his shoulders, causing them to slope, as he stayed silent, apparently gathering his thoughts. He rolled up the sleeves of his white dress shirt and ran his fingers through his hair.

Bolan sipped tepid coffee that was sweet and fragrant. He grimaced. "Chocolate raspberry coffee? You going soft on me?"

Brognola jerked his head toward Bolan and gave him a confused look that slowly morphed into a smile.

"Hey, I don't do the shopping," Brognola said. "I just pay the bills."

Bolan smiled. "Are you going sit and tell me why you called me here? Or just let me die a slow death from drinking this swill?"

Brognola crossed the room and seated himself at the table with Bolan. The Executioner was just winding up a two-day mission, cutting the heart from an extremist group that had planned to dispatch suicide bombers in major cities throughout the European Union for a synchronized terror campaign. The mission had been short and bloody, but Bolan had walked away unhurt.

Brognola, who'd been traveling in Europe on unrelated business, had asked his old friend to hang tight at the safehouse for an impromptu meeting to discuss an urgent problem. That had left Bolan with enough time for a shower, a meal and a few hours' sleep. Brognola had declined to discuss the urgent matter via secure satellite telephone, insisting instead on a face-to-face meeting. The big Fed wasn't given to panic, but his tension had touched Bolan like a tangible force. The Executioner had agreed to the meet, no questions asked.

Brognola pulled the unlit cigar from his mouth and rolled it between his thumb and forefinger. "Striker, what do you know about airborne laser fighters?"

Bolan shrugged. "We've got a handful of 747s fitted with lasers capable of shooting down enemy missiles. They fire at the fuel tank, weaken the metal until the pressure causes an outward explosion and downs the missile. It's hardly a Death Star, but it seems like a step in the right direction."

Brognola nodded. "The ABL program is a good one. Hell, I thought it was state-of-the-art. Turns out I was wrong."

A dark look crossed Bolan's hawkish features. "Explain," he said.

"The ABL is already old technology," Brognola replied. "We're telling the world it's the best we've got. But we've moved well beyond that and we have Trevor Dade to thank for it."

"Trevor who?" Bolan asked.

"Trevor Dade. He's a scientist. He's missing."

"Disappeared? You know I don't do missing persons cases, Hal. Hire a detective."

"Not disappeared, kidnapped and possibly murdered. And his loss could do irreparable damage to our national security."

Bolan took another sip of the coffee. Brognola had his full attention. "Sorry. I'm listening."

"You ever heard of the Nightwind program?"

Bolan shook his head.

"I hadn't either until about twelve hours ago, shortly after Dade went missing."

Bolan was growing impatient. "You're being too mysterious, Hal. Get to the point."

"Sorry, Striker. I'm still trying to digest this myself. The Nightwind is about the size and shape of a B-2 bomber, but it's fitted with a solid-state laser system and some of the most ad-

vanced optics ever developed. No big vats of chemicals, no re-
fraction from clouds and atmospheric disturbances. The lasers
are more portable and more concentrated than anyone in the
world—including our own allies—thinks that we have."

"And Trevor Dade developed the technology," Bolan concluded.

Brognola nodded. "The laser system, anyway. The whole
project began during the cold war. We were so worried about
the Soviets raining nuclear hell on us that the Pentagon and the
White House decided it was best to create the ultimate missile
killer, the Nightwind."

"And they succeeded?"

"Pretty damn close," Brognola said. "To the best of our
knowledge, it's the strongest, fastest thing we've got. They developed it in Nevada at a small base called the Haven. It's kind
of like Area 51 in its mystique."

Bolan grinned. "But without the Martians."

"It's all very earthy stuff, I assure you," Brognola said, smil-
ing. "The whole place is geared toward the creation and test-
ing of the Nightwind. It's a top-tier R&D facility, but you won't
find any little green men getting autopsies."

"So what do we know about Dade's disappearance?"
Bolan asked.

Brognola took a deep breath and exhaled. "He works for
Sentinel Industries, one of the nation's biggest defense con-
tractors. Guy's a genius when it comes to turning lasers into
weapons, but he was a security disaster waiting to happen. The
Man briefed me earlier today, and what he said wasn't en-
couraging. Dade snorts coke by the ton and buys hookers by
the baker's dozen. In his free time, he gambles like hell."

Bolan's brow furrowed. "He got any big debts from it?"

Brognola shook his head. "Dade comes from one of the
richest oil families in Texas. He doesn't care about money. It's
all in the thrill. We're still running the traps on him, but we're

starting to hear some murmurs of possible ties to organized crime."

Bolan felt anger burn hot under his skin. Instinct and experience told him this situation should never have escalated to this level. "His handlers knew all this, but he kept his security clearance. That's bull, Hal."

Bolan knew by Brognola's scowl that the big Fed agreed. "Like I said, Striker, the guy comes from a lot of money. He gets into trouble, he gets bailed out. The people at Sentinel have tried to fire him twice. He has two uncles who are senators, one chairs the intelligence committee, the other the defense appropriations committee. Any time the company leans on Dade, he calls his uncles and they drop the hammer on the company. At least that was the pattern. Recently Dade screwed up so bad that not even his high-powered uncles had enough chits to save him."

"What happened?"

"He makes weekly pilgrimages to Las Vegas. While he's there, he stays in a top-notch hotel and parties. A preliminary audit of the company's books shows he did at least some of it with Sentinel's money. Money out of the Nightwind program funds."

"Which means he did it with taxpayer cash," Bolan said.

Brognola shrugged and shot Bolan a cynical smile. "We've used the money in worse ways. Anyway, about two months ago, he's there for another wild weekend and bam!" Brognola slammed the table with his open palm for emphasis. "One of the hookers overdoses on cocaine and dies. Dade panics, refuses to let the guards call the police. When he finally relents, he gets busted for obstruction, possession and involuntary manslaughter. Within weeks, a grand jury indicts him and the press is off to the races with the story."

"And," Bolan said, "because it's the local prosecutor and not one from Dade's home state, the authorities plan to make it stick."

Picking up his foam cup of coffee, Brognola nodded and

leaned back in his chair. Staring into the cup, he swirled its contents and resumed speaking. "You bet they plan to make it stick. A couple of days later, one of his uncles calls the prosecutor, hat in hand, and asks him to reduce the charges. Maybe even consider dropping them. The senator told him the damage to national security and the state's economy would far outweigh the benefits. The prosecutor told him to take his good old boy politics and shove 'em."

It was Bolan's turn to smile. "Good for him."

"My thoughts exactly. And with a criminal investigation brewing, Sentinel's board of directors finally stopped sitting on its hands and began taking steps to fire the bastard. That was about a week ago."

"And now he's gone. One hell of a coincidence," Bolan replied.

"No coincidence. Whoever took Dade wanted to make it look like a hit rather than a kidnapping. They burned what appears to be his corpse and that of a woman who was in the house when the hit took place. Police identified her with dental records. She was a hooker from Las Vegas."

"What about the man?"

Brognola shrugged. "His head was destroyed with a close-range shotgun blast, so we have no dental records. DNA samples taken from cigarette butts indicate Dade had been in the room. But DNA taken from the man's corpse didn't match up."

"So it was a plant," Bolan stated.

"Right. Whoever did it had to know we'd identify the guy as a ringer in short order. But it did buy them enough time for the trail to go cold."

"Does Dade's family know?" Bolan asked.

"Negative. We're not telling them or the media yet. It helps our cause for whoever did this to think we bought into the ruse."

"What else do we know?"

Brognola let out a big sigh and vigorously rubbed his eyes with balled fists. The man was notorious for depriving himself of sleep, and his red, watery eyes indicated that was the case this day.

"We're getting leads from all over, Striker, but the biggest noise seems to be coming from Sierra Leone. Using tail numbers, flight records and eyewitness reports, we tracked a private plane that left Oregon several hours after the kidnapping and high-tailed it to Mexico. The crew apparently ditched the plane there and took another flight to Colombia, where they switched over to Soviet military surplus cargo planes. A couple of DEA informants there saw the whole thing. We found one of the planes in Sierra Leone several hours ago."

"How do you know Dade was on the flight?"

"A forensics team scoured the thing from stem to stern. We found some of Dade's hair on the craft. So he, or at least his body, was on the plane at some point," Brognola replied.

"I assume the Stony Man cyberteam nailed down the plane's owner."

"They did," Brognola said. Rising from his chair, he retrieved a battered leather valise, opened it and rummaged inside for a moment. Extracting a folder from the bag, he made his way to Bolan and fanned through the contents as he went. Setting a photograph in front of the man, Brognola gave him time to study it while he returned to his own seat.

Scanning the photo, Bolan saw a black man with a shaved head and soulless eyes. The man wore jeans and a tattered camouflage shirt, and carried an AK-47 and a battered hand ax. Bolan committed the image to memory.

Brognola withdrew a sheet of paper from the folder and began reciting its contents. "His name is David Sheffield. He's the son of a British university professor and a Sierra Leonean woman who met back in the 1960s before the country got its independence from the British. Dad split for England in the 1970s, leaving his son and wife to fend for themselves. As a teenager, Sheffield joined the army and actually turned out to be a decent soldier. Then in 1991, he deserted the state's army and joined the Revolutionary United Front, figuring the long-term payout was better. Like most of those guys, he took on a new name—Talisman."

"I guess the names killer and rapist already were taken," Bolan added sarcastically.

"Right. He's a real sweetie. Recently, he's distanced himself from the rebel movement but continues to deal in diamonds, guns and fuel. I guess he thinks that makes him a businessman instead of a killer."

"I don't know, Hal," Bolan said. "The evidence is there, but this just makes no damn sense."

Brognola set down the dossier and nodded. "Agreed. In and of itself the operation is just too big for Talisman to handle. The guy is strictly small-time. Like you said, terrorizing women and children is more his speed. But the facts don't lie."

"Maybe Talisman's working with someone else," Bolan suggested.

"That's the working theory. We just have no idea who."

Bolan took one last nip at the coffee, wrinkled his face and pushed the cup away. "I take it Aaron and the team are trying to fill in the gaps?" Aaron Kurtzman was the computer wizard who fronted the Farm's cyberteam.

"Right. They're working overtime," Brognola said. "Talisman does business with a lot of unsavory characters, so there's dozens of leads to track down. Barbara is riding herd on the cybercrew, so you know we'll get some results."

An image of the honey-blond mission controller filled Bolan's head and a warmth passed through his body. He knew the woman as a fellow warrior and a lover. Barbara Price was a consummate professional, and one hell of a woman. Bolan trusted her.

"Yeah, she'll get results," he said.

Brognola continued. "Whether Dade is a willing participant or an innocent victim matters little to us, Striker. All we care about is getting him back. If the wrong country gets hold of him, it could jeopardize all the work we've put into the Nightwind program. It could set us back a decade or more."

Bolan pondered the big Fed's words for a moment.

"How soon can you get me to Sierra Leone?" the Executioner asked.

2

Freetown, Sierra Leone

Bolan stomped the brake pedal as the figure staggered into the Jeep's path. The car jerked to a stop, the force pushing Bolan forward. The safety harness cut into his shoulder, and he steeled himself by gripping the steering wheel and locking his arms straight. The headlights doused the figure in a white glow, and Bolan saw it was a woman. Crimson eclipsed part of her face. With her right hand, she held her left ribs, which were encased in a Kevlar vest.

She gripped a pistol in her left hand.

The hand hung at her side in plain view, not threatening Bolan. A second pistol was holstered on the hip opposite an empty holster. She staggered slowly toward the Jeep, wincing with each step.

What the hell? Bolan shifted the Jeep into Park, reached for the butt of the Desert Eagle, then opened the Jeep door. Setting one foot on the ground, he kept as much of his body as possible inside the vehicle. Jabbing the Desert Eagle through the space between the door and the frame, he drew down on the woman.

"Drop the gun," he said, "and raise your hands."

The woman shot Bolan an angry look and spoke through gritted teeth. "We're losing Talisman," she said. "We don't have time for this."

Bolan heard a hint of an accent and identified it as Russian.

It was soft, almost like a fading echo, as though she'd trained very hard to lose it. He could guess at her country of origin. Great. But what did she want with Talisman?

"Lady, either you drop that gun and identify yourself, or I guarantee Talisman will be the least of your worries."

The woman gave him a hard stare, but dropped her pistol in the dirt.

"My name is Natasha Rytova," she said. "I'm Russian intelligence. I can tell by your voice that you're American. Let's go."

"SVR?" Bolan asked, referring to Russia's Foreign Intelligence Service.

"Yes, yes. SVR. Of course. Can we go? We might lose them."

Bolan's mind raced as he weighed the situation. The woman was right. The longer they stood sparring, the better the chances Talisman—Bolan's best lead to finding the missing scientist—would slip through his fingers.

The fact was that if she hadn't stumbled directly into the SUV's path, he probably would have blown right past her. She could be lying, ready to hit Bolan when he least expected it. But she could be telling the truth, a prospect Bolan found equally disturbing. He wanted to know why Russia cared enough about either Talisman or Dade to send in an operative. If that country's intervention was about Dade, the implications were even more chilling.

Bolan figured it was in his best interest to keep the woman in his sights.

But he'd do it under his terms.

"Lose the guns," he said.

"And leave myself defenseless? Go to hell." The woman was defiant.

"I'm not asking you, I'm ordering you. You stopped me. You're injured. Drop the guns and I'll help. Otherwise, I'll hop back into this vehicle, get the hell out of here and leave you to fend for yourself."

Rytova wiped some of the blood from her head, studied it for a moment and seemed to consider Bolan's words.

Tentatively, she unbuckled the pistol belt, letting it slide down her hips and legs until it landed around her feet. She raised her hands and shot Bolan an irritated look. "Now may we go?" she asked.

"Yeah," Bolan said.

Climbing into the Jeep, he held the Desert Eagle in his left hand and rested his opposite hand on the gearshift as he waited for Rytova to climb into the vehicle. He'd watched her to make sure she didn't retrieve any of her weapons along the way.

She grimaced as she climbed inside the vehicle.

Bolan shifted and navigated out of the compound. Moments later, the vehicle was racing down one of the main roads into the middle of Freetown.

"You okay?" he asked.

The woman stared ahead. "Someone shot me in the ribs, stomach and kidneys. My vest stopped the bullets, but it hurts to breathe. Another bullet grazed my head."

"Who shot you?" Bolan asked.

The woman shrugged and immediately winced in pain.

"I'm not sure. Some men I have not met before. I believe the shooter's name was Cole. He wasn't one of Talisman's people."

"You know most of Talisman's men?" Bolan was intrigued.

She nodded. "I've been watching him for days. But these were not his men. He's a strong warrior, but his people are unskilled thugs, little boys playing soldier. The men I encountered were professionals. They work for Talisman's boss."

"And that would be?"

"None of your business," she stated.

"Look lady…" he began.

She turned and glared at Bolan. He could tell the effort cost her physically.

"No, you look," she said. "I have no guns. I don't know your name. My information is the only leverage I have."

Bolan clenched and unclenched his jaws. He scanned the

road and guided the vehicle into a sharp turn. He heard the tires squeal, felt a slight slip in the back end as the Jeep cornered. Navigating the vehicle back into a straightaway, he mulled the woman's words and admitted she had a good point.

"When all this is over, you and I are going to have a talk," he said. "A very long talk."

"I do not fear you."

Hell of it was, Bolan could tell she meant it.

"So?" she asked.

"So what?"

"Do you have a name?"

"Cooper," Bolan said, drawing upon an alias. "Matt Cooper."

The woman fixed her gaze through the windshield, nodding and absently rubbing her ribs as she did. "You're American. Are you CIA?"

Bolan shook his head. "Justice Department."

"Interesting. Why does the American Justice Department care about a small-time hood like Talisman?" she asked.

"To quote someone, none of your business," Bolan replied.

Rytova's mouth twisted into a frown. If she had a reply, she kept it to herself. Bolan used the dead air time to check out his surroundings, hoping to catch a glimpse of Talisman.

He reached into a pocket of his combat suit, grabbing a pressure bandage and some packaged alcohol pads. He tossed them into the woman's lap.

"Here," he said, staring straight ahead. "These might help."

"Thank you."

From his peripheral vision, he saw the woman pull down the lighted sun visor and stare at her reflection as she used the pads to wipe away the blood. She winced when the alcohol seeped into the open wound.

"Your vest is matted with blood," Bolan said. "Did you lose a lot?"

The woman continued studying her head wound in the mirror, touching it gingerly with the fingers of her right hand.

"It's not as bad as it looks," she said. "But I do feel a little woozy."

"You going to pass out on me?" Bolan glanced at her.

She gave him an angry look. "I didn't come this far to quit. I'm not some frail thing who faints at the sight of blood. Can we concentrate on finding Talisman instead of my damn head wound?"

"Sure," Bolan said.

The Jeep hurtled ahead, occasionally shuddering as it rolled into an occasional pothole. Bolan passed the burned-out remains of a stately building with columns and domes—left over, he guessed, from Sierra Leone's colonial days—past several smaller buildings and storefronts. Bolan saw occasional clusters of people, the women clothed in colorful dresses, the men in ragged western clothes.

Talisman had gained at least a three-minute lead. That was enough time to disappear into one of the alleys or side roads threading off the main route that led from his compound into Freetown. Or perhaps he'd found refuge in an old warehouse or garage.

Bolan also knew three minutes gave Talisman ample time to call ahead and set up an ambush. The Executioner accepted the risk. Without a doubt, the play had been fraught with danger from the beginning, and he was in too deep to shrink from the challenge.

Glancing into his rearview mirror, Bolan noticed headlights approaching. They began as pinpricks of white interrupting a black background, but swelled in size as they bore down on the Jeep quickly. As the headlights neared the vehicle, they split apart and low rumbles sounded as a pair of motorcycles drove around either side of the Jeep. Both bikers wore black leather jackets and black helmets with clear face shields.

Flashes erupted from either side of the Jeep as the riders caught up with the Jeep and triggered their submachine guns. Bullets drummed hard against reinforced steel as the shooters sprayed the vehicle with autofire.

Bolan glimpsed an approaching biker in his side view mirror and saw the guy fire a burst at the tires with little effect. He guessed that either the man had missed or the tires had been outfitted with special inserts to keep them rolling if punctured.

The other biker came even with the passenger side of the Jeep and loosed a burst of autofire. Bullets collided with bulletproof glass, causing Rytova to flinch and push herself deeper into the seat as she tried to make herself a smaller target.

Trusting his gut, Bolan reached into his shoulder holster, drew the Beretta and handed it butt-first to Rytova. The Russian gave him an uncertain look, then took the weapon. If he'd made a mistake, he'd know soon enough and he'd pay for it with his life.

"Hang on," he growled through clenched teeth.

Cutting the wheel sharply to the left, he nearly swiped the rider closer to him. The shooter veered into an oncoming lane, firing his submachine gun until it went dry. Bullets sparked and whined off Bolan's door. With precise movements, the biker let that gun fall limp on its strap, scooped up a second SMG and continued to fire on the Jeep.

Bolan grimly considered the small knots of African men and women standing on the sidelines. A few ran for cover, but others remained rooted where they stood, unable to turn and run away as the deadly tableau unfolded before them. Years of bloody warfare and abuse had left them too shell-shocked to save themselves.

Bolan had blood on his hands this night, but he'd be damned if he'd add innocent blood to the mix.

He mashed the accelerator, drawing more speed from the Jeep's power pack. He wanted distance from the crowded street, a place where he could reduce the risk to innocent civilians.

As the soldier looked for a side street or an alley, he assessed the situation. Small-arms fire wouldn't cripple the hulking SUV. So, despite their nimbleness and firepower, the bikers had little chance of stopping Bolan. The armored undercarriage would offer at least some protection against a hand grenade or land mine. The hell of it was, if Bolan knew it, so did they. He assumed they had something much more devastating planned for him.

Two more motorcycles, engines whining, appeared from the darkness and joined in the pursuit. Muzzle-flashes erupted around the Jeep and bullets thudded against the windshield, hood and grille. Bolan didn't dare return fire, not while even a single innocent life hung in the balance.

But that didn't mean he was helpless.

Cutting the wheel left, Bolan gunned the engine and again swiped at the motorcycle to his left. The shooter ceased fire, let the SMG fall from his grip and grabbed the handlebars with both hands. The bike engine roared, momentarily drowning out the gunfire, as the rider tried to gain some speed and clear himself from the path of Bolan's vehicle.

The biker never had a chance.

The Jeep plowed over man and machine, causing the SUV to jerk side-to-side, as though crossing over a speed bump. The three remaining bikers fell back and regrouped. Engines thundering, they formed a triangle and roared toward the SUV as Bolan guided it into a nearby alley.

Chattering weapons, squealing tires and roaring engines assaulted Bolan's senses as he guided the SUV through the urban canyon. Coaxing more speed from his vehicle, he locked the steering wheel in a death grip and continued on.

"What the hell do you call this?" Rytova asked.

"I call it improvisation," Bolan replied.

A slight drift to the right and the side-view mirror scraped brick, eliciting a quick shower of sparks. Bolan corrected before the impact sheared the mirror completely from the passenger door.

"You're insane," Rytova said.

Bolan didn't argue the point. Glancing in the rearview mirror, he saw the lead motorbike break away from the pack and close in on the Jeep's tail end. The vehicle shot from the alley and into a cross street. The impact jolted Bolan, and he fought to steady the rocking vehicle as it raced over broken roadways. He heard tires screech and saw headlights as he interrupted traffic flow and caused cars to jerk to a stop on either side of him. He aimed the vehicle into the mouth of the next alley and drove in with the motorcycles following close behind.

Gunshots continued hammering the vehicle. A scrape followed by a loud crack to Bolan's left gripped his attention. The driver's side mirror had struck the brick wall. He watched as it tore free and disappeared from sight.

The Jeep again broke free from the alley and rolled into another cross street. Ahead lay a row of burned-out buildings—drooping heaps of exposed steel, shattered windows and charred brick. The alley had come to an end. Bolan braked hard, steered left. The big tires screamed in protest as the SUV spun 180 degrees before finally coming to rest. The stench of burning rubber and the roar of approaching motorcycle engines filled the SUV's interior as Bolan regrouped.

Slamming the Jeep into reverse, he backed onto a nearby curb, then cut the wheel right to straighten the vehicle. Thumbing the electric window's switch, the warrior grabbed the MP-5's pistol grip, hefted the weapon and jammed it through the open window. Bolan pushed the stock into his shoulder and steadied the weapon. Rytova had opened her own window and aimed the Beretta's muzzle ahead.

The motorcyclists emerged from the alley, weapons spitting flame and lead as they raced their way to Bolan's position. Two more motorcycles approached the Jeep from either side.

The Executioner triggered the subgun, sweeping the muzzle across the alley and hosing down the approaching bikers. Return fire smacked into the windshield and burned past Bolan's arm as he continued laying down sustained blasts of hellfire. Hot shell casings from the MP-5 flew, and bounced across the windshield and hood. Gunsmoke swirled in Bolan's face, stung his eyes.

The night burst into thunder and flames as a round from Bolan's subgun ignited one of the motorcycles' fuel tanks, the resulting blaze immolating the driver in a spontaneous funeral pyre.

Bolan's peripheral gaze caught another of his original pursuers bearing down on the Jeep. Before he could react, Rytova unloaded a 3-shot burst from the Beretta. The Parabellum rounds pounded into the man's chest, and his dead fingers simultaneously released the SMG and the handlebars. The rider fell backward from his two-wheeler while momentum carried the bike onward until it collided with a wall.

The soldier took down two more bikers with the MP-5 before it locked dry. In the same instant, Rytova's weapon ran empty. Bolan extracted two more 20-round magazines for the Beretta and tossed them to Rytova. He reloaded his own weapon. Just as he prepared to resume fire, the remaining attackers turned nearly in unison and fled.

Bolan and Rytova shared confused looks.

"They ran?" Rytova asked.

A sinking feeling told Bolan otherwise.

"More like a strategic retreat," he said. "That can only mean something bad for us."

The beating of helicopter blades in the distance told the Executioner he was right.

3

A sleek black chopper, its landing lights extinguished, crested the jagged skyline of burned-out buildings that walled in Bolan and Rytova and darted toward its quarry. The craft's handlers had ignited searchlights and locked the Jeep under a white glare. Rotor wash kicked up dirt and debris and swirled it about the street. The thrumming noise of the blades and motors threatened to drown out all other sound.

Bolan was already popping open his door. "Get out," he yelled.

He watched as the helicopter closed in on the Jeep. Gunfire blossomed from the helicopter's machine guns, and bullets chewed a path leading straight toward Rytova's side of the vehicle. Stepping from her door would only hasten her death, Bolan realized. The woman froze for a moment as the chopper, which Bolan recognized as Russian-made, sliced its way toward them.

Reaching across the driver's seat, he grabbed her arm and dragged her toward him. His touch broke her paralysis, and she began moving under her own steam to escape the vehicle. Just as she came free, a swarm of bullets thrashed the Jeep, first denting and eventually shredding the vehicle's outer skin.

Bolan knew what was coming next. Rotor wash smacked against him like an invisible fist, threatening to knock him off balance. Pushing Rytova ahead of him, he fired up at the helicopter. Slugs from the MP-5 danced across the helicopter's exterior but were no more effective than pelting an elephant with grains of sand.

Cutting across the street, Bolan tried to gain some combat stretch from the warbird. The telltale whoosh of a missile sounded over his shoulder. Glancing back, Bolan saw the weapon drill into the Jeep. Orange and yellow flames exploded upward from the strike point and rolled through the vehicle.

Bolan shoved Rytova hard into the alley from which they had emerged only moments before. With a gasp, she disappeared into the dark space.

Shock waves smacked into Bolan's back, knocking him facefirst to the ground. He felt the MP-5 slip from his grasp as he went down. Landing in the dirt, Bolan felt solid walls of hellish heat pass over him. A door from the Jeep cut the air a foot above his head before burying itself in a nearby wall.

He gasped to regain the breath stolen from him by the explosion. Even with the greediest pulls, he captured only bits of the superheated air. His ears rang, drowning out all other sound.

As he tried to collect himself, Bolan saw the big predator turn on its nose, seeking him out. More autofire erupted from above. Bullets pounded a trail toward him as he struggled to crawl or roll away.

But even if he did, what then? He had the Desert Eagle, the Colt Python, a combat knife and two stun grenades, hardly enough arsenal to stop an air assault. Even the lost MP-5 would have done little for him.

Slender fingers dug under the straps of his web gear and tugged. Bolan looked up, saw Rytova trying to drag him from the kill zone, grimacing as she did. The effort of yanking his 200-plus-pound frame to safety was agonizing for the injured woman.

Bolan willed muscles to move and, with Rytova's help, he came to his feet and the pair disappeared again into the alley just as a fresh barrage of gunfire rained from the helicopter and dug into the twin structures making up the corridor. Fire from the Jeep had spread to the already shattered structures near it.

Rytova, who had recovered the MP-5, handed the weapon back to Bolan. Maybe his gut had been right about the enigmatic woman.

Thick smoke rolled into the alley as Bolan and Rytova looked for an escape route. Each building stood four stories, but had no ground-level windows or fire escapes. Bolan noticed a wooden door to his left. Moving to the door, he tried the handle, but found it locked.

The helicopter flew over the alley. Wash from the blades cut through the heavy gray smoke and a searchlight scrambled over the walls and ground, scouring the area for signs of Bolan and Rytova.

Fisting the Desert Eagle, the soldier fired three rounds into the door's handle and an accompanying dead-bolt lock. The rounds shattered both mechanisms, allowing the heavy wooden slab door to swing open.

The pair disappeared inside the building.

Holstering the pistol, Bolan raised the MP-5 and turned on a flashlight affixed to the front of his weapon. Running the white beam of light around the room, he saw a pair of deep porcelain sinks, a stainless-steel refrigerator and a stove, all of them weathered. The room smelled of boiled cabbage, fish and dish soap.

"A restaurant," Rytova said.

Bolan nodded, instantly realizing the gesture was impossible to see in the darkened room.

"Keep moving," he said. "More than likely they're going to sink a couple of missiles in this place and burn it to the ground. We need to get the hell out of here before they do."

Rytova didn't argue. She pulled a small flashlight from a pocket and let the light play over the walls and floor. Bolan picked up a few pots and pans hanging from the walls and some large knives arranged neatly on a steel cutting surface.

A chill passed down his spine as he heard the helicopter gain some altitude. The way Bolan figured it, a kill shot from the helicopter into the building could only be moments away. And the aircraft positioning itself farther from the strike zone told him attack was imminent.

Moving fast, they left the kitchen and entered what appeared to be a small dining room furnished with three wooden tables and a few scattered chairs. Bolan ran the flashlight in search of the door and saw a large wooden hutch had been moved in front of it, probably by at least two people. A glimpse of a shattered lock on the door explained the crude security measure. Sweat trickled down Bolan's back and his heartbeat hastened as he realized they'd never get the door open in time.

His gaze settled on a large, rectangular picture window. Bolan peered through the dust-covered glass, but saw no one in the street. Apparently, the fighting had intensified enough to send even the most shell-shocked citizens running for cover. Surging across the room, he fired the MP-5 as he went. Bullets pierced the glass, causing the window to fall in on itself, showering the floor with jagged fragments.

Glass crunching under foot, Bolan and Rytova closed in on the exit, vaulted over the sill and through the opening. Both landed on their feet and continued sprinting, grabbing precious distance from the building as they waited for the inevitable.

Then it came.

With a hiss, the chopper unloaded more of its deadly payload. The explosion rumbled behind Bolan and, checking the reflection in a shop window that lay ahead of him, he saw flame and smoke burst from the windows of the building's top two floors. Bolan threw himself into Rytova, knocked her to the ground and covered her body with his own. Pulverized bits of concrete and brick showered the pair. A piece of concrete the size of a cantaloupe landed inches from Bolan's head. Smaller pieces pelted the soldier's back and thighs as he rode out the blast.

With a low grumble, the building caved in on itself. A tide of smoke and dust rolled across the ground, covering the two in several inches of powdery debris.

The warbird circled overhead, then began its descent.

Bolan rolled to his feet. Figuring himself for a dead man, he raised the MP-5 and drew a bead on the cockpit of the approaching chopper.

A rush of vehicles coming from both directions changed his plans. Troop carriers outfitted with chain guns converged on the war zone. Searchlights scoured the area, settling on Bolan and Rytova. The Executioner found himself blinded by bright lights.

As he raised an arm to protect his eyes, Bolan heard the chopper suddenly gaining altitude. The roaring engine grew fainter as the craft turned and retreated.

"We are Nigerian peacekeeping troops," a voice called out over a loudspeaker. "Drop your weapons, lie facedown on the ground. You will not get a second warning."

Body battered, lungs choked with dust, Bolan didn't need a second warning; he needed several hour's rest, perhaps a hot shower and a meal.

He'd settle for a miracle.

With Dade and his secrets still missing, held captive by an as-yet unidentified enemy, countless American lives hung in the balance. And the involvement by the Russians—if the woman was indeed who she claimed—did nothing to ease Bolan's mind. It all reeked of a much larger conspiracy, one he needed to unravel before all was said and done.

Still covering his eyes with his right arm, Bolan knelt and set the MP-5 gently to the ground. Backing away from the weapon, he laid face down on the pavement and waited to be arrested.

NIKOLAI KURSK EYED the pair of African hardmen with disdain and weighed who should die by his hand.

The men—two of Talisman's flunkies—had arrived from the mainland bringing bad news. They fidgeted in front of him like boys before a schoolmaster, waiting for him to mete out some sort of admonition or punishment. On that front, he decided, he'd not leave them disappointed.

Uncoiling himself from his chair, Kursk came around his desk. Standing with his legs two feet apart, he kept his back rigid and crossed arms across his broad chest. At fifty-two, the man was in better shape than most men twenty years his junior. He ate sparingly, drank alcohol even less. He allowed himself a single vice: ten hand-rolled cigarettes a day.

He began each day with an hour-long run, followed by another hour of yoga and a third of weight training. The former KGB agent knew that in his line of work his body had to remain strong, ready to take on all comers. Everyone wanted to knock Nikolai Kursk from his perch, even those closest to him, and he devoted hours daily to making sure he was ready to fend them all off.

However, he rarely met a challenger with the strength and courage to offer him a real fight, only brief diversions to break up the monotony of running his worldwide gunrunning empire. The world had an overabundance of tough guys and bullies, but very few true warriors. To his way of thinking, that was a shame.

The Russian appraised each man, stifling a yawn as he did. The man in charge stood six inches shorter than Kursk's own six-foot-four-inch height. He wore crisp camou pants and a brown T-shirt. He'd surrendered his pistol belt before gaining an audience with Kursk.

Like most Revolutionary United Front soldiers, he'd adopted a nickname, one that was, under the circumstances, utterly ridiculous. He called himself Iron Man. Kursk considered him anything but.

The second man stood just two inches shorter than Kursk and, the Russian guessed, weighed about 250 pounds. Dressed similarly to Iron Man, he took in his surroundings with a sociopath's dead stare. Unlike his associate, he seemed to sense, perhaps even revel in the violence threatening to explode within the room at any second. Whether from nervous habit or giddy anticipation, he continually ground the knuckles of his right hand into the palm of his left hand.

To Kursk's amusement, the bigger man called himself Blood Claw.

Kursk rested his eyes on Iron Man, waited for him to speak and let him squirm a while longer. After a few more moments of strained silence, Iron Man did so.

"Colonel Talisman sends his deepest regrets."

"His regrets, but not himself," Kursk replied. "He is a coward."

"You misjudge him," Iron Man said. "Even as we speak, he's on the mainland trying to correct the problem."

"He should have corrected it when it first occurred. He had ample warning. I gave him guns, technology and support. Still, he let the whole incident go to hell. Now I must pick up the pieces."

Iron Man took a few steps forward. The plastic tarp surrounding him and Blood Claw crunched underfoot as he did. That they were the only two required to stand upon the protective floor covering hadn't escaped their notice. He looked at the tarp, swallowed hard and returned his gaze to Kursk.

"With all due respect, Mr. Kursk, your own men, Cole and Armstrong, did no better. They had helicopters, missiles and the cover of darkness. Still, they failed. Our men fought in the open. We were only to be bait."

Kursk remained silent, knowing Iron Man's words rang true. The Russian had gotten word of the American interloper shortly after he'd arrived in Sierra Leone. A contact within the State Department had gladly shared what he knew in exchange for a hefty deposit in a Cayman Islands account. Details were spotty: a Justice Department agent was coming into Sierra Leone and was slated to meet with a small group of American agents who were expected to help him carry out a paramilitary operation of some sort.

Kursk's men had fleshed out the details by hunting down the State Department operatives tapped for the mission and sweating the details out of them. Then they killed the men and dumped their bodies in a burned-out building miles from Talisman's compound.

The Justice Department suspected Trevor Dade was in Africa, and the American agent was coming to rescue the scientist. Little did the Americans know that Dade already had been transferred to Kursk's coastal island location. Any sightings linking him to Sierra Leone were old news.

The plan had seemed foolproof. An agent robbed of his backup would most likely turn tail and run rather than tackle an armed camp on his own. Kursk had assumed he'd insured the man's death not only by leaving him to fight Talisman's people, but also by sending a team of his own mercenaries to take the man from behind. By the time the Americans retaliated, Kursk had planned on being gone.

Apparently, he'd been wrong.

"Where is the American?" Kursk asked.

Iron Man shrugged. He gave Kursk a placating smile, spoke in a soothing tone. "Still in United Nations custody," the African said. "That should keep him away from us for a while, anyway. Everything will turn out all right. Leave this to us."

From what Kursk knew of Iron Man, he'd studied political science and diplomacy at a British university before returning to his homeland to rape and pillage. He considered himself the consummate politician, negotiating with the local government and the international community even as Talisman terrorized with his strong-arm tactics.

Without a doubt, Iron Man was good at handling people. But no one "handled" Nikolai Kursk, especially when he smelled fear, as he did with this man.

"I will leave nothing in your hands," the Russian said. "You people fight well against unarmed civilians. You cannot withstand a real battle, with a real warrior."

Iron Man shot Kursk a hurt look. Like everything else with the man, Kursk assumed it was calculated and insincere.

"Again with due respect sir, we are warriors. We can stand anything the Americans can throw at us."

Kursk exploded with pounding, derisive laughter. Iron Man seemed to shrink a couple of inches as the sound bounced around the big room with its vaulted ceilings and exposed timbers.

Kursk collected himself. "You can withstand nothing."

"You are wrong," Iron Man said. His eyes flashed anger as he spoke, retreated to uncertainty as he fell silent. His body stiffened visibly as he waited for the fallout from his words.

Kursk didn't make him wait long.

The Russian gangster looked at Iron Man's companion, who had remained quiet since arriving on the island. The man's bottomless stare recorded the conflict like the lens of a camera, logging all of it and reacting to none of it.

Kursk nodded at the enforcer. "Warriors, eh? Perhaps your man would like to prove that."

Blood Claw didn't give his partner a chance to respond. "I could do that," he said.

Kursk smiled grimly. Unleathering the Tokarev he always carried with him, he tossed it to one of the dozen or so mercenaries ringing the room. He rolled up his sleeves and joined the Africans on the plastic sheeting. With a wave, he dismissed Iron Man and began sizing up his opponent.

The enforcer did likewise for Kursk.

Without averting his gaze, Kursk motioned another guard forward. With his peripheral vision, he saw the guard approach the tarp and set a long-handled machete next to his opponent before backing away. It was the weapon Blood Claw had been wearing when he arrived on the island. A dozen small nicks broke up the blade's otherwise smooth edge. The Russian assumed the imperfections came from chopping the weapon through the bones of countless victims' arms and legs.

Kursk gestured at the weapon. "You can, of course, use the

machete." A smile ghosted his rattlesnake lips. "I don't need a weapon for you."

Never losing Kursk's gaze, the man knelt and gathered the blade from the floor. Gripping the machete with both hands, Blood Claw eyed Kursk, apparently measuring his opponent.

Kursk steeled himself for the attack.

He didn't have to wait long.

The African surged forward, the machete slicing through air as he approached. Kursk sidestepped the attack, drove a sidekick into the man's kneecap and popped the joint. The man yelped, faltered. Stepping behind his attacker, Kursk snagged the man's weapon hand and held it fast. Pushing forward on the shoulder, he pulled on the arm and brought it back at an impossible angle until he felt the gratifying pop of a dislocated shoulder. The machete plummeted to the ground while the man's groans elevated to screams. Kursk buried the toe of a steel tip boot into the man's kidneys. Once. Twice.

Crashing onto the man, Kursk grabbed his head and gave it a vicious twist. A snap of the neck dispatched the man to a one-way trip to hell. His head dropped to the tarp, as his body shuddered one last time before surrendering to death.

Scooping up the machete, Kursk looked at Iron Man, whose eyes widened as he took a couple of steps back. The Russian raised the weapon and brought it down hard, embedding the blade in the floor between Iron Man's feet.

Kursk felt his pulse racing through his charged muscles. He moved toward Iron Man, who flinched.

Growling through gritted teeth, Kursk felt another rage overtaking him. They always came at times like this, threatening to pull him into a black abyss of bloodlust and madness. Just like when he fought the secret wars in Afghanistan. He sucked in a deep breath and forced himself to step away from the edge.

"Bag," he said to no one in particular.

A mercenary stepped next to him and handed a burlap bag to Kursk.

The Russian snatched the bag from his soldier and held it out for Iron Man. "Take it." As he waited for the former RUF man to step forward, Kursk noticed his voice was deeper, almost otherworldly. Iron Man hesitated, then finally retrieved the bag, as though snatching a pearl from the coils of a cobra.

"Take that to Talisman," Kursk said, still struggling to keep his wits about him. "Tell him the next time I fill it with his head."

Iron Man nodded. He gave the dead enforcer one last look. As he backed toward the nearest exit, he kept his eyes locked on the Russian as though the two men were the only ones in the room.

Kursk stepped from the tarp. A pair of mercenaries began to roll up the plastic floor covering, wrapping the corpse inside.

"Dump the body in the sea," Kursk said. "Let the fish feast on it. But bring back the tarp and hose it down. I may need it again before this is all over."

Another mercenary brought Kursk a white towel, which the kingpin used to wipe away his sweat. A voice from behind caught his attention.

"Jesus, remind me never to get you pissed at me."

Had he not recognized the harsh East Coast accent, the cigar smoke would have been a dead giveaway. Kursk greeted his new visitor without turning to look at him. Instead he stared out one of his massive windows and watched the surf crash against the beach.

"I *am* angry at you, Jack Cole," Kursk said. "That display wasn't just for Talisman's benefit."

"So, I'm impressed. Happy? Look, you can bellyache all you want about what happened out there, but you have no idea how it went down."

Kursk clenched his jaws and took a moment to respond.

"Badly is how I'd say it went down, Jack. Very damn badly.

I hold you and Talisman personally responsible. You are supposed to be pros. This American made you look like idiots."

Cole's voice went cold. "Back off, Nikki."

Kursk stiffened when the American referred to him so casually. It was blatant insubordination, the former black ops man's stock-in-trade.

Kursk spun on a heel, dropped the sweaty towel at his feet and glared at Cole.

The former CIA man was decked out in a pair of camou pants, an olive-drab shirt and black combat boots. He carried a Beretta 92-F holstered on his belt in a cross-draw position. A .44 Magnum Ruger, also in a cross-draw position, balanced things out on his opposite hip. The red-haired American stood about five feet six inches. Kursk knew Cole's small frame, like his ever-present lopsided grin, disguised his ability to kill with deadly efficiency.

"Treat me with respect," Kursk said. "Otherwise, I'll take two lives today."

Cole shrugged and his grin never wavered. But his eyes narrowed and his cheeks flushed, betraying the rage bubbling beneath the surface. His hand rested on the butt of the Beretta as he addressed the Russian.

"Look, Kursk, you can stand back here on your cushy-ass island playing armchair quarterback all you want. But I don't want to hear it, okay? I never saw anything like this guy. And don't bore me with another of your stupid war stories about Afghanistan, 'cause you never saw anything like this guy either. We clear?"

Kursk hated insubordination, but couldn't help but respect Cole's backbone. It was almost refreshing after dealing with Talisman's band of cowards.

Almost.

The gunrunner pinned Cole with a cold stare.

"Do not overstep your bounds," Kursk warned. "My patience is waning. This operation is too important for me to tolerate your bullshit."

Cole held his ground. "Hey, I've got a stake in this, too. All I'm saying is there were too many variables. The whole mission was like a dam exploding. The water spilled over, and next thing you know we're drowning."

Pausing, Cole dug deep into his pants pocket, withdrew a lighter and reignited the cigar that had gone cold in his mouth. Exhaling a white-gray cloud of smoke, he peered at Kursk through the haze. Absently, he rubbed the stubble along his cheek.

"I guess Talisman told you the woman showed up again?"

White-hot rage pulsed through Kursk. He clenched his fists and felt the nails digging into his palms. His jaw muscles ached as he ground his teeth together, trying to maintain his composure. Dammit, he didn't want his soldiers to see how much the woman worried him.

"No, Talisman didn't tell me that," he said finally. "You mean the woman from Moscow? Natasha Rytova?"

Cole nodded. "One and the same. You ask me, she's crazy."

Kursk walked to his desk and dropped heavily into his contoured leather chair. He stared straight ahead and thought of the monster he'd created.

Two months earlier, an explosion had leveled one of his weapons warehouses, costing Kursk a small fortune. His Kremlin contacts had identified Rytova as the culprit. Before the disaster, he'd known she was gunning for him but had underestimated her resolve to settle the blood debt that existed between them.

Afterward, he'd sworn never to repeat that mistake. But, regardless of his increased vigilance, the woman had destroyed assets in Brighton Beach and Tel Aviv. She'd left behind minimal body counts, but destroyed what Kursk cared about most—weapons, vehicles, diamonds and cash. Each time he almost could hear the woman laughing at his misfortune.

Kursk was strangely subdued as he spoke. "She's not crazy, Cole. She's driven. Driven to kill me."

Kursk watched as a smile tugged at the corners of Cole's mouth.

"I'll admit it's an admirable goal, Nikki, but why does she want to nail you so bad?"

Kursk ignored the question. "Trevor Dade arrived a few hours ago. I must see him. We have many details to attend to before we make our move overseas."

"Your people in Moscow still interested in buying that damn plane?" Cole asked.

"Yes, along with Iran, China and North Korea."

"Fuck North Korea."

It was Kursk's turn to smile. "You're thinking like an American intelligence agent, Cole. In my organization, that's a fatal flaw. We are arms traders, not politicians. Our allegiances go to the highest bidder—period. If you cannot stomach that, perhaps you should leave. I'll keep your portion of the sale proceeds for myself. I hired William Armstrong because he caused me so many problems in Afghanistan. I brought you on because he spoke highly of you. Don't disappoint me."

Cole shot the Russian a hard stare. Kursk felt his muscles tensing, his breath shortening, as he prepared to launch himself at Cole.

The men had worked at cross purposes for many years—Kursk with the KGB and Cole with the CIA. Their alliance was an uneasy one.

With two fingers of his right hand, Cole reached into his breast pocket and withdrew a pair of aviator shades. Flicking them open, he slipped them on without averting his gaze from Kursk. "I'm cool, Nikki. No worries here," he said.

"Tell Talisman to hunt down the American and kill him. And I want the woman dead, too. Talisman must not fuck this up. There's too much at stake here."

"Gotcha, Comrade," Cole said. "I've got a two million dollar payday coming when all this is over. Hell, I'd sell out the entire Western world for that kind of cash."

Turning, Cole left the room. Kursk stared after him and wondered if the CIA man knew just how prophetic his words really were.

4

Mack Bolan kept his cool. Stuck in a hot, cramped room at the American Embassy, Bolan had spent the last half an hour trying to get Natasha Rytova to tell him what she knew of Talisman's boss.

She'd told him to go to hell.

With the help of Hal Brognola, Bolan and Rytova had been freed from the peacekeeping soldiers and returned to the embassy in a matter of hours. Bolan's alias had immediately passed muster, but the Russians had disavowed any knowledge of Rytova. A little more muscle flexing by Brognola had resulted in the woman being released into Bolan's custody as a material witness in a kidnapping case. The appropriate paperwork had been sent electronically to Sierra Leone before Bolan had finished claiming his belongings. The peacekeeping troops had released Bolan's and Rytova's weapons to the embassy personnel.

The pair sat across from each other at a small table inside a windowless cube. The table, two chairs and a security camera were the ten-foot by twelve-foot space's only furnishings. Bolan had disconnected the security camera at its source before entering the room.

He had changed into a pair of black denim jeans, a black polo shirt and leather athletic shoes. He'd left his weapons locked in another room within the embassy. Rytova had washed the blood from her face and scalp, but still wore the same clothes as she had during the assault at Talisman's compound.

Occasionally, she'd grimace as she moved, gingerly touching her ribs, jaw muscles bunching up as she held in the pain.

Bolan leaned back in his chair and pinned her under his icy gaze. The clock was ticking, and he had little time for verbal fencing. Unfortunately, she was the best lead he had in finding Trevor Dade. And she wasn't talking.

"Back at the compound, you said you know who Talisman works for," Bolan said. "Who is it?"

She glared at him, repeating what had been her mantra during the short, tense meeting. "I'll tell you nothing."

A satellite phone on the table buzzed and Bolan answered it. "Striker?"

Bolan recognized the voice as that of Aaron "The Bear" Kurtzman, leader of Stony Man Farm's cyberteam. "You still got the lady with you?" the Bear asked.

"Right," Bolan said.

"If she still works for the Russians, we can't find any evidence of it. We've done some major hacking into the SVR and the Kremlin's computers but found only limited information. We can't stay in their system too long because of the threats of a reverse trace."

"What did you find?" Bolan asked.

"She worked for the SVR but resigned several months ago. Had a family tragedy, went on leave and never came back."

"What happened?" As Bolan uttered the words, Rytova looked at him and scowled, but remained silent.

"Lost her husband and her dad in an explosion of some kind. The case began as a suspicious death, but within days was closed out as accidental. Press accounts from the time pretty much follow the same line of thinking. One reporter quoting unidentified sources said investigators were examining a link between the deaths and organized crime figures. But it stops short of naming anyone."

"Any other mentions of organized crime in any of the other stories?" Bolan asked.

"Nada," Kurtzman said. Bolan could hear keys clicking on the other end of the phone. Excitement nudged the timbre of Kurtzman's voice up a notch. "But get this, within days of that story running, the reporter disappeared. There was no body found, so all anyone can do is point fingers. The Committee to Protect Journalists says the guy is dead and was killed in retribution for the story. Russian authorities say he left Russia and went underground. Anything else is just journalistic histrionics, they say."

Bolan felt his gut twist with anger. He knew better than that. "I'm inclined to believe the press on this one," he said.

He watched as Rytova began to shift nervously in her chair. She looked up at the camera positioned in the corner of the room. She absently ran her fingers through her hair, drawing it back from her cheek and tucking a lock of it behind her ear. As she did, Bolan noticed a long white scar that began at her left ear and snaked down the line of her left jaw before coming to a stop under her chin.

She saw him looking, covered the scar with a hand and glared.

Bolan didn't break his gaze. "What else you got for me, Bear?"

"The organized crime ties don't stop with the mysterious Miss Rytova," Kurtzman replied. "Seems our scientist friend had his own dealings with the Russian Mob. Albeit a bit more friendly."

"Friendly how?"

"Besides not being able to keep his pants on, Dade also likes to gamble. Seems he made weekly pilgrimages on a private jet to Las Vegas. He'd whoop it up at a couple of strip clubs and casinos owned by one Sergei Ivanov, a Russian mobster who holds considerable power in Las Vegas and Denver. Dade lived like a high roller and lost lots of money to the house."

"Dade couldn't have been in debt," Bolan said.

"No. Family's got too much money for him to end up under water. But according to the FBI, he and Ivanov were getting awfully chummy along the way. Pretty sordid, huh?"

"Sordid," Bolan agreed. "But it makes sense. The Russian Mafia runs a lot of guns in Africa, so we might be closer to connecting Talisman to Dade. I'm assuming Ivanov isn't the top of the food chain."

"Both FBI and DEA think Ivanov has a handler. *Who* is the question."

Bolan stared at Rytova. "I think I have an idea where to find out," he said.

"You figure it out, Striker, you let me know," Kurtzman said. "Hey, the big guy wants to talk with you. You got a second?"

"Go."

The line went silent for a moment, then Brognola's booming voice sounded. "How you coming along, Striker?"

"Slowly," Bolan told his old friend. "It was a set up from the word go. Dade may have been here at some point, but it was before I ever set foot in Freetown. If he's still in Africa, he's not at Talisman's place and I'd guess he's not in Sierra Leone. But if we can find Talisman, we might still have a chance of locating Dade."

Bolan heard Brognola take a deep breath and exhale.

"I think you're right," Brognola replied. "While you were in jail, the local police found the bodies of the U.S. agents who were supposed to get your back at Talisman's compound. They'd all been bound with wire and shot execution style."

The soldier rubbed his forehead with the thumb and forefinger of his left hand and stared at a spot on the desk. A sick feeling seized his stomach. "Sorry to hear that," he said.

"Damn shame," Brognola agreed.

Bolan felt himself getting impatient. The mission thus far had produced dead ends and more questions. He began to scan through what he knew, trying to see what angle he might be missing.

Brognola interrupted his thoughts. "The Man's worried. Telling him that you ran into a possible Russian intelligence agent didn't do much for his mood. Nor did finding out America's top laser scientist has Mob ties."

"They should have known about the Mob ties way before I came on the scene," Bolan growled. "As for the disappearance, tell him I'm working on it."

"Already did, Striker. It's probably the only thing keeping him sane. Or me for that matter."

"The first step is finding Talisman. Do we have anyone here who might know how to get me connected?"

Brognola paused for a few seconds. Bolan heard him shuffling through some papers.

"Ronald Moeller," Brognola said. "He does a lot of ground intelligence work for the State Department. Listens for seismic shifts in public opinion for or against the United States. Monitors for potential threats against the embassy. That kind of thing."

"You got an address?"

Brognola gave it to Bolan. He wrote it down in his war book.

"Stay in touch Striker."

"Will do." Bolan severed the connection and set the phone on the table.

"We need to talk," he said, "about what happened to you in Moscow."

Rytova's eyes softened for a moment. Then the steel returned and her cheeks burned red.

"I'll tell you nothing. In fact, I demand to be let go. You have no jurisdiction over me," she said.

Bolan put an edge in his voice. "Lady, that wasn't a question. You know who Talisman works for and I need that information."

"I'm Russian intelligence," the woman insisted.

"Moscow says otherwise. They've disavowed any knowledge of you, period."

Bolan figured it was time to bluff. "So I guess if you were to disappear, no one would be the wiser," he said.

"You do not mean that."

"You saw me in action earlier," Bolan replied. "I'm here for a reason, and I'll take it all the way to reach my goal. I'd rather we work together, but I can have you on a military flight to the United States within an hour. With one phone call, you're off to a federal prison, locked up under a sealed indictment. That would definitely cramp your style."

Rytova rubbed at an invisible spot on the table and stared at her hand as she did. She seemed to draw within herself and her voice flattened as she spoke.

"His name is Nikolai Kursk," she said.

Bolan ran the name through his mind and came up blank.

"Never heard of him," he said.

"No reason you should have," Rytova replied. "He was one of the KGB's best covert operators—a government-sanctioned killer. He had more than 150 confirmed kills in Afghanistan alone. But he's much more than an assassin. He's a brilliant behind-the-scenes player, what you would call a power broker. He owned people in the Kremlin. Everything he had, he got through intimidation and blackmail. When the Soviet Union fell, he funneled huge sums of money out of the country, enough to last him five lifetimes."

"Okay, so what's your tie to him?" Bolan asked.

"Until five months ago I was with the SVR," she said. "So was my husband, Dmitri. I was an analyst, he was an agent. Kursk had already left government service and was smuggling weapons and uranium out of the country. Dmitri heard about it and started an investigation. He pushed harder than anyone within the agency to bring Kursk down. But everywhere he turned, he hit a wall, most of them erected by the government."

Her voice caught for a moment. She continued staring at the table, almost unaware Bolan was in the room. Her eyes softened with a deep sadness.

"He kept fighting. That was Dmitri. He was a warrior. He would do the right thing, even if it killed him. Eventually it did."

Bolan knew where the story was going, and his heart went out to the woman. But he kept his expression stony. "What happened?"

She shrugged, brushed a lock of hair from her eyes. "My father was a police officer in Moscow, and Dmitri respected him very much. The two met in a tearoom to discuss Dmitri's problem. Kursk was tailing Dmitri, but Dmitri had become too obsessed to notice. He got that way sometimes, you know."

She never looked at Bolan, but a smile played across her lips for a moment as she apparently got lost in memory. Bolan had noticed her curves earlier, but her innate beauty became glaringly obvious when her features softened. An instant later, the vulnerability drained away, replaced by the hardened battle mask to which Bolan was accustomed.

Her voice again flattened as though she were reading from a book. "Anyway," she said, "Kursk's people threw two fragmentation grenades into the tearoom. The blast killed Dmitri, my father and ten other people."

"And no one believed Kursk was involved," Bolan said.

The woman stiffened. "Many believe it. They just won't admit it. Through either money or intimidation, Kursk owns lots of people. And so I am alone in this mission."

The woman's story reminded Bolan of the searing losses he suffered several lifetimes ago.

"I'm sorry," he said. Even as the words came out, he realized how insignificant they sounded.

She shrugged again. "I'm sorry, too. But I will feel much better when Nikolai Kursk is dead."

"I won't discourage you from that path," he said. "But you might want to think twice before you devote your life to it. It's a hard road to walk."

The woman gave him a cold look. "You cannot know how I feel."

"I have a better idea than you know."

"Have you been married?" she asked.

"No."

The woman crossed her arms over her chest and gave him a cold look. "Then you know nothing of my loss."

Bolan decided to let it go. He didn't have time to play counselor. "You got any other names?" he asked.

The woman thought for a moment. "Cole. The man who shot me. He sounded American. I heard him speak on the radio set I stole from one of the men at the compound."

Bolan grabbed the satellite phone, raised Kurtzman again and gave him the new information. "I'll check back later," Bolan said and killed the connection.

"So where's Kursk now?" he asked.

"I don't know."

"Look, lady…"

Rytova's eyes narrowed. "I really don't. He has safehouses all over the world and moves a great deal. He's hard to pin down. But I am hearing disturbing things about him."

"What kind of things?"

"My sources say he's got something big in the works. Perhaps it was taking this Dade you speak of, perhaps something else. I know nothing about that matter. But I do know that Kursk has been amassing troops for months."

"He has to have a place in Africa."

"Somewhere, yes. He also spends a great deal of time in Colombia and Israel. But he's extremely active in this continent's diamonds, weapons and fuel trade, so I'm sure he has a hideaway somewhere."

"Would Talisman be able to point us in the right direction?" Bolan asked.

"I had hoped so. That's why I was at the compound," she replied.

Bolan nodded. His head still hurt from the glancing blow from the rifle butt. Otherwise his body felt like it was in fighting shape. He hoped the same was true for Rytova; he might need her knowledge of Nikolai Kursk and he wanted to take her with him.

"You okay to look around a little?" he asked.

"Of course."

He stood and started for the door. "Then let's go find Talisman."

RONALD MOELLER STUFFED the unloaded Uzi into his suitcase, covered it with a mateless white tube sock and a wadded red T-shirt. He'd grab a couple of magazines for the weapons later, but first things first. He needed to pack up and get the hell out of Freetown.

The message from his handlers had been brief: expect company. A U.S. intelligence agent probing a recent executive kidnapping was on his way. The guy apparently wanted to pick Moeller's brain about a local weapons and diamonds smuggler, learn anything he knew. So he was to sit tight and wait for the guy's arrival.

Like hell. That was all the excuse Moeller needed to start packing his things and get out of Dodge.

The way he figured it, the Feds were coming for him. To complicate matters, Talisman was due to make his final payment of rough diamonds to Moeller for his services over the past few days. Moeller had considered telling him to stay away, perhaps even warn him about the U.S. agent coming to call, but had decided against it, figuring Talisman would just use the information as an excuse either to kill him or skip the final payment.

Moeller planned to get out of this sinkhole before morning and maybe put a bullet in the maniac's brain—just out of principle. But he'd have his diamonds in his pocket before he left. Those little bits of rock had been the only things keeping him going the past few days.

He stared at the suitcase and asked himself for the fifth time in as many minutes whether this was a good idea. Disappearing was risky. The caller had purposely been vague, and Moeller wasn't sure his bosses knew of his indiscretions. If they didn't yet, they'd figure it out damn quick when he came up MIA. Sierra Leone had become too hot to think otherwise.

Fuck them. Even if they did realize he was a turncoat, they'd never find him.

For the past several months, Moeller had risked his career and his life to get to this point, and he wasn't about to let it all turn sour on him. So he'd take his meager belongings, his recently acquired wealth and flee this armpit of a country. Several cigarette cartons stuffed with rough diamonds held the promise of a lazy life. Moeller just needed to get to Antwerp, Belgium, where he could trade the gems for currency. From Belgium, he'd travel to the Caribbean, hook up with a plastic surgeon who specialized in identity changes, put on a new face and surround himself with sun, daiquiris and women as he healed. Then he'd spend his remaining days as a rich man.

Screw the God-and-country routine. Out here it was every man for himself.

Some might call it treason—Moeller considered it self-preservation.

He pulled a handkerchief from his back pocket and sopped up the sweat from the bald crown of his head. With the first two fingers of his left hand, he pushed his glasses farther up the bridge of his nose, clenched his jaw and wondered what else he should pack. Guns came first in Africa. He pulled a SIG-Sauer from a desk drawer, checked the load. He sheathed and secured the pistol in his shoulder holster and slipped extra clips into the pockets of his baggy jeans. Pulling a light Oxford-style shirt from the couch, he slipped it on so it covered the pistol.

The weight of the handgun felt reassuring to Moeller. He preferred murder by proxy, of course. But he'd draw blood if it came to that. He had already fingered the State Department agents so that Kursk's bloodthirsty jackals could take the men down. And he considered the intelligence agent's trip more than an unhappy coincidence.

To hell with them. The State Department had driven him to this point, sending him to this cesspool. During fourteen months, he had grown to hate Freetown.

He grabbed a laptop from his desk and stuffed it and some cords into a black nylon carrying case. Before he left, he'd torch his PC, reduce it to a pool of molten slag, destroying any incriminating evidence it might contain. He'd burn down the apartment building and everyone in it if it meant getting out of here.

Moeller retrieved a final cigarette carton from his bedroom and slipped it into the suitcase. He zippered the bag shut, hefted it and the computer case, lugged both to the door, then set down the suitcase to free a hand. He cracked open the door, peered into the hallway, saw it was empty and pulled the door open the rest of the way. He'd store the luggage in his car, be back upstairs before Talisman arrived. He could get his final diamonds and be gone before the American arrived.

The PC chirped behind him. Moeller swore. Another e-mail.

He considered ignoring it but decided not to. If the message was urgent, a delayed answer might raise an eyebrow. Or maybe not. He'd missed other e-mails. Was he getting paranoid? Maybe. That didn't mean they weren't out to get him.

Jesus, he was thinking like a fool. He'd better check his e-mail just to put his mind at rest.

Slipping the computer case from his shoulder, he set it on the floor and pushed the door shut without latching it. He returned to his desk and seated himself.

As he gripped the mouse, swiped it around the mouse pad, he felt the hairs on the back of his neck rise and scratch the collar of his shirt. A door hinge squeaked from behind, betraying someone's approach. Moeller's hand shot underneath the shirt, fingers scrambling for the SIG-Sauer.

A cold voice, almost certainly American, said, "Don't do it, Ron."

Moeller stopped in midreach.

"Hands up. Then turn toward me," the voice said.

Moeller complied. A cold feeling in his stomach told him he wouldn't like what he'd see.

His gut was right.

NIKOLAI KURSK SMELLED fear and it satisfied him. He watched as Trevor Dade fidgeted in his chair, relentlessly wringing together his hands and crossing and uncrossing his legs. His expensive but dirty clothes hung loosely from his emaciated frame. Puffy, bloodshot eyes peered through thick glasses resting slightly askew on the man's nose as he cautiously regarded his Russian host.

Kursk displayed a nasty gash of a smile. "Welcome, Trevor Dade."

"Cut the crap, Kursk. I've hardly slept since I left the United States. I've been stuffed into helicopters, planes and trucks. Flown all over the damn world. Ivanov promised me first-class treatment. I end up stinking like a pig. Tired. Pissed off. This better not be how you treat the talent."

Kursk feigned concern, his voice taking on a placating tone. "You are displeased? How very unfortunate."

Dade scowled. "Whatever. You got any blow?"

"Yes, I do. But that will come later."

Dade stared at Kursk like a hungry dog entranced by a steak. "I want it now."

"Later. First we must talk."

Dade narrowed his eyes at Kursk, but dropped the subject. The scientist nodded at Kursk's cigarette. "You got any more of those?"

With precise movements, Kursk rolled a cigarette for the American and pushed it and a stainless-steel lighter across the desktop with his fingertips. Dade grabbed both, ignited the cigarette's tip with the blue-yellow flame and consumed it in greedy drags. He fired a column of smoke across the desktop that momentarily shrouded Kursk's head in an eye-stinging haze. The Russian's gaze hardened and he felt his muscles tensing, ready to propel him forward.

Kursk took a deep breath and stood. Walking around the desk, he leaned against it and towered over Dade. The son of a Russian army commander, Kursk had inherited his father's love of discipline, and he worshiped routine and self-development. Fortunately, the fates hadn't burdened him with his father's failings—patriotism and loyalty—traits that had left the old man a penniless buffoon so depressed and disillusioned that only shooting himself in the head could cure his crippling malaise.

With forensic detachment, Kursk recalled finding the old man's body, slumped over in a chair, his head cocked at an impossible angle, eyes propped open in the same pitiful look of surprise that had haunted them since the fall of the Soviet Union. The pistol and an empty bottle of vodka—each symbols of things the old man held most dear—lay to either side of the chair. His father had a blood-splattered picture of himself in dress uniform, posing before the Soviet flag resting in his lap. A single bullet had torn away the back of the man's head.

Before police had arrived to haul away the body, Kursk had snatched away his father's pistol. He carried it with him, a grim reminder not to repeat the follies of a sentimental old fool. Besides, Kursk hated to waste a perfectly good pistol.

The big Russian crossed massive arms over his chest and stared down at Dade. Fear flashed in the scientist's eyes as Kursk's shadow overtook him.

"You have concerns about your treatment?" the Russian asked.

Dade's lips worked for a moment before he found his voice. When he did, it sounded small and whiny. "I brought you the Nightwind plans. I want my money. And I want a little respect from you."

"You'll get your money," Kursk said.

"And?"

"Do you know of the mujahideen?" Kursk asked. Dade gave Kursk a blank stare, but the big man continued. "When Russia invaded Afghanistan, men who considered themselves holy warriors—the mujahideen—fought us guerrilla style and eventually drove us from their country. They were primitive, but remarkably tenacious. With covert help from your country, they brought a superpower to its knees. Our soldiers, even our elite troops, respected these fighters. Perhaps even feared them."

"What's that have to do with me?"

Kursk made a small sound of disapproval, stood and began to pace his office. Dade shifted uncomfortably in his chair as the Russian passed within inches of him. Kursk considered it a good sign that he already had instilled such fear in the man.

Kursk walked to a window, stared through it at one of the high walls surrounding his compound. "I was an operative in Afghanistan. Lived there for three years. By day, I slept. By night, I raided their strongholds, killed them. Sometimes I killed entire families—mothers, sons, daughters. I left that dirty little country with 150 confirmed kills to my credit. I believe that number is low by about 50. I spilled much blood before returning to Russia. Given the chance, I would gladly have spilled even more."

Dade squirmed and stared at his lap. "Is that supposed to scare me?"

Kursk turned toward Dade and shrugged. "Perhaps. But not to worry. If I wanted to intimidate you, you would know it. I'm just trying to—educate you." He gave Dade a wicked smile.

The scientist squirmed a bit more.

"The point is I killed these men, killed their wives, their children, but not because they threatened my country's security or made Russia look foolish. I did it for myself. I wanted to be a big deal in the KGB. Killing made me a big deal. So I did it often, and it took me where I wanted to go. And their fighting prowess meant less than nothing to me. I killed them without struggle or remorse. I did it because I've found killing is the most expedient way for me to get what I want."

Dade shuddered. Kursk sat behind his desk, spread his hands and smiled.

"Let's not have this conversation again. Rather, I want to speak of Nightwind. Yes?"

Dade nodded, only too glad to change the subject.

"I looked at the schematics this morning," the Russian said. "They are brilliant. Surely, I will have no problem selling them."

The American exhaled a puff of smoke. Whether from fear or cocaine withdrawal, his shoulders and hands trembled.

"It's my best work," Dade said. "I spent two years fine-tuning the lasers so they won't get warped by atmospheric conditions. Maxed out, they could punch a hole through a ship's hull. Or an aircraft skin."

"And depressurize the cabin," Kursk said.

Dade shrugged. "I guess so," he said. "I didn't design Nightwind for use against commercial jets. It's meant to shoot missiles from the skies. Not airliners."

Kursk made a dismissive gesture. "We don't determine uses," the Russian said. "The customers do. If they can pay for the craft, they can do what they want with it. A customer asked me if it could be damaging to commercial jetliners. "

"Sounds like a terrorist," Dade said.

"He considers himself a freedom fighter."

"Whatever," the scientist replied. "This is highly technical. Even if the guy could foot the bill for the plans, he'd never have the resources to reproduce it. Sentinel has billions of dollars, and they still needed help from the U.S. government to make the plane. It'd take a sovereign government with untold billions and a first-rate military establishment to make another Nightwind. Most nations can't figure out how to build a nuclear bomb, let alone a tactical laser fighter. Even your country couldn't reproduce it."

Typical American arrogance, Kursk thought. "I have no country," the Russian said, correcting him. "Only customers."

Dade rolled his eyes. Talking science, he was in his element and less intimidated. "No one can reproduce this plane. That's why I figured it was okay to sell the plans. Let some despot drop half a billion dollars and end up with the equivalent of a screen saver. Lots of pretty pictures, with no real value. I couldn't care less."

Kursk smiled. "You assumed I would sell my clients a—how you say—pig in a poke."

"You knew that," Dade said. "I told you as much."

Kursk shrugged. "I changed my mind."

"What?"

"My business is built on trust. I cannot sell someone faulty merchandise. It would not be right."

"What the hell do you care?" Dade asked. "You make this score and you can retire. Get out of the blood trade for good. Besides, your customers are crooks, for God's sake."

"You, too, are a criminal now. This you must not forget."

Dade looked down at his lap and studied his hands. "Bull. I just wanted to get back at my company. Get the hell away from everything. I wasn't going to jail for anyone, especially some stupid hooker."

The man was a bottomless well of self-pity and whining, Kursk thought. "I must ask more from you before all this is done."

"What the hell do you mean?" Dade replied, startled.

"I want the plane. I am going to steal it, and you're going to help me do so."

Dade looked stunned. "You're crazy."

The smile drained away from Kursk's face. He leaned forward, rested his big forearms on the desktop and trapped Dade under his gaze. "It's quite simple, my friend. You either help me or I kill you. I already have the data. The world already thinks you are dead. I have nothing to lose if you die for real. It might even make my life easier in the long run."

To punctuate the point, Kursk reached behind his back, drew the Tokarev and set it on the desktop within easy reach.

Dade's blood-etched eyes widened, his cheeks flushed and anger flared. "This wasn't part of the deal, and you know it. Besides, the plane is heavily guarded. You'd never get to it. It'd be a bloodbath."

"You let me worry about that. You said it yourself, I work in a blood trade."

As if reading Kursk's mind, Dade said, "I don't know anything about the security. I'm just a scientist."

"You're an extremely intelligent man," Kursk said. "You

notice things. Despite your little problem, eh?" Kursk squeezed his thumb and index finger together to approximate the tip of a spoon, stuck them to his left nostril and snorted.

Dade's face flushed red. "You bastard, I ought to—"

Kursk held up a hand for silence. "You ought to calm yourself, my friend. Put away your pride. It's no secret you enjoy cocaine, alcohol, women. Whether you are addicted is of no consequence to me. I just want to provide you with as much of all three as you can handle. I do that for business associates all the time."

"What about my money?" Dade whined.

"You'll get that, too. But you must help me steal the plane. I have ideas, and I have a contact within Sentinel's research and development facility, the Haven. But I need you to confirm what I know and give me specifics about the aircraft."

Dade leaned forward in his chair, grabbed the edge of the desktop. Kursk noticed the scientist's fingers whitened as he held it in a death grip. Dade looked side-to-side before speaking, as if they were about to share a secret.

"Look, I'm dying for some blow," the scientist said. "You get me that and we can work things out. I'll help you get Nightwind."

"Consider it done, my friend. Tell me what I need to know and you can have all the drugs and money you want."

KURSK SHOVED ASIDE the aerial photos and drawings that had been scattered across his desk. A wave of disgust cascaded over the Russian as he looked at Dade. Sweat beaded the scientist's forehead and his hands shook violently. His attention was becoming increasingly unfocused as his withdrawal symptoms deepened.

Kursk decided that he'd learned enough for now. He dismissed the scientist with a wave of his hand. "Please, go to your room. I believe you will find it suited perfectly to your particular tastes. And be assured you will have company this evening. You are my guest and shall be treated as such."

Dade shot him a wary look, which pleased Kursk. Scared

people were compliant and Dade's fear pulsed through the room like waves of energy.

"We will speak further of this later," Kursk assured the man.

A pair of guards escorted the scientist from the room. With a wave of his hand, the Russian dismissed the rest of his security force, too. He needed time alone to consider the challenges that lay before him.

That the American and Natasha Rytova were still alive worried Kursk. He couldn't tolerate another debacle like the one at Talisman's compound. If those two weren't dead by morning, he would send his army of former Spetsnaz and special forces troops to Talisman's compound to eliminate him and set an example for others within the organization.

Kursk would have killed Trevor Dade in a heartbeat if he didn't think the man would fetch so much on the open market. Rogue nations and those engaged in uneasy alliances with the United States alike would gladly take custody of the man and his secrets.

But Kursk had other plans in the works. With a brilliant flash, he'd reduce America's premiere weapons-development facility into a crater measuring a half mile in radius.

Freetown, Sierra Leone

As THEY APPROACHED the building, a skinny boy dressed in a sweat-stained, sleeveless T-shirt and shorts, stepped from the doorway and thrust forward an AK-47 knockoff.

The young African held up the rifle with two hands, diagonal across his chest, muzzle pointed skyward, as though blocking throngs of rioters. Bolan guessed the child was about fourteen. A faded necktie converted into a rifle strap hung loosely from the gun. A dead-eyed stare appraised Bolan for a moment, Rytova even longer.

"Where are you going?" the boy asked. He brought the rifle down, leveled at Bolan's chest. The boy's index finger rested on the outside curve of the trigger guard.

"I'm going inside," Bolan said. "We're here to see a tenant."

"Who?"

"You the security here?" Bolan asked.

The boy nodded. "You want to go inside, you have to go through me."

Bolan had no doubt he could. He just didn't want to.

"We really need to get inside," Bolan said. "Maybe we can make a deal."

"No deals. Who are you here to see?"

"I've got money," Bolan said. He dug in his pocket, extracted the equivalent of $40. He held the money just out of the boy's reach.

The boy stared at the money but said nothing. Bolan kept the cash front and center, entranced the boy with it as he shifted slowly to one side.

The boy grinned. "I could kill you and take the money."

"Suit yourself," Bolan said. He flicked the cash through the air to the boy's right. Small eyes followed it as it exploded into a cloud of several small bills wafting toward the ground. The rifle followed the boy's line of vision, moving the muzzle precious inches away from Bolan's center mass.

The big man stepped in, grabbed cold steel and cleared the muzzle from his kill zone. Rock-hard muscles tensing, arms acting in concert like pistons, Bolan gave the assault rifle a hard yank with one hand, the boy's chest a rough shove with the other.

The boy fell back and yelped when his rear collided with concrete.

Bolan raised the rifle, ejected the magazine and handed it to Rytova. With practiced movements, he stripped the weapon, heaving components in different directions. He removed the weapon's recoil mechanism, held it up so the boy could see it, then handed it to Rytova. He tossed the knockoff AK-47's remains aside.

"You're out of business, son."

Pulling himself up from the pavement, the boy balled up his fists, surged toward Bolan and snapped out a sloppy left. Bolan

stepped aside and let the punch glide past him. Snagging the
kid's wrist, Bolan wheeled at the waist and yanked him forward. The force stole the boy's footing. Grabbing at the young
man's upper arm with his free hand, Bolan pushed him to the
ground. He kept the movement as gentle as possible so he
could maintain control without hurting the boy. Laying him flat
against the pavement, Bolan twisted a slim arm up behind the
youth's back.

"You don't want to fight me, and I don't want to hurt you if
I don't have to. So take your money and go. Understand?"

The boy nodded.

Bolan eased off. The boy got to his feet, rubbed his shoulder and gave Bolan an angry look.

"This isn't over," the boy said.

"Between you and me it is," Bolan said.

The boy agreed to unlock the building's front door, and gave
Bolan and Rytova a wide berth as they entered the sagging
building. Looking over his shoulder, Bolan saw the boy col-
lecting pieces of his rifle. A clattering noise sounded from behind, prompting the soldier to turn. He saw Rytova had stepped
behind the desk and dumped the recoil mechanism into a trash
can. He watched as she shoved the container inside a cabinet
underneath the lobby desk and closed the door.

Bolan scanned their surroundings as Rytova walked to
the elevator and summoned the car. The lobby was devoid of
people. A pair of bare bulbs burned overhead, illuminating
the dingy area. White wallpaper stained brown from water
leaks separated from the wall in several spots and hung down
in large curls. Bullet holes and scorch marks blemished the
walls. The stink of mildew hung heavy in the air, nearly
overpowering the weaker smells of coffee, cooking grease
and exotic spices that drifted from the building's upper
reaches.

A muffled ring announced the elevator's arrival and the door
slid open. With a gesture, Bolan ushered the woman into the

car, took a last look behind them and followed her inside. As the car ascended, Bolan's combat senses began to sound, and he felt the pit of his stomach tighten.

He had the Beretta in his hand before the elevator halted at the sixth floor. As the door slid open, the warrior poked his head out and glanced down the hallway. A shaft of light shone through a partially opened door farther down the hall. Taking a quick inventory of room numbers, Bolan figured the open door was Moeller's.

They made their way down the hall and Bolan peered through the door while Rytova, armed with a SIG-Sauer P239, watched his back. He saw the suitcase and the nylon computer bag setting on the floor near the apartment entrance. Computer keys clicked from deeper inside the room. Bolan stepped into the doorway, chanced a look inside and saw Moeller dressed and seated at the computer desk. He noticed the bulge in the guy's left armpit almost immediately.

Bolan locked the Beretta on the man and nudged the door with his free hand. Rusty hinges protested as the door swung open.

Moeller gasped, jumped to his feet and whipped around, knocking the chair to the floor in the process. His hand stabbed inside his shirt.

"Don't do it, Ron," Bolan said.

Moeller didn't. Instead, he raised his hands and smiled.

"Hey, you're American," he said. "You're Cooper, right?"

Bolan kept his face impassive. "Maybe."

"Bull," Moeller said. "You're the guy I was told to expect."

Bolan didn't respond. Instead he cocked his head at Moeller's suitcases. "Looks like you didn't want to be here when I arrived. Where are you going?"

Moeller's lips tightened for a moment, a sheen broke out on the crown of his head.

"I got orders to move tonight," he said. "I've helped the locals stop a couple of diamonds-for-weapons deals around here. Somebody figured it out, put a price on my head. The bosses in Washington told me to haul ass and go home. Hey, man, can I put my hands down?"

Bolan ignored the request. "Interesting," he said. "Now try telling me the truth."

"That is the truth," Moeller said, looking serious.

Instinct told the Executioner otherwise.

Bolan scanned the room and spotted a tattered cigarette carton resting on a scarred wooden coffee table. The plastic wrapping had been stripped away and a couple of bands of clear tape held the box closed. Bolan noticed the room had the same rotten stench as the rest of the building—years of sweat, backed-up sewers, mildew—but no cigarette smoke. There wasn't even an ashtray in sight.

"You a smoker, Ron?" he asked.

"Nah, man. Nasty habit, right? Got enough people trying to kill me already. You know what I'm saying?"

Bolan nodded toward the cigarette carton. "Holding those for someone?"

Moeller's lips tightened again. Bolan assumed that meant he was trying to think of a new lie to tell. Brushing past him, the soldier stepped to the table and grabbed the carton.

Moeller stepped toward Bolan, clenching his fists as he did. The Executioner's gun hand snapped forth and leveled out as he planted the Beretta's muzzle on Moeller's forehead.

The State Department agent stopped cold.

Bolan pushed the Beretta harder into the man's face, forcing his head to tilt back at an uncomfortable angle. "Sit," Bolan said.

Moeller folded his legs and fell into the couch.

Bolan pointed his pistol at the agent's armpit. "Two fingers," he said. "Take it out. Hand it butt first over your shoulder to the woman behind you. If I get nervous, I'll put one in you and apologize to your bosses later."

Moeller retrieved his pistol and handed it to Rytova, who had shifted to the side to get out of the line of fire. Rytova snatched the SIG-Sauer, cocked back the hammer and pointed it along with her own pistol at Moeller's head.

The agent jerked in his seat. He shot her a frightened glance. "C'mon, guys," he said, "you've got the wrong idea."

"My mistake," Bolan said. Holstering the Beretta, he ripped open the cigarette box and emptied rough diamonds into his palm. Faced with the suitcases and the jewels, Bolan's worst fears had been confirmed. "You doing some freelance work?" he asked.

"Screw you, man," Moeller responded.

"Is this for fingering the other State Department agents?" Bolan asked. He closed in on the man. "You the reason they're dead, Ron?"

Moeller's eyes bulged, and he backed up against the couch until the wood frame stopped him. "I don't know what you're talking about, man. I was holding them for someone. Actually, one of my sources must have left them here. He was here earlier tonight, I swear. Hell, that's the closest I've been to rough diamonds since I arrived in Africa."

Moeller managed a weak smile, an even weaker shrug. Bolan pocketed the diamonds and drew the Desert Eagle from behind his back. He centered the big-bore hand cannon's muzzle on Moeller's chest.

"Ron, I'm a better shot than you are a liar. What say we start playing straight with each other?"

It was Bolan's turn to lie. He knew he couldn't kill an unarmed man looking like he was more ready to cry than to retaliate.

But he would indulge in a little psychological warfare. The gun's muzzle stayed rock steady.

"You know Talisman, Ron?" Bolan pressed. "You the guy who sold us out? Where can we find him?"

From the hall, Bolan heard the elevator bell ring and the door slide open. The furtive scrapes of boot soles striking bare floor were followed by the metallic click of a weapon being cocked.

Bolan glanced back at Moeller and saw a look of relief

wash across the guy's features. Apparently he figured help
was on the way. That could only mean something very bad for
the Executioner.

TALISMAN THREW the two-way radio to the floor of his red
BMW sports car and stared out the car's window. Artificially
cold air blew against the exposed skin of his face and arms,
making them feel clammy. But an angry fire consumed his
stomach, and breath whipped in and out of his lungs in long
pulls. He sounded like an enraged rhinoceros preparing to
charge a hunter.

He looked down at the radio and mentally replayed his dis-
cussion with Iron Man.

Nikolai Kursk had insulted him, called him a coward and
killed one of his people. Not that Talisman cared particularly
about Blood Claw. But he did consider the man property—his
property. As far as Talisman was concerned, you didn't kill his
people any more than you'd steal his car or burn down his
house. Doing such things were blatant acts of war.

But Talisman knew he could never wage war against Kursk.
To do so was suicide. Kursk had handed him a do-or-die mission, and he had no choice but to comply. So he'd get his re-
match with the American, and this time he'd walk away a
winner. First, though, he had another loose end to tie up. Ronald
Moeller had outlived his usefulness, and Talisman no longer
trusted the squirrely bastard. The guy might have an attack of
conscience and turn himself in, or worse, dump his guts to
some drinking buddy who, in turn, sold the information to a
U.S. intelligence agent. Talisman knew it would all come back
on him, and he didn't need the headache.

He wheeled the BMW into the parking lot next to Moeller's
apartment building, a former luxury hotel. An armored Mercedes sedan followed. Kursk had provided Talisman with a
fleet of armored cars and trucks so he could shuttle the kidnapped scientist around the country in safety.

The hardman shifted the car into Neutral, yanked up the emergency brake and killed the lights. He waited for his boss to exit the car before doing likewise. A ten-foot-high fence topped with curls of razor wire surrounded the pockmarked parking lot.

The building had begun to sag under the weight of the civil war's tireless onslaught. When bombings, gunfights and kidnappings took hold of the country, the tourism trade evaporated. From what Talisman knew, this particular structure had been abandoned and later transformed into an apartment building for the army of bleeding heart aid workers infesting his country.

The young guard approached Talisman and held out a hand. Talisman reached into a jacket pocket, withdrew a half-burned joint and handed it to the boy.

"Watch the cars," Talisman said. "If I find a scratch on them, I'll cut off your arms."

Talisman patted the head of the battered ax shoved inside his belt and smiled. The boy scowled and nodded his understanding.

"Someone already is here," the boy said. "A man and a woman, both white, came earlier. I've not seen them before."

Talisman frowned. "You let them in?"

The boy shrugged his frail shoulders. "They forced their way in. I confronted them, but the man snatched my weapon and broke it. Told me to go home." The boy leaned toward Talisman and stared intently as he spoke. "My rifle is no good. Perhaps you could fix it or give me another one?"

"The man, was he American?" Talisman asked.

"I think so. He was big. Not as big as you, of course, but big."

Talisman gave the boy a hard shove that knocked him against the fence. "If someone tries to hurt my cars, you hit them with your empty rifle. Do whatever you have to do or it's your ass."

Heart hammering in his chest, Talisman started for the main door. His earlier buzz had worn off after the battle at his compound and he felt edgy, ready to pound somebody. He'd considered lighting up, but had decided against it. He needed his senses sharp for the task ahead. The marijuana had caused him to hesitate and run out the door after he'd hit the American with the rifle. He wouldn't repeat that mistake.

He'd lost his AK-47 during his escape and had replaced it with a Galil assault rifle. He snapped off the ambidextrous safety and canted the weapon by its pistol grip as he tugged the hotel's front door open. If everything went his way, he could kill three enemies and lord it over Nikolai Kursk.

5

Mack Bolan was on the move even as the first shadow approached the doorway. He turned to Natasha Rytova who nodded, indicating she too saw the impending danger. The woman raised her SIG-Sauer and brought it down hard, cracking it against Moeller's skull. The State Department agent groaned and rolled to the side, unconscious.

Bolan leveled the .44 Magnum hand cannon in front of him as he closed in on the door. An African trooper, his Galil assault rifle snug against his shoulder, filled the portal and swung the weapon in an arc toward Bolan.

The Desert Eagle roared once in Bolan's hand. The bullet pounded into the man's skull, tore away part of his head and knocked him backward into the hallway. Rytova fired two shots from her weapon, planting both in the man's torso. His weapon fell to the ground. Even as the reverberations from the Desert Eagle's last blast died down, Bolan was again in motion, seeking another target.

A devastating wave of 5.56 mm tumblers punched through the doorway and into the apartment, splintering wooden furniture and fixtures, piercing drywall and shredding upholstery before sawing through Moeller's inert form.

Bolan cursed himself as he bolted for cover. He hadn't meant to get the agent killed, even if the man was dirty.

A second gunner had twisted himself around the door frame and raked the room with sizzling autofire. The Desert Eagle

barked once in Bolan's hand, but the round whizzed harmlessly past the intruder. The soldier adjusted his aim, fired
again. The bullet caught the man in the right eye, and he collapsed to the ground in a heap.

The gunfire halted for a moment as the remaining shooters saw
the second of their two comrades fall. At best, Bolan knew, the
respite was temporary. He also knew his good fortune thus far
was just that. He'd need better firepower to finish the job at hand.

The warrior ran in a crouch to the abandoned weapons lying
on the floor. Grabbing the fully loaded Galil dropped by his first
kill, he slid it across the floor to Rytova who was closing in on
his position. She held the SIG-Sauer in both hands and extended
it forward, covering the shattered doorway as she came up beside him. Holstering the handgun, she hefted the Galil and
checked its load.

Bolan grabbed the second corpse's ankle and dragged him
inside the room. The movement reignited another deadly surge
of firepower more fierce than the last. Bullets lanced through
the air and drove Rytova back behind a heavy wooden chest.

Furiously, Bolan continued to tug at the Galil's strap, which
had become entangled in its owner's arms. After the weapon
came loose, Bolan stripped the man of his web belt and moved
off the firing line. He strapped the seized belt crossways over
his chest like a bandolier.

The gunfire lessened for a moment as more than one of
Bolan's attackers apparently reloaded their weapons. He continued to hold his fire, though, not wanting to send wild sprays
of autofire into the corridors of a crowded apartment building.
Instead, he used the time to scan his surroundings and formu-
late a survival plan.

Then things got worse.

A chorus of fire bells rang throughout the building, followed seconds later by screams and thundering footsteps as already panicked residents bolted from their apartments in search
of safety. Whether activated by the rolling gunsmoke or one of

Talisman's foot soldiers, the alarm bells had just opened a floodgate of human shields that would cramp Bolan's style and make the job that much easier for Talisman and his band of exterminators.

Bolan caught Rytova's eye and nodded toward a sliding glass door at the other end of the living room. He crawled backward toward the glass door, propelling himself with his elbows. Regardless of whether she understood his idea, Rytova followed suit.

She slid the door open, and they both slipped through it and onto the balcony. Even Freetown's humid, fetid air felt fresh and cool compared to the smoke-and-cordite laden atmosphere of Moeller's apartment.

Strapping the Galil across his back, Bolan moved to the balcony railing. Peering down, he saw dozens of people already pouring from the building's entrance. Rytova gave him a questioning look. "Where are we going?"

"Up. Then we get them from behind. I'm not leaving this damn place without Talisman."

Balancing himself on the balcony railing, Bolan reached up and over the balcony platform above him. Running his hands along the concrete surface, he searched until he found the posts securing the railing. Gripping one in each hand, he pulled himself up to eye level with the next balcony. For long moments, his legs dangled five stories above the streets. Ignoring the burn in his muscles, Bolan hoisted himself high enough to swing a leg onto the platform and complete the climb. Moments later, he was on the balcony, inside the railing and reaching below for Rytova. She fired a short burst into Moeller's apartment, then climbed onto the railing and looked up at Bolan.

"They're trying to storm the room," she shouted.

"Take my hand," Bolan said.

She complied, and he pulled her to him. As soon as she was able, she slid a leg onto the balcony, grabbed hold of the railing and pulled herself the rest of the way up.

Bolan peered into the apartment, which seemed empty. He tried the door and found it locked. A quick burst shattered the handle and the locking mechanism, and he slid the door open.

A quick sweep revealed the apartment was empty, and Bolan made his way to the front door. He stopped and listened. Stragglers shouted at one another over the fire alarms. There was a lot of noise and panic, but nothing to indicate an immediate threat to Bolan or Rytova.

Stepping into the corridor, the soldier nearly collided with a woman in a robe, who screamed when she saw him. Others began to raise their hands and stop when they saw the armed intruders.

"Go," Bolan said.

The people raced into the stairwells at either end of the floor.

"You take the stairs at that end of the hall," Bolan said to Rytova. "I'll take these. We converge on Moeller's apartment. Catch them from behind."

"Right," she said.

Bolan returned to Moeller's floor and stepped from the stairwell into the corridor. Screams sounded from elsewhere in the building and a cold sense of unease gripped him. He decided to stand his ground. Another distraction might cost him a chance to take down Talisman, and he couldn't allow that.

As he closed in on the wrecked apartment, Bolan could hear Talisman inside, screaming at someone. "The troops, the police, they're everywhere. We have no air support. Grab me hostages before the building empties, or we'll never make it out of here."

Bolan heard the creak of leather and the pounding of boot soles as someone approached the corridor. Whispering across the floor like a wraith, Bolan squeezed into the recess of a nearby doorway and drew down. A hardman exited Moeller's apartment, AK-47 held at the ready. The Beretta coughed twice and the twin Parabellum rounds broke through the man's ribs and tore into vital organs. The gunner's eyes widened in surprise as crimson wounds blossomed across his chest. He struggled to scream, but only managed to conjure up a sickening gurgle as he staggered back.

His handgun held at the ready, Bolan stepped into Moeller's apartment and found Talisman standing among the ruins. The big African had pushed the agent's corpse onto the floor and dumped the contents of his suitcase on top of him. Talisman was kneeling next to the mess, picking through the scattered clothing.

Thankfully, the blaring fire alarms went quiet.

"If you're looking for the diamonds, forget it," Bolan said.

Talisman stiffened, but raised his hands. He stood and turned toward Bolan.

"Not bad, American," Talisman said. "Take away that gun, though, and my guess is you're a whole lot of nothing."

Bolan eyed his opponent and considered the challenge. Talisman was wasting his time trying to goad the Executioner into a fight by attacking his ego. Bolan had survived too many hellgrounds to feel a need to prove himself.

Still, Talisman might have valuable intel to share about Nikolai Kursk or Trevor Dade. And if Bolan could sweat it out of the guy, so much the better.

"There's only one way this will work," Bolan said. The Beretta remained locked dead center on Talisman's forehead.

Talisman nodded. He dug into his holster, drew his handgun with two fingers, tossed it aside. Sliding his ax from his belt, he thrust the weapon into the floor. The razor-sharp steel buried itself in the wood with a dull thud.

Bolan lowered the Beretta. Unloading the weapon, he threw it behind the couch and pocketed the empty magazine. He did the same with the Galil and the Desert Eagle.

A guttural cry escaped Talisman's lips as he surged toward Bolan. Cold steel glinted in the larger man's hand and the Executioner found himself fighting for his life.

NATASHA RYTOVA WADED into the wave of panicked residents as they scrambled downstairs in a desperate search for safety.

Fire alarms blared in her ears and caused her head to throb as she pushed her way though the people, her SIG-Sauer held at the ready.

A baby cried, and the noise transported Rytova to a place she didn't want to go. Back to Moscow and before she was drummed out of the SVR. She'd been in the early days of her second trimester when Kursk's thugs had killed Dmitri and her father.

When they died, she went numb for what seemed like weeks as she waited for the shock to wear away. When the ice briefly began to melt, it had been thanks to the smoldering rage that permeated her every cell and jolted her back to life. Her anger drove her to work hours, days on end without sleep or food as she began petitioning the SVR to track down and arrest Kursk.

After two weeks, she collapsed and woke up later in a hospital. The baby was gone.

The loneliness had been almost unbearable. She came to realize that Nikolai Kursk had killed her husband and father, but it had been her rage that had caused her baby to die.

She had gone cold at that realization. And when the rage seeped through it came in the form of a self-hate that burned inside and, at times, threatened to consume her.

The crowds had thinned, and Rytova reached for the doorway leading onto Moeller's floor.

Footfalls thundered overhead. The Russian spun and brought up the SIG-Sauer in a two-handed grip. An African hardman stopped short, staring at her over the barrel of his AK-47. Her heart quickened, her breath went shallow. Emotion clashed with training as she fought to control her racing mind. She could run, sure, but she needed to draw blood first or take a bullet in the back.

A small cry from below diverted her attention.

She knew what was coming, but looked anyway.

A woman was climbing the steps. Sweat and tears rolled down the coffee-and-cream complexion of her face. Breath intermingled with frightened sobs. A gunner had snaked his sinewy arm around her throat. He had turned her neck hard, forcing her to walk on her toes. The woman had arched her back to relieve the pressure on her neck. The pair came to a rest on the landing just one flight below Rytova. Another flight below that was the doorway leading into the next floor.

The gunner flashed Rytova a smile. Buried an Uzi's snout into the woman's side, just inches from the baby she carried.

Rytova had no delusions. The woman and the baby were as good as dead. So was she. Unless she got all three of them out of this.

The fire alarms ceased their incessant wailing and the contrasting silence seemed almost stunning. Finally, one less distraction and one more thing going in her favor. A door below Rytova opened. She heard more footsteps as people began to file into the stairwell.

"Sir, put down the weapon. Let the woman go. Let her go," someone ordered.

The gunner from above kept his weapon trained on Rytova, but his eyes darted wildly as he tried to ID the new variable in the standoff. The man with the hostage whirled violently toward the voice. His gun drifted about six inches from the hostages. It wasn't much, but perhaps it was enough.

Intervention by what Rytova assumed were peacekeepers had opened a window of opportunity. A small, brief opening. But an opening, nonetheless.

She took it.

TALISMAN DROVE the razor-sharp steel toward Bolan's throat with a vicious roundhouse swing. Bolan stepped inside the arc of the blow and blocked it with his left arm. He stabbed at Talisman's Adam's apple with a knife-hand strike and threw his hip into the blow to give it more power. Talisman's upper body whipped back and Bolan made only glancing contact with the bigger man's throat. His adversary took three steps back, clutched his throat and gagged but didn't fall. Bolan wanted to press the advantage, but Talisman continued to wave the knife in wide patterns in front of him.

Bolan kept the man in soft focus, not concentrating on the arms or the legs, but on the whole body, and prepared for his next move.

Talisman moved forward, slashing the air with the knife and driving the soldier back. The blade's tip caught the front of Bolan's jacket, sliced a three-inch gash through the material but missed the flesh underneath. Talisman continued forward trying to crowd Bolan with his greater bulk.

The Executioner cracked his opponent hard in the face twice, flattening Talisman's nose and causing the bigger man to drop back and give him a wider berth. Hitting Talisman was like striking granite.

The African snapped a kick for Bolan's groin. The Executioner spun and bore the brunt of the impact on his hip. It struck Bolan like a gunshot and knocked him backward. His hip and thigh went numb, but Bolan knew pain would kick in after the shock and adrenaline wore off. He covered the distance between the men with a snap kick that plunged into Talisman's solar plexus.

Bolan let his momentum propel him deeper into the fray. As Talisman bowed at the waist to protect his midsection, the Executioner grabbed the African by the ears, yanked down on Talisman's head as he drove his knee into the man's face.

Talisman ran an arm across his mouth, wiping at the torrent of blood that cascaded down his lips and chin from his broken nose. He stared at the blood staining the back of his hand. Swaying a bit, he flashed Bolan a smile.

"I'm going to kill you for this," he said.

The gunrunner threw a punch at Bolan's head. The Executioner rolled with the blow, but gave up ground as Talisman closed in. A glint of steel registered with Bolan. He threw down a low block that stopped his adversary's knife strike cold while also shooting an uppercut into the African's jaw.

Talisman staggered back against the wall, but used the surface as a launching pad for another strike. Careening toward Bolan, he slashed at the air and let out a thunderous shout. But he was shaky enough that Bolan sidestepped the attack and drove a fist into the bigger man's kidney as he sailed by.

Talisman groaned, sank to his knees. Rolling onto his back, he sliced the air with wide strokes. The blade kept Bolan at bay, but the unfocused swings told him that the man had lost most of his steam. A kick from the soldier knocked the knife from Talisman's grip, sent it skittering across the floor.

Clearly defeated, Talisman did the unexpected: he laughed.

Bolan retrieved the Beretta, reloaded and charged the weapon, drawing down on Talisman's head.

The gunrunner's laughter degenerated into coughing, and blood began to froth at his lips. When the hacking subsided, he regained his composure and his smoldering eyes bored into Bolan's own.

"You've won the battle, but you lost the war," he said.

"What the hell does that mean?"

Talisman smiled. "You'll find out. There are things in motion that you just can't stop."

Bolan wasn't in the mood for games, especially from this murderer. "I'll find out now," the soldier said in a graveyard voice. "It's the only way you're leaving this room alive."

"If I talk, my life's not worth a damn. Kursk will see to that."

"We can give you protection from him," Bolan said.

Talisman stared at him for a long moment, then shook his head. "There is no protection against Nikolai Kursk."

"At this moment, I'd say he's the least of your worries," Bolan replied. "Where is he?"

"He has an island."

Bolan tightened his finger on the trigger and never let his gaze waver from Talisman's bloodied face. He was bargaining with the one chip he had—Talisman's life—and he was ready to take it all the way. "Where?"

Another pause, a last bit of token resistance, and then Talisman gave him the coordinates.

Footsteps sounded in the hallway, catching Bolan's attention. The Executioner kept the Beretta trained on Talisman, but peered over his shoulder and saw an assault rifle's muzzle protrude through the doorway. An anxious Nigerian soldier wielded the weapon.

"Put down the gun and slide it toward me," the soldier shouted.

Bolan complied. The soldier yelled that the room was all clear and a second figure, a Nigerian officer with a red beret, appeared in the doorway. He scowled at Bolan, and the Executioner realized he'd met the man earlier in the aftermath of his previous battle.

"You? I'll be damned if I let you walk away from this, too. I don't care who you are," the peacekeeper said.

Suddenly the foot soldier's eyes widened and his weapon's muzzle shifted a few inches to Bolan's left. At the same time, something scuffled behind Bolan. An icy sensation washed over him as he realized he was unarmed.

The assault rifle cracked three times. Bolan watched as the slugs pounded into Talisman. Two ripped open the man's chest while a third pierced his left shoulder. Talisman had produced a stubby automatic pistol from somewhere, and his dead finger tightened on the trigger once in a final reflexive move. The small pistol's report filled the room, and a bullet tore into the floor inches from Bolan's feet.

Keeping his hands partially raised, the big American stepped to the corpse and kicked the weapon away. It seemed like the only thing he could do.

NATASHA RYTOVA PITCHED to the side and drew down on the gunman with the hostage. The weapon bucked twice in the Russian woman's hand, and the twin reports echoed through the narrow chamber. Slugs ripped open the gunman's cranium and covered the woman and the walls with a crimson spray. His weapon slipped from his grasp and clattered to the floor.

The woman fell to the ground, clutching her child and sobbing. She curled up on her side and wrapped her body around the baby to shield it from harm. At the same time, she screamed and tried to kick the gunman's corpse away from her.

Rytova wanted to help but knew the second gunman remained at large. A Nigerian soldier brandishing an AK-47 bolted up the stairs and inserted himself between the young mother and any potential danger. The muzzle of his kalashnikov rifle centered on Rytova's midsection. A second soldier also sprinted up the stairs and drew down on her, rooting her to the spot.

"Put down the gun," one of the soldiers ordered.

Rytova hesitated for a moment. The scuffle of footsteps and a slamming door caused her heart to sink.

"The other man," she said, "he's getting away."

The soldier's voice got louder. The second soldier shouldered his assault rifle and centered it on her head. She knew only too well the damage a round from the rifle could inflict on unprotected flesh. "The gun," he said, "now."

She set down the SIG-Sauer and raised her hands.

6

The army of killers was ready to move.

Inside a hangar on the island's southern tip, Nikolai Kursk stared at the two dozen fighters assembled before him in three neat rows of eight. He plucked the cigarette from his mouth and tossed it to the concrete floor. Despite the early-morning hour, heat and humidity already permeated the island, dampening his short-sleeved shirt against his thick torso.

None of the men were armed, but canvas bags stuffed with MP-5s, AK-47s, Uzis, Berettas, web gear, night camouflage and other tools of war lay at their feet.

They all knew the plan, had drilled it mercilessly for months.

"The helicopters will take you to the mainland," Kursk said. "You'll disperse and take separate flights from different countries and converge on America. You'll travel completely unarmed and will do nothing to arouse suspicion. If you are caught, I promise you'll not survive a single night's incarceration. Do you understand?"

"Yes, sir," the soldiers shouted in unison.

"We reconvene in Nevada in two days. You will meet with our liaison and his team at 2100 hours. He has gathered two Black Hawk helicopters. You will use them to storm the base. The facility has six Apache helicopters, two in the air at all times. The advance team will disable the grounded choppers, communications and radar before you land. Securing the base is your problem. So is getting the pilot to the airplane. If he gets caught in the crossfire, scuttle the entire mission."

He paused, leveling his gaze at the men.

"And if that happens, don't bother coming back. I'll find you. Trust me."

The men stayed inscrutable, but Kursk could sense fear rising up from them like mist from the ground.

Kursk continued. "You'll have to kill people. The base is full of civilian workers. We want no witnesses. You will have to murder what some would call innocent people. Can you handle that?"

The mercenaries shouted as a single chorus. "Yes, sir."

Kursk smiled. Greed made men malleable, allowed them to rationalize otherwise abhorrent behavior. They were selling their souls to him in exchange for a few million dollars.

"Make this operation seamless. Kill anyone who could compromise our success. That includes one another. Otherwise you stand to lose what has been promised to you. Would that be acceptable?"

The response rattled the hangar's metal roof. "No, sir."

"Just remember," Kursk said, "the plane gets off the ground first. You stay behind until it has gotten away safely. Then and only then will the helicopters return to pick you up. You have a very short window of time in which to make this happen. If any one of you fails, we all fail."

He passed his gaze over the front row, pinning down select soldiers as he did. He sensed their discomfort, reveled in the rush he gained from intimidating others, especially warriors such as these men.

Many of these same men had been inside his study when he killed Blood Claw. They knew he was cold and ruthless. Gallons of blood stained his hands and would never wash away.

Every man was only as good as his last mission, ultimately expendable.

He paid them handsomely when they succeeded.

They paid in blood if they failed.

This time they'd pay with their lives, regardless of the outcome. He'd set in motion a plan to make sure that happened.

He dismissed the troops and watched them scramble from the hangar to the choppers awaiting them on the tarmac.

This mission would end in a firestorm. One that would tear at the heart of America, and bathe in hellfire anyone unlucky enough to come in contact with Kursk, the Nightwind or the Nevada base.

It would be a horror show. And the Russian knew he'd enjoy every last minute of it.

JACK COLE STOOD outside the island's main house, watching as screeching gulls reached the apex of their flight and dived just out of sight behind the security wall surrounding the compound. The tide crashed steadily against nearby rocky beaches, but as Cole listened he felt anything but soothed. Instead, his jaws clenched tight like a pit bull clamping down on a rag, and acid churned in his stomach.

Cole didn't consider himself a tree hugger, and most days he all but ignored the wealth of natural beauty that surrounded him. But with Nikolai Kursk's death threat still booming in his brain, he couldn't help but pick up the rhythmic sounds, sniff the brine-tinged air with new attention. Every little sound, every move, every smell, registered on his internal radar like a fleet of enemy aircraft carriers moving within striking distance.

Despite his cool demeanor, Cole hadn't taken Kursk's threat lightly. Without a doubt, the Russian was a psychopath, and one of a short list of people Cole couldn't charm or intimidate. That made the man doubly dangerous. It also hastened the moment when Cole would have to tender his resignation either by flashing Kursk the middle finger or putting a bullet in his psychotic head.

Leave quietly or escape soaked in Kursk's blood, it mattered little to Cole.

He just wanted his damn money. The promise of a big payday tied him to Kursk and his organization. Once he got the two million dollars the Russian had promised him, he'd pound sand. Preferably, he'd saunter away with Kursk's death rattle reverberating in his ears.

Cole plucked the cigar from his mouth, absently flicked some ash from the smoldering tip and smiled at the image. There was little love lost between himself and the Russian. But Kursk did respect Cole's prowess for psychological warfare and black ops. Since joining Kursk's organization, Cole had enjoyed Kursk's ear and a blank check whenever he needed it. Or at least he had until yesterday's debacle at Talisman's compound.

The American's intervention had cost Cole more than a couple of fighters. It had cost him credibility.

The big American had made Cole look like a moron. Left him to fret about saving his own ass and preserving the biggest payday of his life rather than enjoying the downhill ride as the merc team traveled to America to handle the heavy lifting.

But death seemed to follow this guy everywhere. Word was Talisman and four of his guys had died at the apartment building while a sixth escaped. That weasel Moeller bought it, too. Cole felt goose bumps rise along his skin and a chill passed down his spine.

Enough, he told himself. You're acting like a scared old woman. If that bastard came here—and Cole had no reason to believe he wouldn't—then he'd burn the guy down. With that done, he might mutiny against Kursk, solve two problems in one day....

A voice sounded behind him. "Jack, we've got a problem."

Cole turned and saw Daniel Emmett approaching. Emmett was reed slim. He kept his reddish hair cut well above the ears and collar. A neatly trimmed red beard peppered with white and gold covered the lower half of his face.

Cole exhaled acrid cigar smoke, peering through the cloud at the man. "What the hell's gone wrong now?" he asked.

"Iron Man contacted us. The American has disappeared from Sierra Leone. He and the Russian bitch are coming this way."

"They using air or sea?"

"We're thinking the sea. Guys have been watching the airports and haven't seen a damn thing. They could have him on a boat and near the island in a couple of hours. Probably dump him off in a rubber raft and let him paddle or swim the rest of the way here."

Cole nodded. "Makes sense. You get any more intel on the guy?"

Emmett grinned. "Not from Iron Man. Nobody talks to that son of a bitch, especially now that Talisman's dead."

Cole returned the cigar to his mouth and spoke around it. "But you got something."

"Yeah. Our contacts told me he's U.S. Justice Department. Name's Matt Cooper. At least that's what he told the peacekeeping troops."

"You don't buy it?"

Emmett shrugged, scratched his beard absently as he spoke. "I sent the name to Washington. And I gave it to Armstrong to run. No one could find the first thing on the guy. But he's obviously got connections. He whipped through Freetown like a hurricane and walked away. Not many have that kind of clout. We were both with the Company long enough to know that. Personally, I don't think there is a Matt Cooper."

"He exists," Cole growled. "Trust me."

"Agreed. I just don't think his name is Cooper."

"Does it matter?"

Another shrug, more scratching of the beard. "Depends on who he really is, who sent him and how much they know about Nikolai Kursk and Trevor Dade."

A handset clipped to Emmett's belt trilled for a moment. He plucked it, raised it to his mouth and began to speak. The deeper into the conversation Emmett went, the more his forehead creased, the more his scowl deepened. He killed the connection and let the hand holding the walkie-talkie hang by his side. "We had a boat stop about two miles out from shore, stay long enough to dump someone off and then leave. Guy's probably coming here even as we speak."

"How soon?"

Emmett shrugged. "Thirty minutes. Maybe longer."

Cole nodded grimly. "Gather the troops. Let the dumb bastard come to shore. Then take him down. I want confirmed kills. Both of them."

"Right. You got any ideas on the guy's next move? Any thoughts on how to get him?"

Cole's forehead creased for a moment as he thought. He imagined himself in the Justice guy's position. A scenario unfolded before him in his mind.

He grinned. "Bet your ass I do."

As HE AWAKENED from a fitful sleep, Trevor Dade sucked in a deep breath of air fouled by stale smoke, spilled whiskey and body odor.

Rolling onto his back, the scientist wiped grit from his eyes, then shielded them from the slivers of yellow sunlight slicing into the room from around heavy drapes. He tried to raise himself from the bed, but found flaccid muscles unwilling to respond. He decided to stay put and have a cigarette.

Another day in paradise, he thought.

He heard soft breathing next to him and looked over at the dark body sharing his bed. One of Kursk's whores had fallen asleep with her feet on the pillow next to his and her head resting at the foot of the bed. Another hooker lay on the floor, immersed in a drug- and alcohol-induced slumber.

An image of last night's party filled Dade's head and he allowed himself a smile. The Russian was a bastard, but he did know how to treat a guest.

Dade almost laughed out loud at that one. Guest? When he'd first arrived in his room, the door slammed behind him and a dead bolt had been thrust into place with the startling report of a rifle shot. The scientist had drawn back the drapes and been treated to a gorgeous ocean view interrupted by five vertical steel bars.

Kursk could talk all he wanted about the two of them being partners. But Dade was a realist; he was a prisoner. Forget that he'd agreed to fake his own kidnapping and had willingly let Kursk's people spirit him away from his home. He'd been duped, and now he found himself under the Russian's yoke.

It had seemed like a good idea at the time. Kursk had promised him a fresh start and enough money to make his bulging trust fund seem squalid. And, of course, the scientist had jumped at the chance to stick it to Sentinel Industries before company officials could fire him.

Screw Kursk and Sentinel Industries. Dade decided he'd show everyone just how destructive one man could be.

He crushed the cigarette's glowing red tip against the tabletop. With a grunt, he brought himself to a seated position at the edge of the bed, set bare feet against the plush carpeting. Standing, he crossed the room stiffly, plopped himself onto a couch and turned on a small table lamp.

"What the hell?" the woman on the bed said. With a bare arm, she shielded her eyes from the intrusive light. Dade recalled her saying something about being from Las Vegas. Kursk and Ivanov shipped women here to entertain the troops, let them do short tours of duty for big bucks. A sleazy USO tour for an army of bloodthirsty psychos.

The hooker's voice softened. It was her professional voice. "Turn that light off, baby. Come back to bed."

Enraged, Dade picked up an ashtray and heaved it across the room at the woman. The heavy glass object hit her square in the back, causing her to yelp.

"Shut the hell up, woman," Dade yelled. "I'm trying to think here."

An unsure grin played on the woman's lips as she studied Dade's face. Grabbing a sheet from the bed, she wrapped herself in it and walked over to the second woman. She nudged the woman with the toes of her left foot, but kept her eyes locked on Dade. The other woman finally stirred.

"Get up, Cindy," she said. "Nikki stuck us with another freak."

Still groggy, the second woman got to her feet and wrapped herself in a blanket. After two sharp knocks on the door accompanied by some yelling, a guard opened the door, allowing both women to leave. Still intoxicated, the second woman had to lean on the first for support as they walked out.

The guard slammed the door shut, sealing Dade back inside with the dead bolt.

Finally, he was alone.

The longer he considered Kursk's plans, the more the scientist seethed. Ultimately, Dade didn't care whether Kursk stole the plane or committed mass murder. Fine, he could live with that. But Kursk thought he could play Dade—one of America's greatest minds—for a fool.

Let him try. No one played Trevor Dade for a fool, period.

From a vial, he dumped some white powder onto a small mirror. Steadying the rectangular piece of glass with the thumb and index finger of his left hand, he picked up a razor blade with his other hand. As he ran through his plight in his mind, he absently began chopping up the cocaine.

A guard posted outside the door coughed, and Dade scowled. He had no money with him, but had millions stored in offshore accounts that he could get his hands on with a few phone calls or access to a computer. More than enough to get a couple of these gun-toting morons to help him get off the island, get away from Kursk.

A pang of fear passed through his stomach. Trying to turn Kursk's men against their boss was risky. They could turn him in, maybe for a better reward, and he'd die at Kursk's hands.

Dade snorted the cocaine, went to the bathroom and spent twenty minutes under a steaming shower. By the time he had shaved and slipped into fresh clothes, the nagging fear had dissipated. The cocaine always took the edge off. He felt confident, ready to make the guard an offer too good to refuse.

He knocked on the door.

MACK BOLAN STOPPED the Swimmer Delivery Vehicle one hundred yards from the shoreline. Disengaging himself from the craft's built-in oxygen supply, he grabbed the regulator, stuffed it in his mouth and cleared it of excess water. He began taking long, steady pulls of air from the twin-cylinder scuba system attached to his back.

A dark shadow moved overhead, prompting him to look up. He saw Rytova had unhooked herself from the SDV and was distancing herself from the conveyance. Bolan patted down the weapons he carried in watertight containers. He was ready to take the war to Nikolai Kursk.

Inflating the buoyancy control device, careful to compensate for the weight of the weapons and tools on his body, Bolan pushed off from the SDV. Pulling the craft to a rock ridge about fifty feet below the surface, he secured it against some rocks. He unhooked a small weapons bag outfitted with an air bladder from the SDV and kicked away from the vehicle.

As he took in air with measured breaths, bubbles roared around his lips and rushed past his ears. He'd wanted a bubbleless rebreather system for the infiltration. Unfortunately, because of time constraints and meager equipment offerings, he'd been given two options: use scuba or hold his breath.

About twenty yards from the island, Bolan signaled Rytova and pointed at a large pipe that extended from a gentle slope of rocks positioned over their heads and about twenty feet below the surface.

According to intelligence nailed down by Stony Man's cyberteam, the island had been a small, but expensive resort a decade or so ago before Kursk's people had swooped in and forced the corporate owners to sell.

The cyberteam had hacked around until they found a series

of drawings detailing the original structure and its water system. Any changes made by Kursk were a wild card and rendered the intelligence questionable at best. A fresh set of satellite photos supplied Bolan with information that qualified as better than nothing, but only barely.

He cut across the currents and came up to the entrance. As expected, Kursk had realized the vulnerability created by the tunnel and had sealed it with a thick mesh of steel bands interwoven with sensor wires.

Bolan weighed whether to risk the time and effort necessary to infiltrate the tunnel. He assumed Kursk, Cole and anyone else who mattered knew he was coming. Bolan had figured all along that the gunrunner was receiving intel from people both inside and outside the law in Sierra Leone. The State Department's dead security team and the equally dead Ronald Moeller underscored that grim point.

The best Bolan could hope for was that Kursk was expecting his arrival, but wasn't sure when or where the fireworks would start.

Bolan planned to start them soon. But he needed some time. Signaling Rytova to watch his back for him, he began working to bypass the alarm hooked to the grate.

JACK COLE MOBILIZED a dozen well-armed soldiers as he steeled the island for a visit from the man known as Cooper.

Cole rode shotgun in the Land Rover, while Emmett drove. Neither man spoke. There was no need; Cole had already laid out the plan. Instead, he cracked a clip into the Colt Commando assault rifle, chambered a round and stared ahead. He felt his teeth clamping together, his heart pounding as the vehicle neared the water-treatment plant. Adrenaline rushed through him, making his vision seem clearer and giving him a rush that was downright euphoric. He'd take this son of a bitch, he decided. Or at least die trying.

As the vehicle passed down the hand-hewn trail it kicked up

roiling clouds of tan dust. Dirt and rocks popped underneath the tires as the vehicle crept along the path. A pair of hardmen walked point about ten feet from the Rover's grille, scanning the surrounding foliage. A fifth gunner manned the mounted machine gun in the back of the vehicle. A pair of divers seated in the back seat performed last-minute checks on their equipment.

In brief, measured statements Cole had alerted Kursk to the impending infiltration. Kursk had greeted the news with stony silence. His rage spoke for itself, a silent but tangible force—a force Cole knew would be directed at him before all was said and done.

He had sought to reassure Kursk, but to no avail.

Cole had spent ten years as a U.S. Army Ranger before working for the CIA where he specialized in staging secret paramilitary operations. He was a professional soldier, and he thought he deserved some respect from that coldblooded thug.

Emmett brought the vehicle to a stop.

Cole noticed that his anger was causing him to grip the Commando's pistol grip so tightly that his knuckles had turned white and begun to ache. He pushed it away and cleared his head, knowing he had to stay sharp until the danger passed. One of the soldiers walked to the gate, unlocked it and swung it open. The second gunner covered the first, then moved inside the fenced area, followed by the first. The two men continued to leapfrog covering each other's approach until they disappeared from view. Thirty seconds later, the soldiers returned to the gate and motioned Cole and his people into the area housing many of the island's electric generators and the water treatment plant.

Back at the compound, Cole had figured the utility area as the island's weakest point, making it the most likely place for an enemy insertion. A large tunnel brought in thousands of gallons of sea water to be processed for use in toilets, showers, sprinklers and the like. Weekly shipments of bottled water were used for drinking and cooking. But with a few dozen people living on the island at any one time, the demand for water was endless.

A series of cameras positioned on the outcroppings surrounding the entrance monitored the area. More cameras positioned inside the tunnel offered a view of its interior, but were used primarily for maintenance purposes such as identifying blockages. Cole sat at a large console and began watching the screens for activity.

It didn't take long to find some.

He saw what he assumed was the Justice Department agent working to slice through the grate with a set of cutters. The woman watched Cooper's back while he worked. Cooper had disabled the alarm system before he began cutting at the grate. Not surprising, considering the level of skill the agent had exhibited thus far.

Cole had switched to a headset communicator before suiting up for battle. "Predator One, this is Command, do you read?"

"Predator One, go."

"You in position?"

"Almost, sir. What's the target's status?"

"He's at the grate, just like we expected. You ready to put in the divers?"

"Affirmative. Another two hundred yards and we can drop them in. Cut off the rear flank. You got them if they make it into the tunnel?"

"Right. We knew this damn tunnel was a liability. Kursk has outfitted it with a few surprises in case they get too far. You let me handle this end."

"Clear, Jack." The headset went dead.

Cole watched Cooper work on the gate for another minute, before a shadow filled the picture and the monitor went black. Damn, apparently the Russian woman had found the camera and—judging by the speed with which it winked out—had deactivated the damn thing by yanking it free or smashing it.

No matter, he decided. If things went south and one or both

of them got past the first set of attackers and made it inside the tunnel, they'd find themselves surrounded by cameras and things a whole lot deadlier.

Either way, they were screwed.

Metal scraping on metal sounded behind Cole, prompting him to turn. He saw a pair of his gunners sliding a steel cover from the top of a large cylinder. The strain caused their muscles to bunch under their shirts and their faces to redden to the shade of cooked lobster as they hefted the cover and set it to the floor.

Cole knew the cylinder, which measured about four feet in diameter, was the access tower leading into the tunnel. Originally, it had been installed so divers could safely enter the passageway and clear blockages.

The divers who'd accompanied Cole in the Land Rover entered the room, masks poised on their foreheads, hoses tipped with mouthpieces dangling over their right shoulders. Each man fisted a speargun and carried a pair of combat knives, one on the hip, one on the right strap of his scuba tank.

Cole held up his hand to stop them and called over his shoulder, "You girls hold on a minute."

The cigar wagged between his lips as he spoke, shedding bits of ash on the control board. "If I have my way, these stupid bastards never will get close enough to warrant putting you guys in the water. Chances are, they'll never get past our first underwater team."

"And if they do?" one of the divers asked.

Cole stared at the man and grinned. "Then they're just delaying the inevitable."

GET FREE BOOKS and a FREE GIFT
WHEN YOU PLAY THE...

SLOT MACHINE GAME!

Just scratch off the silver box with a coin. Then check below to see the gifts you get!

YES!
I have scratched off the silver box. Please send me the 2 free Gold Eagle® books and gift for which I qualify. I understand I am under no obligation to purchase any books, as explained on the back of this card.

366 ADL D34F   **166 ADL D34E**

FIRST NAME   LAST NAME

ADDRESS

APT.#   CITY

STATE/PROV.   ZIP/POSTAL CODE

7	7	7	**Worth TWO FREE BOOKS plus a BONUS Mystery Gift!**
🍒	🍒	🍒	**Worth TWO FREE BOOKS!**
♣	♣	♣	**Worth ONE FREE BOOK!**
🔔	🔔	🍒	**TRY AGAIN!**

(MB-04-R)

DETACH AND MAIL CARD TODAY!

The Gold Eagle Reader Service™ — Here's how it works:

Accepting your 2 free books and mystery gift places you under no obligation to buy anything. You may keep the books and gift and return the shipping statement marked "cancel." If you do not cancel, about a month later we'll send you 6 additional books and bill you just $29.94* — that's a saving of over 10% off the cover price of all 6 books! And there's no extra charge for shipping! You may cancel at any time, but if you choose to continue, every other month we'll send you 6 more books, which you may either purchase at the discount price or return to us and cancel your subscription.

*Terms and prices subject to change without notice. Sales tax applicable in N.Y. Canadian residents will be charged applicable provincial taxes and GST. Credit or debit balances in a customer's account(s) may be offset by any other outstanding balance owed by or to the customer.

7

Using a pair of long-handled cutters, Mack Bolan severed the grate's final supporting strut and let the barrier fall free. It kicked up thick clouds of brown, and etched jagged lines in the vegetation blanketing the rock wall underneath the tunnel's mouth as it sank into the murky depths.

He'd spent two minutes deactivating the alarm and another minute slicing through the grate. Bolan assumed more alarms and other security devices remained inside the tunnel.

Rytova, in the meantime, had discovered a camera lens about the diameter of a pencil inside some nearby rocks and smashed it with the butt of her knife.

Bolan's combat senses suddenly came alive, warning him of impending danger.

Long shadows circled overhead and began descending toward him. A pair of divers, each armed with a carbon dioxide powered speargun bore down upon them. Bolan slid his war bag from his shoulder and jammed it into the mouth of the tunnel. Kicking fiercely and drawing a combat knife from his harness, Bolan rocketed up to meet the challenge. A spear flew past him, missing his head by inches and smacking harmlessly into the rock walls at his back.

Motion to Bolan's right caught his attention. With his peripheral vision, he saw Rytova also darting upward.

While the first shooter reloaded his speargun, the second drew down and fired at Bolan. The Executioner whipped to the side, and the spear's trident-shaped tip razored inches from his chest as he closed in on the hardmen.

Bolan rose face-to-face with the closest of the two men and drove an open palm under the diver's chin, pushing back the man's head and knocking him off balance. The speargun slipped loose from the man's fingers and he grabbed at Bolan with both arms, trying to get hold of his attacker. With his other hand, the Executioner brought up the combat knife and drove the blade into the man's rib cage between the third and fourth ribs, letting it bite deep into the man's heart. He watched life drain from the man's face. The diver's regulator came free as his mouth opened to utter a final cry of pain.

Grabbing the speargun and twisting his knife free from the corpse, Bolan sheathed the knife and reloaded the gun with the dead man's last spear.

Bolan turned and darted to the right, sharklike in his movements as he crossed the distance with sweeping kicks from his legs.

Just ahead, Rytova struggled with the second diver. The pair was at a stalemate as Rytova gripped the wrist of the man's shooting hand. Likewise he had caught her wrist in midlunge, fingers encircling her small wrists and holding her knife at bay. The fighter was a good deal larger than Rytova, and the fight seemed to be shifting in his favor. She had no solid surfaces to give her the leverage she needed to take the man down.

Raising the speargun, Bolan drew down on Rytova's opponent, but the pair's thrashing quickly caused him to lose his clear shot. He rushed forward through the water, ready to grab another shot or ditch the speargun and go hand to hand.

But Rytova turned the fight in her favor before Bolan got close enough to help.

Twisting her knife hand down, she drove steel into the man's wrist, slicing skin, tendons and muscle as she did. The move surprised the diver and he opened his mouth to scream in pain, letting the regulator slip free. Trying to grab some distance between himself and his opponent, the man began whipping his body about and eventually drove a foot into Rytova's gut to force her to loosen her grip on him.

Breath exploded from her lungs and she lost her own regulator and her grip on his arm loosened. The man slipped away. The hardman gathered up his regulator and shoved it back into his mouth, then surged back toward Rytova.

As the woman gathered her regulator and jammed it back into her mouth, her opponent was raising his speargun, ready to skewer her with the three-pronged spear.

Now less than five feet from the struggle, Bolan triggered his own weapon. The spear whizzed through the brackish water and bit into the man's back at the base of his neck. He thrashed around for a moment, simultaneously trying to assimilate the searing pain raging through his body and to retaliate against his attackers. Stabbing between the flailing arms, Rytova drove her blade into the man's Adam's apple and held it there until he concluded his death spasms.

Seconds later, Bolan and Rytova slashed apart their dead opponents' inflatable vests and let the corpses, weighted with lead belts and other equipment, sink like stones into the depths. Bolan also ditched the empty speargun.

Descending again, occasionally equalizing the pressure in his ears as he went, Bolan slipped into the tunnel with Rytova following a few feet behind.

Two down and how many dozen to go? Bolan wondered as he pushed farther ahead into the darkness. He had wanted to gather more intelligence on the island before hitting it, but that kind of recon took time. He didn't necessarily trust the numbers gathered by the satellite surveillance photos. If he was lucky, he might get a chance to do some observation on Kursk's main base before hitting it, once they got on the ground.

The numbers were falling too fast to sit back and try to gather a reliable head count. He was operating on Kursk's timetable, not the other way around. That meant he had to hit fast, hit hard, hit sure.

And make it out alive.

As he continued on, Bolan played the flashlight's beam over the cylindrical surface. Something metallic winked back, standing out in stark contrast against the grimy walls. He halted and held up a hand for Rytova to do likewise. Slipping the weapons bag from his shoulders, he passed it back her and closed in on the shiny object.

Worried that the tunnel had been rigged with an explosive trap, Bolan felt tensed muscles loosen when he saw the apparatus was a camera lens.

A hiss, followed by the thunder of metal striking concrete sounded behind Bolan, with the water magnifying the sound. Turning, the warrior saw a steel grate had dropped from the ceiling, separating him from Rytova and his weapons bag.

Bolan felt his breath quicken and his heartbeat accelerate as he realized he was trapped. He quickly brought both reactions under control while he decided on his next move.

He studied the grate for a moment. The barrier was composed of two-inch-thick steel bands that his cutters would never penetrate. Even trying to dismantle the gate would burn time and air, neither of which was in surplus. He estimated he had another hundred yards to cover before he could exit into the water-treatment plant's control room. Most likely, the path would be fraught with danger, and he needed air and energy to make the journey. He had no other choice but to proceed. And do it alone.

Using hand signals, he told Rytova to retreat. She hesitated for a moment, and Bolan guessed it was because she didn't want to leave him behind. Then she nodded, turned and shot back down the tunnel, eventually disappearing in the darkness.

With powerful kicks, Bolan thrust himself forward and prepared himself for his next encounter with death.

AS TREVOR DADE WATCHED, the guard pressed his thumb against a smooth pad built into a wall and waited for the reader to process his prints. After a second or so, the machine chirped and the steel door slid open with a hiss.

Dade felt the guard's fingers dig into his biceps and yelped in spite of himself. Blood flushed his cheeks as embarrassment washed over him. The bigger man shot him a disparaging look and hurled him through the open doorway like a sack of garbage.

After he regained his footing, Dade took in his surroundings. The massive room extended upward three stories, the entire height of Kursk's luxury home. A series of massive processors were positioned throughout the ground floor, their cooling fans humming in unison as the machines crunched mounds of data.

One floor up, a mezzanine stretched around three of the four walls, and two pairs of computer workstations sat on the east and west mezzanine ends. Four workers stared into their screens, apparently unaware of the intrusion.

Fucking geeks, Dade thought. So damned absorbed in their little digital fairyland that they didn't realize death had come calling for them.

Dade glanced at the guard, whose soulless eyes were scanning the room even as he raised his weapon. The scientist shuddered, but the Russian either didn't notice or didn't care. The muscles of the guard's angular jaw bunched and released as he looked around and identified his first kill.

The guard had been more than happy to turn on his boss for the promise of five million dollars to be deposited into a numbered account in the Cayman Islands.

Security cameras were positioned in every corner of the room. Dade turned to the guard and spoke slowly. "Did you deactivate those cameras?"

The big man gave him a hard stare. "Yes. And do not treat me like a moron. Or I will kill you."

For emphasis, the guard pointed the pistol's muzzle at Dade. "Right," Dade said.

The guard turned his back to the workers and screwed a sound suppressor into the pistol's barrel. Dade felt sweat break out on his forehead.

"Hey, what the hell are you two doing in here?" a voice called from above. "Ivan, you know this is an eyes-only facility. Get that guy out of here now."

Ivan turned and brought the small black gun up in his massive paw. The weapon coughed and a red hole appeared in the space between the speaker's eyes. His face froze in a death mask of shock as he stiffened, folded in on himself and tumbled down the stairs.

Before the death registered with any of the other occupants, the guard was sprinting across the room, bridging the distance between himself and the stairs in long strides. His bulky body moved at such a fast clip that it reminded Dade of those charging grizzly bears he'd seen on more than one nature documentary. The guard rocketed up the stairs, taking two steps at a time, homing in on a new target as he reached the apex of the stairs.

The gun coughed four more times, and Dade heard thumps as bodies hit the floor. One of the computer operators fell against the rail, a bullet wound clearly visible between his eyes. The man's glasses had been split in two and hung from the ear pieces as his sightless eyes locked with Dade's own gaze.

Witnessing a second murder snapped Dade from his shock. He felt his stomach convulse and tasted bile as it pushed its way to the top of his throat. Averting his gaze, he swallowed hard and began greedily inhaling and exhaling to keep from vomiting. Dade had seen corpses before, but never carnage like this. He wondered if he was about to pass out.

"Come," the guard growled.

Dade turned and saw the Russian holding a heavyset man by the collar of his green polo shirt. Like Dade, the man was struggling to catch his breath. Shiny patches of blood covered his clothes and face. His skin was colorless, either from fear or blood loss. Or both.

"I said come," Ivan repeated. This time, he underscored his orders by giving Dade a hard shove to the back.

Dade moved to the stairs and ascended with less vigor than his counterpart. As he neared the captive man, he realized the man hadn't been injured but instead had been showered by the blood of his comrades.

"He operates the computers," Ivan said. "He can get you past the security devices."

Dade looked away from the crimson-splattered man and pointed at a workstation. "Put him there."

The man sat down and let his fingers hover above the keyboard. He looked at Dade and the Russian expectantly.

"Find the files marked 'Sentinel Works,'" Dade said. Grabbing a pen and paper, he scribbled an address onto a piece of scratch paper and slipped it to the man. "When you find them, ship them to this address."

"These files are huge," the man protested. "You know how long this will take?"

"I don't care," Dade said. "Send them to this address and purge them from this system. Otherwise, you join your friends—fast."

Sweat had beaded on the computer operator's bald, freckled pate as his fingers danced across the keyboard, punching in a series of commands that even Dade had a hard time following. Windows flashed open, warning boxes presented themselves, but were quickly dismissed by the man as he dug deep into the computer's recesses to locate the secured files and send them out.

"Now destroy the system," Dade said. "The whole thing. I don't want Kursk able to send a simple goddamn e-mail when you're done."

The man gave Dade a hard look. "No way, man. That's suicide. None of us want to do that."

A hot wave of anger cascaded over Dade. He hated to be told no, especially by some workaday moron like this. He looked at the Russian guard, nodded at the computer operator. Ivan stuffed the sound suppressor into the man's left ear, eliciting a sob from the guy.

Dade moved in close to the man. "You want to tell me no twice?"

The man's fingers resumed their fast movement as the man began a meltdown sequence for the computer system.

"Will this affect Kursk's computers at other sites?" Dade asked.

The operator shook his head. "No way. When we destroy the system in one place, redundant systems at Kursk's other locations go on alert and seal themselves against all outside contact. They become self-contained until Kursk punches in a series of codes that reverse the process. That way, if someone hits one of Kursk's sites, the overall security of the organization's system won't be compromised."

Dade grudgingly admitted to himself that the Russian mobster was smarter than he had figured. But Dade knew he was the smarter of the two. And he'd stick it to the thug before all was said and done.

A security door leading into the mezzanine hissed open. A pair of guards bent themselves around the doorframe. Ivan turned and aimed his pistol at the men. Before he fired off a shot, their assault rifles blazed out twin lines of death that slammed into his chest. The onslaught shoved the guard against a rail and jerked his body around as lead burrowed into his chest and exploded from his back. The shooting continued, tearing the computer into shards of glass and plastic and showering the workstation with sparks. The stingers continued, ripping into the chest and head of the computer operator.

The fusillade stopped just inches short of Dade.

It was only after the room went silent that Dade noticed a hot wet sensation in the crotch of his pants and realized he'd pissed himself. Adrenaline and fear caused his body to tremble and made it hard to breathe.

Weapons held at the ready, the gunners walked through the haze of gunsmoke and closed in on Dade. He raised his hands without being told.

One of the men said, "Turn and face the rail. Clasp your fingers behind your head where we can see them."

Dade complied.

"Trevor Dade." The scientist's heart sank as he recognized Nikolai Kursk's voice. "You have made two very tragic mistakes, here my friend. You have betrayed me and underestimated me."

"Fuck you, Kursk," Dade said. His words had sounded strong in his head, but his voice sounded small and brittle as he delivered them.

"If you wanted to steal the damn plane, you should have told me up front. Truth was, you wanted both the plans and the plane. And didn't plan to split the fucking money with me. You were going to kill me."

"Turn to face me, Trevor Dade," Kursk said.

The scientist complied but kept his hands locked behind his head. Kursk apparently noticed that Dade had soiled himself and a grim smile creased his face.

"You're pitiful, Dade," Kursk said. "You wanted revenge on your employers so bad that you were willing to believe anything. This all goes so far beyond the plane and beyond your stupid little designs. It's much, much larger than you and your petty problems."

"What the hell do you mean?" Dade asked.

"It's about crippling a nation. Striking a blow so devastating that it will demoralize and frighten America and its allies. One of several blows, I am sure. It's about emboldening other countries to attack the United States, its allies and their interests by showing just how vulnerable they really are."

A smile ghosted Kursk's lips. "It's about chaos, really."

Dade tried to wrap his mind around the Russian's words.

"Are you talking about restoring Russia to superpower status?" he asked.

Kursk shook his head. "No, no. I have no allegiance to Russia. I have no illusions of world conquest or new world orders. I'm a businessman. Unrest, chaos and lawlessness breed war. I sell the instruments of war. The more chaos I create, the greater the demand for my wares. So I will wreak havoc on American soil. Scare the hell out of the United States and rock the world economy, all of which trickles down to fear, unrest and wars, both big and small. At the same time, I get the ultimate weapon to sell to the highest bidder. It's really that simple."

Fire lanced into Dade's stomach even before the gunshots echoed in his ears. He stumbled backward and collided against the ragged workstation, before pitching forward and landing on all fours. As his mind raced to assimilate what had happened, he touched his belly, brought up his hand to look at it, saw his own blood glistening on his palm.

The pain finally registered and he fell facedown against the ground, screaming and writhing, waiting for death to claim him.

MACK BOLAN'S COMBAT senses cried out, alerting him to danger before he heard or saw a thing. Killing his flashlight, he hovered in the darkness for a moment and stared at a bend in the tunnel twenty feet ahead of him. Seconds later, he saw white beams of light playing over the surface and heard the roar of air bubbles expelling from regulators out of time with his own breathing.

His opponents had to know he lay in wait for them. If he could hear them, it stood to reason that reverse was true.

Fisting his knife, he waited until the men rounded the corner, one right after the other. Each was armed with a speargun and wore a light affixed to his forehead. Bolan surged forward, slicing in a downward arc and skimming along the tunnel's bottom. As he descended, a pair of spears fired overhead, cutting through the space he formerly occupied before disappearing from view.

Bolan didn't give the men time to reload.

He rocketed toward the nearer man. The diver dropped his speargun and grabbed for a knife sheathed in an upside down position on the harness of his scuba gear. The man's fingers encircled the hilt, but before he could clear the scabbard Bolan came upon him. Pressing the man's knife hand firm against the scabbard, Bolan plunged his knife into the man's lower abdomen, ripped upward until the blade struck against bone. An inky cloud of blood filled the water between the men and temporarily obscured Bolan's vision. The man thrashed about, and the Executioner gave him a hard shove to free the blade. Bolan's knife hand stabbed out again and he scored a lucky hit to the rib cage that caused the man to go limp. Bolan tried to free the blade, but it had become stuck in the man's rib cage.

White light grew more imposing from behind Bolan, signaling the second attacker. Setting his feet on the tunnel floor, the soldier grabbed the dead man by the straps of his air tank, whirled him around and brought him up as a shield. The dead man's bulk moved slowly against the water, but the Executioner succeeded in bringing him around far enough to catch a spear slicing through the water in Bolan's direction.

A metallic thud sounded as Bolan's opponent dropped his spear gun and began scrambling for a knife.

The hardman lunged forward, steel jetting straight for Bolan's solar plexus.

The Executioner moved to the side, letting the blade pass just inches from his torso. Bolan's hands exploded forward, fingers digging into the man's neck and gripping his forehead. Arm, chest and shoulder muscles coiling, Bolan dragged the man in close and twisted until he felt the man's neck snap. The man's body went limp and Bolan let him go.

He negotiated the bend in the tunnel and saw a shaft of light beaming down into the water from above. He assumed it marked the exit; he had entered the final stretch. Another twenty yards and he'd be able to exit this tunnel. If they didn't seal the damn thing off and leave him in there to drown.

Bolan still had the Desert Eagle and the Beretta 93-R strapped to him in watertight cases. He also carried another piece of ordnance that might help him survive.

Might.

JACK COLE GROUND the edge of his cigar between his teeth as he stared at the video monitors and watched the intruder kill two more of his men.

Looking over his shoulder he saw two of his fighters standing next to the small tower that led into the tunnel. Turning back to his video monitor, he watched the diver nearing the tunnel's exit. The man paused for a second and looked directly into the camera lens. His image grew as he neared the glass eye and knelt by it. He pulled a spare air canister from his gear, raised it up and then brought its curved bottom down like a sledgehammer. For a moment, the blunt object filled the screen, causing Cole to blink.

The screen went black.

Matt Cooper was quickly making the odds even in what had started as a very lopsided game. Cole knew the next several minutes would determine who would walk away from the island and who would be carried off or dumped in the water as fish food.

"We lost visual," Cole called over his shoulder.

The men standing next to the tower shouldered their rifles and aimed into the hatch leading to the tunnel. Laser sights shot small red beams into the cylinder as the men swept their weapons around, trying to acquire a target.

A clanging sound emanated from within the tunnel, soft at first but growing in volume as it neared them. Cole swiveled in his chair and locked eyes with one of his men.

"Sir? Should we close the tower? Just leave the guy in there to drown?" the merc asked.

"Stand fast," Cole said.

Uncoiling from his seat, he crossed the room. He fisted a Beretta 92-F as he closed in on the cylindrical opening. The clanging continued.

Cole stepped to the tower and looked down. He heard water dripping somewhere in the system. Peering into the tunnel, he saw the surface smooth and unbroken, like black ice.

They'd turned off the pumps to reduce the risk to his men. Grilles covered the pipes drawing dirty water into the filtration system, so the men couldn't have been pulled into the cleaners. But the suction made it hard for a diver to control himself. It could even pin someone to the wall, leave them there to watch helplessly as they burned up the last of their air.

A lopsided grin creased his face as an idea hatched in his mind. What the hell had he been thinking?

"Seal the tunnel," Cole said. "I got an idea."

Slinging their weapons, the men bent and grabbed the lid by its carrying handles.

As they did, Cole decided to chance one last look in the tunnel. Afterward, he'd return to the control board and fire up the pumps. He peered into the dark hole and saw bubbles popping as they reached the top of the water line. Son of a bitch! He pointed the Beretta's barrel into the tube and fired off a quick shot.

Even as the echo of the 9 mm round died down, he yelled, "Move it."

An arm shattered the water's surface. A cylindrical object flew up the tube.

All hell broke loose.

MACK BOLAN KNEW he only had one chance to make it happen.

The warrior knelt several feet from the exit tower, watching as an occasional shadow fell across the shimmering column of light that shone down into the tunnel. He'd smashed the surveillance camera, so the soldiers up above had to know he was coming. A ladder, its surface slick with plankton and sludge, offered the only means of escape.

Bolan knew he'd need to make a hell of a racket to draw attention away from the tunnel so he could clear it without taking a bullet. He also knew just how to do it.

He removed his fins and weight belt, then drew in a final breath from his scuba tank before abandoning it, too.

Reaching behind him, the warrior grabbed a small, watertight case from his belt, brought it around front and ripped it open. From within the bag, he withdrew a small device—a fragmentation grenade designed by Stony Man armorer John "Cowboy" Kissinger. The weapon was small enough to hide in a pocket, but powerful enough to clear a room full of killers in the space of a couple of heartbeats.

Bolan stayed in the shadows, but positioned himself as close as possible to the exit tower. He felt his air burning down to nothing and knew he needed to pick up the pace if he was to make his plan work at all. Grabbing a second sealed bag from his belt, he ripped it open and withdrew his Desert Eagle.

Orange and yellow flashed down into the tunnel, and even through the layers of concrete and steel the explosion was impressive.

Ripping off his mask, Bolan shot up out of the water and gasped for air. Gripping the Desert Eagle tightly, he raced up the ladder, but stopped inches from the access tube's steel rim. He listened for a moment, trying to determine just how much damage the explosion had wrought.

Smoke stung his eyes and he could hear the moans of at least one gunner. The Desert Eagle leading the way, Bolan popped up from the tunnel, looking for targets and surveying the damage. He saw two men, one lying on either side of the tower. The blast had ripped open one of the hardmen from thigh to forehead, his body savaged by countless shards of stinging steel. A second man lay to Bolan's left, curled into a bloodied ball.

The growl of an engine starting caught Bolan's attention. He crossed the room in seconds and headed toward the door. He exited the building in time to see a Land Rover disappearing down the trail in a cloud of dust.

The soldier pegged the departure as a strategic withdrawal rather than surrender. Within a matter of minutes, he knew reinforcements would arrive, hoping to bring his time on the island to a quick, bloody end.

Checking the two bodies, Bolan recovered a Colt Commando undamaged by the explosion and several extra clips from both men. He also stripped one of the men of his pistol belt, which carried a Beretta 92-F and extra magazines.

Bolan exited the control house and tried to get his bearings. From his vantage point, he could see the main house's roof which towered above the trees a half mile to the northwest.

In between Bolan and the stronghold lay an untold number of troops fully aware of his presence and ready to gun him down. Unconsciously, he tightened his hold on the Colt Commando as he disappeared in the surrounding foliage. Sticking close to the towering palm trees and inserting himself into the shadows they cast, he padded deeper into the jungle. The reinforced soles of his scuba boots protected his feet from sharp-edged stones and other obstructions as he traveled.

His mind flashed to Rytova's welfare and, for a moment, he reconsidered his decision to include her in the mission. Someone had done a masterful job of separating them.

Divide and conquer.

Like hell.

Bolan took his first step onto a trail soon to be soaked with blood, fully prepared to walk his final mile, if necessary.

He vowed to not walk it alone.

8

The guard wasn't supposed to hear the Executioner coming.

But as Bolan emerged from the jungle the stout stalk of a plant snapped underfoot, diverting the man's attention from his cigarette to the soldier closing in on his back.

The guard had ventured too close to the jungle. Bolan had hoped to take the man down quietly, perhaps interrogate him and gather valuable intel regarding troop strength, perhaps even garner the man's help in breaching the compound.

Instead, the noise had ignited the hardman's combat reflexes and set him into action. In a single fluid motion, he turned, firing his Galil and trying to acquire a target as Bolan approached.

The Galil's snout was homing in on Bolan's chest, but he had the other man in his sights. The Beretta chugged once, spitting out a single 9 mm round, which burrowed deep into the man's cheek before ripping out the side of his head in a spray of blood, bone and brain matter.

As the man tumbled to the ground, Bolan continued on. He exchanged the Beretta for the Colt Commando as he went. The Galil's chatter had shattered the stillness along with Bolan's hopes for a quiet insertion. People already knew he was somewhere on the island. The Galil's burst just told everybody where.

It was time for the bigger firepower. The Colt carried a 30-round magazine of 5.56 mm and had a four-inch flash suppressor attached to the barrel's tip. Bolan switched the Colt to full-auto as he glided along the wall, eyes darting about, scouring the area for the next threat.

The intel had indicated the island's nerve center was located within a single sprawling compound positioned at the landmass's highest point. Satellite photos provided to Bolan by Kurtzman indicated the main complex included Kursk's home, dual helipads, the motor pool and several smaller, unidentified buildings. A twelve-foot-high security wall protected most of the compound's perimeter, while a sheer cliff plunged down the back side, making entry from that direction all but impossible.

If he wanted to locate Dade, Bolan had no other choice but to enter the main compound. He'd lost his climbing gear along with most of his other equipment back in the tunnel. That left him with a single option, and not a very good one at that: he had to go through the front door.

A flash of movement ahead caught Bolan's attention. A gunner popped up at the corner of the security wall, exposing his head, part of his upper torso and an Uzi submachine gun. Muzzle-flash blossomed from the SMG's barrel and autofire buzzed a path toward Bolan.

The Colt cracked out a smooth line of return fire that struck the wall just inches from Bolan's target. The rounds chipped away at the concrete and forced his opponent to take cover. Bolan bolted to the right, returning to the dense foliage that lay nearby. He emptied the Commando's clip on the run, peppering the wall with an angry swarm of slugs and keeping his opponent pinned down.

When the gun went dry, Bolan ejected the magazine and grabbed another from his seized combat webbing. As he recharged the weapon, the hardman braved the corner and came into view. He had his right arm raised overhead and appeared ready to lob something in Bolan's direction.

Fluidly, Bolan aimed the Colt and stitched the man from hip to shoulder with a quick burst. Even as bullets pulped the man's midsection, the grenade flew free from his fingers and arced in Bolan's direction.

The fragmentation grenade's smooth surface caught the sun's glare as it arced overhead and began its descent about ten yards from Bolan. The warrior ran the numbers in his head as he turned and ran. If the egg had a standard fifteen-meter kill radius and a four-second fuse, Bolan had two, maybe three seconds to get some cover.

The warrior sprinted for the nearby trees and underbrush. As the doomsday numbers plummeted to zero and the grenade boomed behind him, Bolan thrust himself into a tangle of plants. He landed on his belly, the impact driving out his breath. Though he had distanced himself from the kill zone, bits of razor wire whistled overhead, shearing the tall grass and plants and slicing the skin of the palm trees.

As the grenade's thunderclap died down, Bolan rolled onto his back and stared up at the emerald leaves of the palms. He took a moment to regain his breath while his right hand patted the earth, searching out the Colt Commando, which had slipped from his grip when he hit the dirt. He found it and let his fingers move over the smooth finish until they reached the pistol grip. He pulled the weapon to him and brought himself upright.

Moments later, Bolan was crossing the clearing. Hoping to scavenge more weapons, he knelt beside the corpse and stripped the guy of two fragmentation grenades. An access card with a magnetic strip hung from the man's neck by a thin chain. Bolan grabbed the chain and ripped the access card free.

The rumble of an engine, the grind of earth under wheels caught Bolan's attention. The noise originated from an opening in the trees to his right and about thirty yards away. At the same time, he also heard gunfire emanating from within the compound at his back. An image of Rytova in trouble flashed across his mind faster than he could will it away.

As Bolan got to his feet, a Land Rover rocketed out from the jungle and roared down a trail toward him. The arms and heads of shooters protruded from the vehicle's windows, and weapons rattled as they spit a hail of deadly fire in Bolan's direction.

The warrior spun and ran for the gate, feet pounding hard against the red earth. Staying close to the security wall, he dug the access card out of his pocket. From behind, he heard the Land Rover's driver red-lining the engine as he mashed the accelerator to the floor.

Bullets whistled as Bolan sprinted up the incline leading to the front entrance. Looking over his shoulder, he saw the Land Rover weaving back and forth as it struggled over deep ruts worn in the road. Bolan figured the jostling caused by the rough terrain probably was throwing off the gunners' aim and consequently saving his ass.

At least for the moment.

He knew Kursk's mercenaries were pros.

Ahead, a pair of hardmen bolted through the stronghold's front gates. Even as the gunners started to raise their own weapons, Bolan raked them with long bursts from the assault rifle, cutting down both men where they stood.

Bolan crested the hill, ran past the dead men and reached the gate, which was closing. He wedged himself between the two ends of the chain-driven gate as it slammed shut behind him.

The main house—a luxurious three-story structure—stood to his right about thirty-five yards away. Three other buildings, all single-story painted aluminum structures about twice the length of a suburban ranch home, stood in a row to his left. Bolan guessed the area contained the barracks and other utility buildings.

The soldier heard the steady whir of helicopter blades before he saw the craft. Looking toward the house, he glimpsed the whirling rotors as they peeked just above the roofline for a moment before the chopper came in to full view. The aircraft hovered for a moment and machine guns erupted, raining down a punishing volley of slugs that shredded the house's exterior.

Before Bolan could react, the helicopter shot farther up, whirled and winged its way toward the Atlantic Ocean.

He cursed under his breath. If Dade was on the chopper, the

mission had been a bust. From the start, Bolan had had serious misgivings about pulling the scientist's fat from the fire, considering his fast and loose lifestyle and how he'd jeopardized national security. But the warrior had agreed to do it for a greater good. Thus far, he'd gotten zilch in return.

A mechanical growl sounded behind Bolan. He whirled in time to see the Land Rover, knobby tires kicking up long plumes of dirt, as it carved out a collision course for the gate. Steel clashed against steel. The barrier bowed under the battering but didn't give. The driver slammed the Land Rover into Reverse, grabbed some running room and accelerated again. A glance at the twisted metal gate told Bolan it wouldn't withstand a second strike.

He needed to get some combat stretch. The sprint to the house was too great to make before he became a hood ornament. He'd have to make a run for the aluminum buildings. Bolan raced over the expanse of barren earth and headed for the nearest of the three buildings.

At the same time, the Land Rover broke through the gate and roared into the compound. It immediately swerved in Bolan's direction and, with engines whining, bore down on him.

A brick wall rose about four feet from the ground and surrounded the group of buildings. Bolan willed his legs to move faster as he closed in on the barrier and without breaking stride, he vaulted over it and sprinted between two of the buildings.

The Land Rover ground to a stop, and Bolan heard doors snap open as a group of gunners disgorged from the vehicle. Two of the men pursued Bolan into a valley between the buildings while the third went MIA. On the run, the warrior plucked a frag grenade from his web gear, yanked the pin and lobbed the weapon behind him.

As he raced out from between the buildings, he thrust himself into a deep rut and burrowed in for cover. The grenade discharged, raking the area with shrapnel and flame and cutting anguished cries short. Holding the Colt Commando close to his body at waist level, Bolan checked the blast site and found what appeared to be the remains of two men.

Stepping back into the open, Bolan spotted a slender, red-haired man sprinting for the main house. Recalling the intelligence photos supplied by Stony Man Farm, he identified the guy as Jack Cole.

Bolan knew the rogue CIA agent had been part of the team trying to ambush him at Talisman's compound. Chances were he'd had a hand in the murders of the State Department agents. That made Cole a traitor of the highest order. And, even if Bolan had lost Kursk and Dade, he'd consider the mission a partial success if he could eliminate Cole.

It was better than nothing.

But not by much.

Yeah, he'd hunt the guy down, lean on him to find out what he knew about Kursk's plans. He'd make sure the treasonous agent was served justice.

HIDDEN IN A TANGLE of tall grass, Natasha Rytova rested her gaze on the sentry standing several yards to her left and thought about how best to take him down.

Sheathed in a Kevlar vest, eyes obscured by mirrored aviator shades, the man stood a foot away from the security wall, an AK-47 canted across his chest.

Fear fluttered about Rytova's stomach like a moth circling an exposed light bulb as she decided her next course. She guessed the man outweighed her by at least one hundred pounds. And he was heavily armed with an assault rifle, a pistol and a combat knife in plain view and who knew what else hidden on his person.

Even with her training, she could end up losing if she undertook a head-on clash with this man.

Undoubtedly, the quickest path to survival was to exterminate him with a bullet to the brain. Clean, neat, precise.

The question was could she do it? Not could she kill; she'd already done that many times over, but always in self-defense.

Could she shoot an unsuspecting person, even one she considered a murderous thug? That posed a whole new dilemma for her.

And what about Nikolai Kursk? The question had nagged her since she'd started this quest months ago. What if he raised his hands and surrendered? What if the same man who'd killed her father and husband in cold blood begged her for mercy? What then?

Finally, she shoved the conjecture away.

She bracketed the big guard in the sights of her SIG-Sauer and tightened her finger on the trigger.

A crack, distant and muffled, broke the stillness. The guard turned, looking in the direction of the noise. As chatter broke out on his headset, he cocked his head, listened.

He replied in Russian. "Yes, yes, I understand," he said. "I will stay at my post."

Almost as soon as he said the words and killed the connection, he began running along the length of the security wall and heading for the fight.

The guard made Rytova's decision for her. Breaking cover, she drew down on the man. If Cooper was waging war elsewhere on the island, she couldn't stand by while this man went to join the fray.

"Stop!" she yelled in Russian.

The man halted.

"Drop your weapon."

The AK-47 thudded as it hit the ground.

"Turn toward me."

The man did. He stared at the Russian woman.

"I hope you can shoot that pistol well. It's much bigger than you are." A grin spread across his features. "I am much bigger than you are, for that matter."

Hot rage flushed Rytova's face.

"The other weapons," she snapped. "Drop them now."

Unsheathing the knife, he chucked it several feet away, then unholstered his pistol and set it lightly on the ground.

"Turn and lie facedown on the ground. Put your hands behind your head."

The man turned, dropped onto one knee. He kept his left biceps level with his shoulders, while his forearm shot up at a ninety-degree angle and his palm faced forward. His right hand drifted out of sight. He whirled at the waist, clutching a small, black pistol and hastily tried to acquire a target.

The SIG-Sauer bucked twice against Rytova's palm as she cored two shots into the man. One hammered into his throat, a second into his mouth.

The guard's body convulsed for a minute as his overloaded nervous system worked in vain to understand the trauma gripping his body. He went still and pitched forward, dead.

Rytova noticed her hands trembled, and she bit hard on her lower lip. Fighting to regain her professional detachment, she turned to the wall and appraised it, shoving the image of the dead man from her mind. Solid. Poured concrete. No hand- or footholds. Fifteen feet high. Ornate iron lamps positioned along the top ledge every fifteen feet or so. A small rail ran the length of the walls.

Reaching into her bag, she extracted a length of nylon rope tipped with a black rubber-coated grappling hook. Tossing the rope up and over the wall, she pulled back on it until one of the claws caught under the railing. She tugged at the rope, checking to see whether it would bear her weight, found that it would and began to climb.

By the time she reached the top of the wall, her shoulder and arm muscles burned from the effort. She ignored the discomfort, relying on the anger surging through her body and her countless hours of conditioning to shore up her stamina. Dmitri would have made the climb, she knew. He'd have walked through hell for her and never complained. Could she do any less? The answer was obvious.

Pulling herself onto the top of the wall, she dropped the rope down the other side, and rappelled quickly to the ground.

Moving into an angular shadow cast by the wall, Rytova checked her surroundings. An unmanned helicopter gunship sat nearby. The house was a luxurious three-story structure with a stucco exterior and a roof covered in ceramic tiles. Potted palms filled balconies running the lengths of the second and third floors. A tennis court and a swimming pool were set in back of the house.

A pair of women clad in bikinis lay in the sun, roasting their already dark skin to what seemed to Rytova to be the color and consistency of beef jerky.

Rytova guessed the women were hookers; she knew from Kursk's profile that he rarely surrounded himself with any other type of woman. Rytova also knew from her contacts in Moscow that it galled him to no end that a female was methodically damaging his criminal empire piece by piece.

A pair of gunners sprinted from the house, and Rytova burrowed deeper into the shadows. Instead of coming for her, though, they turned, headed around the front of the house and went to the front gate. One man swiped a card, opening the barrier, while the second man covered him. They disappeared from the compound, the gate sealing behind them.

Rytova made her way to the house, using the sweeping shadows cast by palm trees for cover wherever possible. She holstered the SIG-Sauer and replaced it with an Uzi. She slipped up behind the women, drawing within a few feet of them before her shadow betrayed her approach. They turned in unison and one started to speak. Rytova held up a finger to silence her.

"I'm not here to hurt you," she said in a low voice. "Please be quiet. Things here are about to become very unsafe. You must go somewhere else. Do you have such a place?"

One of the women nodded and pointed west. "Nikki keeps a house for his ladies on the west beach. It's where we entertain."

Rytova nodded. "Have you seen a man, an American?" she asked. "He's a scientist."

The woman scowled. Rytova noticed her words were slurred

and she seemed to struggle as she put together her thoughts. "Oh, yeah, we seen him. Spent the night with the guy. He's a freak. Not a freak like kinky. But just a freak, you know?"

Rytova felt adrenaline-fueled anger ready to spill over. She glanced at the pool and watched as sunlight danced on small breaks in the surface. She sucked in a deep breath. "Please. Is he in the guest house?"

"Aww no, honey. He's in here." The woman nodded at the main house. Her voice went quiet, almost reverential. "Nikki says he's a real important guy. I still say he's a freak. Nikki always sticks us with the freaks." She said it as if she were sharing information with a close girlfriend. The woman's glassy red-rimmed eyes and constant sniffing indicated strong cocaine use.

"So he's in here?" Rytova asked.

"Yeah. He's on the third floor."

"Is there a cell in there?"

"A cell?" The woman paused for a moment. "Oh, you mean like a prison cell? Hell no. He's Nikki's guest."

"What?"

"Oh, yeah. All last night he was talking about him and Nikki this and him and Nikki that. How Nikki had promised him a big score, but ended up giving him the shaft. How 'he was going to get even with that big Russian SOB.' He's not a gnat on Nikki's ass, you ask me."

Gunshots sounded from within the house.

"Go," Rytova said forcefully.

The women stood and began gathering their things, but Rytova stopped them and ordered them to get moving immediately. As they padded across the grounds, Rytova switched her attention to the house.

Pulling back a sliding glass door, she entered a kitchen. She cleared that room and two other small spaces before passing into a dining room and a massive sitting room. Impossibly big crystal chandeliers were suspended overhead, and dark wood paneling seemed to suck the light from the room's interior, which was filled with leather-covered couches and chairs, and heavy oak tables.

Rytova felt an even deeper disgust for Kursk as she saw how well he'd been rewarded by his blood trade. While his "clients" slaughtered thousands—mostly the world's poor and down-trodden—Kursk lived in obscene luxury.

A circular staircase led to the second and third floors. Rytova had cleared most of the ground floor without incident. Uzi pointing the way, she started up the stairs.

As she stepped onto the second floor, a door ten feet to her left swung open and one of Kursk's soldiers emerged, a 40 mm Glock clutched in his right hand. Catching the movement in her peripheral vision, Rytova whipped toward the man and was locking the Uzi's muzzle on him as he came into view.

The man spotted Rytova, spun toward her and brought up his own weapon. Before he could squeeze off a shot, Rytova's sound-suppressed Uzi coughed out a burst that killed him almost instantly. She stepped over the body and continued deeper into the house.

Two wooden doors to her right were shut, and their handles didn't budge when she tried to open them. A sliding steel door at the end of the corridor opened, and a burly guard carrying an AK-47 stepped through the portal. Seeing Rytova, he squeezed off a hasty round in her general direction as he backpedaled for cover.

Rytova was already in action, unleashing a quick burst from her Uzi. The shots slammed into the man, digging into his body armor and causing him to stagger backward.

Even as that man reeled back, a second gunner armed with an Ithaca 37 bulled past his comrade and snap-aimed at Rytova. As he triggered the riot gun, his comrade fell against him and threw off his aim. Thunder echoed throughout the enclosed space as the shotgun blast tore through wood paneling and caused plaster to rain down from the ceiling.

The man who'd taken the hits to his chest clawed at his side arm as he dropped into a crouch in front of Rytova. She triggered the Uzi and planted another burst in the man's face.

The woman swung her weapon toward the gunner, caressed the trigger and came up with nothing. The gun was empty.

The gunner worked the shotgun's slide again, brought it to bear on her. As he did, Rytova wheeled and hurled herself through an open doorway. An instant later, the shotgun roared. The blast ripped through the wall, showering her with wood shavings and plaster dust.

Fear and adrenaline overtook Rytova, causing her to feel light-headed, her hands shaking as she tried to reload her weapon. Cracking the clip into the SMG's pistol grip, she heard the intimidating snap of a fresh round slamming into the shotgun's chamber. The shooter appeared in the hole in the wall, his eyes ablaze with anger. A shadow passed from behind as the gunner raised his weapon at Rytova.

"Fire," the shadow said. "Kill that stupid bitch."

Rytova's blood froze.

The voice belonged to Nikolai Kursk.

Rage replaced fear, and she brought herself up and began pounding her attacker with autofire. The man on the other side grunted as 9 mm Parabellum rounds thumped against his body armor, lanced through his head and hurled him away from Rytova.

Her submachine gun leading the way, she moved through the door. She heard Kursk's shoes clicking on the tiled floors below as he fled. Outside the house, she could hear the thrumming of an engine, the whipping of helicopter blades as somebody started up the gunship. If Kursk made it out of the house, she'd lose him for sure.

As she headed for the stairs, she heard groaning coming from within the room behind the steel door. A corpse lay on the sliding door's track preventing it from drawing shut. She dismissed the noises, figuring they came from one of Kursk's dying soldiers.

Then another thought seized her: it might be the American scientist. She had not yet seen him and he was supposed to be here.

Forget it, she told herself. The hookers said he was working with Kursk. That made him just as bad as Kursk, didn't it? But what if they'd lied to her? What if he was a hostage?

She wanted Kursk so bad she could taste it. He'd cut out her heart when he'd killed her family. Getting even had been the only thing that had kept her alive since her husband and father died violently. Now the bastard was within her grasp, and she wasn't sure what to do.

She made up her mind. She had to do the humane thing, while she still had some humanity left in her. Turning on her heel, she started toward the noise but held the Uzi at the ready. As she moved, she heard the chopper begin its ascent and she clenched her jaw to hold back the tears of frustration welling up inside her. She'd made the right decision, she told herself. It was really the only decision. This was all bigger than her and her vendetta. It had to be.

A cold pit of fear opened up in her stomach as she realized the chopper was hovering, rather than getting the hell away from the island. Driven by instinct and intuition, she burst into a run, vaulted over the dead man blocking the steel doorway and landed inside the cavernous room. She found herself on a mezzanine, surrounded by shattered machines and more corpses.

She saw an emaciated man laying on the floor, struggling for breath and gripping his abdomen, which was stained with blood. She started to say something to him, but the chatter of machine guns cut her off. A withering fusillade rained down from the helicopter, punching through the front of the house and chopping through furniture, walls and corpses like the blade of a buzz saw. Autofire blazed through the door and pounded into the mezzanine, tearing a path toward Rytova. Then as suddenly as it began, the shooting stopped and the sounds of the engines grew increasingly distant.

JACK COLE STEPPED carefully through the debris and made his way to the shattered front of the house. Bolan had double-timed it to catch up with him and watched as Cole slipped into the house, his Colt assault rifle leading the way.

Bits of glass, plasterboard and other debris lay in heaps around the ragged building, which only moments before had been lashed with a storm of hellfire. The concentrated assault had ripped doors from hinges and chewed large holes in the structure's facade. Two of Kursk's soldiers bobbed facedown in the pool, apparently sacrificed by the chopper as it escaped. The water around them was turning dark with their life fluids.

Rounding the corner, Bolan advanced in a crouch toward one of the gashes in the wall and peered inside. The assault by the gunship's chain guns had ripped large holes in the interior walls, allowing him to see large portions of the first floor from a single vantage point.

He saw Cole sneaking through the house, looking from side-to-side for potential threats. Bolan watched as something gripped the former CIA man's attention and he froze next to the circular stairwell. Holding the Colt in both hands, Cole launched himself up the stairs.

The Executioner stepped through the frame of a shattered sliding glass door and found himself inside a kitchen. The floor was a field of broken bottles, jars, plates and bowls, smeared sauces and spices and bullet-scarred woodwork. Bolan stepped on a curved shard of glass, heard and felt it pop under his foot. Even the small noise in the otherwise dead quiet house set his teeth on edge. He moved quickly through the rooms and made his way to the stairwell.

From above, Bolan heard a male voice shouting and assumed it was Cole.

"Son of a bitch got what he deserved," the man was saying. "If he'd just played ball, he'd be fine right now. Hell, we'd all be fine. Now we're just fucked. I was going to walk away with millions, and now I got nothing. I'm going to at least get the satisfaction of shooting this son of a bitch. And, honey, you're next."

Rytova's voice replied. "Stop and think. I'm armed, too."

"I guess I'll just have to shoot you first, then."

Bolan bounded up the stairs, two steps at a time. The rubber-soled scuba boots made only a slight scuffling noise against the oak steps. The noise didn't seem to register with Cole in his agitated state.

Bolan cleared the steps and saw Cole's frame standing in a doorway, back toward him. The warrior lined up his shot and said, "Freeze, Cole."

The other man stiffened. "Cooper. You going to shoot me in the back, Fed? Just what I'd expect from one of you Justice Department jerks."

"I'll show you the same kind of mercy you showed those State Department agents," Bolan said.

He was fishing and Cole took the bait.

"That was pretty sweet work, wasn't it? Nikki didn't think I'd do it. He thought I'd get all teary eyed about killing some Feds. But I popped those bastards right in the back of the head."

The Executioner had to stifle an urge to core a bullet through Cole's head. He needed to get Rytova out of harm's way.

"It doesn't have to be this way, Cole. You hurt that woman, and I kill you. You back off, and we'll take you into custody."

"So I can be charged with treason and killed with a lethal injection? Thanks, Cooper. You're all heart. But just go screw yourself, huh? You want to saddle someone with treason? Talk to this rich boy scientist here. He's the one who sold the Nightwind plans to Kursk. Just wait until you see what that Russian bastard has planned for the United States. Makes me glad I'm out in the middle of the Atlantic on this shitty little island."

"It's your call," Bolan said in a graveyard voice.

Cole had to have sensed the change in the warrior's speech. Whirling, he tracked for Bolan with the muzzle of his assault rifle. Bolan's own weapon cracked once. The slug ripped into the former spook's right ear, burrowing through his skull before exiting from the other side in a spray of gore. Cole crashed to the ground. His weapon came free from his grip and skittered across the floor.

Stepping over the body, Bolan entered the room and found Rytova kneeling on the floor. A slender man, sweating profusely, eyes screwed shut in pain, lay next to her. She had stripped the man of his shirt, wadded up the clothing and pressed it to an abdominal wound, trying to staunch the bleeding. She looked relieved when she saw Bolan fill the doorway.

"He's lost a lot of blood. It looks like two bullets entered at nearly the same point and ripped through his insides. I was going to call for help, when Cole showed up," she said.

Bolan knelt beside the stricken man. The floor was slick with the scientist's blood, and his face was pale. Rytova lifted the makeshift compress and let Bolan scan the wound. A glance told him the man was hovering close to death.

Dade locked eyes with Bolan, tried to stare him down. The soldier's steel-blue eyes registered no emotion.

"About time you people showed up," Dade said.

Bolan put some ice into his voice. "What did Cole mean? You gave Kursk the plans for the Nightwind?"

"Cole's full of shit," Dade rasped. The effort cost him and he winced in pain. He took a moment to collect himself. When he spoke again his voice had gone hoarse. "Why don't you just get me out of here? I'm the victim."

"Sure you are," Bolan said. "Why did Kursk shoot you?"

"I tried to escape."

"Bull. He'd have just put you back in your room if that was the case. He needed you to interpret the plans. You pissed him off, didn't you? What happened? You talk and I'll call for help."

"I'll have your job," Dade said.

"What happened?" Bolan said coldly.

Dade looked at Bolan. His pallor was almost grotesque in its intensity, but he was still clinging to the fantasy of surviving. "He screwed me," Dade said. "We were going to work together. But he made a deal with someone else, changed the plans. He made me look foolish."

"Who'd he make the deal with?"

"I don't know."

"Wrong answer."

"It's true."

"What's his angle?"

"Find out for yourself." Dade stared at the ceiling and gasped for air.

Bolan scanned the blood-splattered room for a satellite phone or other communication device. Finding one on a nearby table, he called for help. Fifteen minutes later as a team of helicopters descended on the island, he heard a rattle escape Dade's lips. The scientist shuddered one final time and slipped into death.

9

Nevada

Jon Haley settled into the soft living room couch and listened
as the grandfather clock chimed out the hour. Tipping his head
back and squeezing his eyes shut, Haley let the sounds carry
him away for a moment. He'd inherited the clock from his
mother when she died three years ago. But the sound always
took him back to his boyhood home in Arkansas when his par-
ents paid the bills while he played football and chased girls.

Now he and Monica shouldered the responsibilities. And
sometimes they seemed overwhelming, even with his pay as a
test pilot. Monica, a certified teacher, schooled the children at
home while he worked for Sentinel Industries. It had been a mu-
tual decision, and Haley considered his family a true blessing.
But just as often he felt as though he were running to stay in
the same place.

This was one of those days. The washing machine broke and
the transmission went in Monica's 1992 Chevy, both problems
clamoring for immediate attention—and money. This just after
they had paid for a new roof.

So he did what he always did: settle into the couch and
crack open a beer and listen to the chimes sound. Monica had
volunteered to put the children to bed and had promised to
return as soon as possible. She'd already come downstairs
and was bustling around the kitchen. As her image filled his

mind, he thought of the swell of her hips and the way her skin had darkened to a honey gold under the Nevada sun, highlighting her coral lips and chestnut brown eyes. A swelling in his groin pressed against the fabric of his jeans and he wondered—

"Honey?" Monica called. "Come in here, please?"

Haley's eyes popped open. Her voice sounded taut, perhaps even close to panic. Had something happened to one of the children?

Grunting, he raised himself from the couch. He walked from the living room through the dining room, both of which were dark, and into the well-lit kitchen. He stepped into a nightmare.

A thug wearing a brown leather bomber jacket clutched Monica. She gripped at the man's forearm with her small hands, trying in vain to ease the pressure against her throat. Her eyes were wide, her face pale and tears streamed down her cheeks. Another man pointed a gun at her head and stared at Haley, grinning.

Haley's fear quickly turned to anger. "What the hell's going on here?" he said.

A third intruder stepped in from the side and cracked Haley in the jaw, catching him by surprise. Haley's head swam, and the taste of blood registered with him as he reeled from the sucker punch.

If it had been an old-fashioned street fight, he would have jumped in with both feet. But this involved his family's safety, guns and an unknown enemy. Haley's training kicked in. Assess the threat and choose the best response, he told himself.

He touched the inside of his lower lip with his fingertips. They came back covered in blood. "I repeat," he said, "what the hell is going on here?"

A hulking guy with a vampire's complexion and receding white hair stepped into the room. His forehead was a mass of even whiter scar tissue. Snakeskin cowboy boots thudded against the floor as the man moved around the room, sweep-

"I'm listening," Bolan replied.

"Hang on." Brognola reached across his desk, grabbed an intelligence report gathered by Aaron Kurtzman and pulled it in front of him. He leafed through a couple of pages until he found the section he wanted.

"Here it is. I already told you about Dade's buddy, Sergei Ivanov. We've been running the traps on him. The guy runs casinos, adult bookstores and strip clubs in Vegas. Those are his legitimate businesses, and he probably uses them to launder massive amounts of money. But Bear dug deeper and found confidential ATF and DEA reports accusing the guy of running guns and drugs worldwide. A check with Interpol confirmed it."

"Any ties with Kursk?"

Brognola shifted a couple more papers around, refreshed his memory on a couple of facts.

"Most of the ties are old," he said. "They served together in the Soviet army back in the 1970s. After that, Kursk joined the KGB, and he all but disappeared. Ivanov immigrated here in the late 1980s, allegedly because he was fleeing religious persecution in the motherland. Within a year, he'd opened his first strip club just outside Washington, D.C."

"Welcome to the land of opportunity," Bolan said.

Brognola cracked a smile. "Theory is he was being propped up with Soviet money, though no one could ever prove it. According to old classified documents that Bear unearthed, some FBI agents started frequenting his strip club. One of the special agents in charge finally had to smack the guys across the knuckles for it."

"So chances were he came over here as a spy," Bolan said. "And if so, he might have been in contact with Nikolai Kursk."

"That's my line of reasoning," Brognola said. "We know Trevor Dade was one of Ivanov's regular customers. My guess is the connection goes even deeper. And here's another interesting wrinkle."

"Go."

"We're hearing rumblings about a former CIA agent named

William Armstrong. He could be very important. He conducted black ops in Afghanistan during the Soviet invasion. He supplied weapons and communications equipment and trained the mujahideen in combat techniques. Did that for several years. Then he just disappeared."

"Disappeared?"

"Disappeared. During the final days of the war, the Soviets shelled an Afghan command post that was supposed to be secret. Ended up killing several of the locals. Allegedly Armstrong was there, but they never found his body. Flash to the present and some CIA guy who knew Armstrong back in the day is in Vegas on vacation. He's playing the slots at a casino when suddenly he sees what he swears is an older version of William Armstrong. He tries to track the guy down, loses him and files a report the next day. Since he was three sheets to the wind at that point, the Company dismissed it as the ranting of a drunk."

"I guess it's not a wild leap to assume that Ivanov owns that particular casino," Bolan said.

"You stole my punch line, Striker."

"So where's Ivanov now?" Bolan asked.

"We don't know."

"What?"

"I figured you'd want to know, so I asked the FBI's Vegas field office to track him. He was under surveillance for a while, but then he and a cadre of his lieutenants disappeared. The guy's still connected. So he probably leaned on the right people, got them to turn their heads while he took a powder. The special agent in charge is investigating the incident, of course."

"Rearranging deck chairs on the *Titanic* is more like it," Bolan said. "I assume security for the Nightwind project has been stepped up, too."

"Right. Sentinel is doing all it can on that front. We've offered to bolster their security with some military support, but thus far the company has declined."

"Why?"

"They don't want a contingent of troops flooding the base and setting their people on edge. They also don't want an overnight military buildup drawing undue attention to the facility. The Man hasn't taken the option off the table, but he also isn't ready to commit to it, either. Sentinel's former chairman is a member of the presidential cabinet and, in my opinion, is exerting some undue influence over the situation."

"Nice," Bolan said. "I'll let you handle the political sensitivities. That's not my strong suit."

"Agreed," Brognola said. "You just find Kursk. Or at least figure out what the bastard's up to. That means tracking down Ivanov."

"Don't worry," Bolan said, "I know precisely how to bring Sergei Ivanov out of hiding. I'll just hit him where he lives."

Las Vegas, Nevada

"I APPRECIATE THIS," Natasha Rytova said. "Your letting me come with you, I mean."

Bolan gave her a tight smile and nodded before returning his gaze to the world passing by outside their rented Firebird. The pair had arrived at Nellis Air Force Base after what had seemed to be a never-ending string of flights. They'd barely spoken to each other during the trip, opting instead to sleep or put new dressings on old wounds.

Bolan sipped some coffee from a foam cup. It tasted like sewer water, but he took another drink, knowing he needed the caffeine.

"It goes against my better judgment," he said. "I prefer to work alone. Partners usually mean more people to worry about. But you proved yourself in Africa."

"As did you."

Bolan grinned at her. "Touché."

The lady had guts and the soldier was starting to like her in spite of himself. He shifted a bit as pressure from the car's seat caused the Desert Eagle to dig into his side. A Justice Department agent had met them at the air base and provided them with fresh civilian clothes, additional weapons and identification, all courtesy of Brognola. Both were traveling as Justice employees; Bolan as an agent, Rytova as an interpreter.

Along with the Desert Eagle, the soldier carried his Beretta 93-R in shoulder leather. Both weapons were hidden beneath a light windbreaker worn over a black T-shirt. He also carried a pair of throwing knives and some lock picks in special pockets in the jacket's lining. His other combat gear—an M-16/M-203 combination, an Ithaca shotgun, an Uzi submachine gun, thermite grenades and other explosives—were locked in the Firebird's trunk.

Dressed in black denims and a matching T-shirt, Rytova had gathered her ash blond hair into a ponytail and stuck it up under a navy blue baseball cap. Per Bolan's request, the Justice agent had supplied her with a pair of SIG-Sauer P-239s and the necessary accessories. She carried one in a shoulder rig and the other on her hip and had filled her pockets with extra magazines.

Bolan needed to get Ivanov's attention. And he'd learned a long time ago that the best way to get an audience with a mobster was to hack at the guy's lifeline—his money. With the cyberteam's assistance, Brognola had located several of Ivanov's businesses and passed the intel on to Bolan. Brognola was also working to freeze all of Ivanov's personal and business bank accounts.

The soldier parked the car along the curb of the small, suburban industrial park, killed the lights and the engine.

"Let's go," he said.

He exited the car, grabbing a small satchel as he went and slinging it over his shoulder. Bolan locked the car and set the alarm via remote control. The car chirped when he did, and he gave the vehicle one last look before walking away. If the numbers fell the way he hoped, they'd only have to leave it and its lethal contents unattended for a few minutes.

He unleathered the Beretta and held it in close to him as he started into the industrial park.

Making their way through a maze of small warehouses and manufacturers, he and Rytova came to a two-story warehouse surrounded by an eight-foot fence. Most of the grime-streaked structure sat dark, though lights burned in a couple of the first-floor windows.

Like a dark wraith, Bolan silently scrambled up and over the fence with Rytova following. Coming down in a crouch, they ran across the parking lot and sought refuge behind a pair of large trash bins. The pungent odor of warm, rotting garbage assailed Bolan's senses, and he involuntarily wrinkled his nose in a vain attempt to repel it.

An ocean of broken, oil-splotched asphalt surrounded the warehouse. Street lamps posted in three corners of the fenced area cast whitish cones on the property, and Bolan watched as swarms of insects danced in the light.

A shoe scuffled against the asphalt. Once. Twice. It was the halting gait of a bored sentry performing his rounds by rote. The footsteps stopped and Bolan peered around the steel trash container, trying not to create a silhouette as he did. The guard sat on concrete steps leading up to a door illuminated by a single light bulb. The man peeled the golden skin from an apple with a switchblade and occasionally slapped at bugs. Those two acts seemed to demand all his attention.

A trilling noise caught the man's attention, stopping him in midslap. Pulling a digital phone from his jacket, he opened it, uttered a greeting and listened, occasionally interjecting something. After a few more seconds, the man clicked off the phone and hauled himself to his feet. Pocketing the phone, he dropped the apple, ascended the stairs and disappeared inside the building.

Bolan looked at Rytova who nodded back at him. They waited several moments and then surged across the asphalt until they came to the door. Rytova tried the handle while Bolan watched their backs, but she found it locked. Bolan handed her a set of lock picks from his jacket pocket, and she went to work on the handle. Within moments, it yielded.

Keeping the Beretta out, Bolan fisted the Desert Eagle as they entered the building. The warehouse's storage area rose the full two stories and covered most of the building's footprint. Cardboard boxes marked Peas, Lima Beans and Cereal were stacked five or six high on pallets positioned all over the room. Light cast a dull sheen as it reflected off the plastic sheeting holding together the stacked boxes. Two forklifts sat idle.

A small, rectangular structure stood in the warehouse's southwest corner, shades drawn, lights burning inside. Bolan ran his gaze over the building's interior, but saw no security cameras or other equipment that might betray their presence.

Leaving several feet between them, Bolan and Rytova silently closed in on what the soldier assumed was an office. As he neared the structure, he overheard a heated exchange between two men speaking Russian. Bolan understood enough of the language to know the argument involved division of labor.

Rytova came up next to Bolan and whispered in his ear. "Apparently, this is the guard's fourth night walking the grounds. He's not happy about it."

"It's about to become the least of his worries," Bolan said. "Are you ready?"

Rytova nodded. Ducking under the shaded windows, the Executioner ran in a crouch along the length of the office. Once he passed the door, he brought himself to his full height and glimpsed through a slit between the blinds and the window, trying to determine the strength of his opposition. Thus far, he'd only heard two distinct voices and saw two silhouettes, arms waving dramatically as they argued.

He had expected more gunners and the opposition's apparent strength—or lack thereof—didn't sit well with him. His combat senses were telling him something. A phone rang inside and one of the hotheads answered it. His voice almost immediately dropped to an inaudible level.

It came to Bolan more as a feeling, an instinct, than a thought. Someone was watching him from overhead.

He wheeled and caught a pair of gunners coming into view on a series of catwalks that crisscrossed above him. Each man cradled a submachine gun and was acquiring a target, ready to deal out death.

"Go!" Bolan yelled.

Chugging in unison, the Beretta and the Desert Eagle spit flame and lead. The warrior's first shots sparked off the metal catwalk, careering into the darkness. As the hardmen began to fire at Bolan and Rytova, the Executioner tapped out a pair of tribursts from the Beretta that shredded one of the attacker's legs. The man convulsed under the onslaught before falling over the railing, plummeting headfirst to the concrete floor. At the same time, Rytova was moving in a crouch, acquiring her own target with one of the SIG-Sauers. Bolan heard the gun crack twice, the echoes nearly drowning out the cries of pain as 9 mm rounds drilled into flesh.

More gunfire erupted from behind Bolan, tearing through the walls of the office. He whirled and returned fire as he backed away to get some cover. The Beretta locked open, and the Desert Eagle had two shots left. Hurling himself behind some boxes, the warrior reloaded both weapons. He heard the steady crackle of Rytova emptying the SIG-Sauers.

His opponents continued peppering the room with a hail of autofire. The wild hails of gunfire were fast eroding the office's facade and shredding the warehouse's interior. Bullets hammered into the boxes of food surrounding Bolan, slicking the floor with vegetable juices. Judging by the undisciplined shooting, Bolan guessed he was facing untrained thugs rather than the elite troops Kursk threw at him in Africa. These guys seemed to rely more on the spray-and-pray method than real combat shooting techniques.

Digging in his satchel, Bolan palmed a flash-stun grenade but waited to throw it until after he located Rytova. He caught a glimpse of her about twenty feet to his left, hiding behind an overturned desk as she reloaded her pistol. The din of gunfire had died, and from within the office Bolan could hear the metallic clicking of weapons being locked and loaded.

Coming around the side of his protective barrier, Bolan tossed the grenade into the sagging office and returned to his cover behind the boxes. A flash of white was accompanied by a peal of thunder at his back. He was on his feet and cautiously moving on the office. Gunshots rang out, punching wildly through the walls and heading at an upward angle.

Bolan waited out the hostile fire and heard someone swear as his gun went dry.

The Executioner moved in low, taking in the scene as he went. The man who'd been closest to the stun grenade lay on the floor, pressing his fists against his eyes and groaning. The other hardman, the guard who minutes ago had been eating an apple, was blindly trying to put a new clip into his pistol. The Beretta whispered once and Bolan cored a round through the guy's shoulder. He screamed, dropped his weapon and grabbed at his shoulder. Blood stained the white shirt crimson and trailed down the good fingers of the man's hand as he applied pressure to the wound.

Bolan crossed the room in quick strides and kicked away the gun. Rytova came in just behind him, both pistols leveled rock steady as she scanned the room. Bolan grabbed the wounded shooter and tried to roll the man onto his stomach. The Russian shooter wasn't about to give up easy and kicked wildly at the Executioner to keep him at bay. His patience worn to a frazzle, Bolan caught the swinging leg and drove the edge of his own foot into the man's wounded shoulder with bone-snapping impact. A scream erupted from the shooter's mouth and he rolled onto his uninjured side, whimpering in pain.

Bolan pocketed the man's weapon and glimpsed Rytova securing her prisoner with plastic handcuffs.

"Watch them," Bolan ordered.

Sliding the Beretta back inside his jacket, the warrior returned to the warehouse and made his way through the maze of stacked pallets. He passed them by, figuring they were a smoke screen for the real prize. Glancing down the length of the warehouse, he spotted three trailers that had been driven into the loading bay and sealed inside the sprawling building.

Bolan knew the clock was ticking. The nearest occupied building was a plastics manufacturer located in the same industrial park but four blocks from the warehouse. He'd noticed cars parked outside it and lights on inside the building when they'd passed by earlier.

If he was lucky, machine noise and distance had conspired to mask the gunfire. If not, Bolan could expect police intervention at any minute. He could find himself face-to-face with nervous street cops, or an entire SWAT team, for that matter. He considered both scenarios unacceptable.

Moving to the trailers, he inspected all three and found each locked.

At the last trailer, Bolan aimed the Desert Eagle at the steel padlocks sealing the trailer door. The big bore pistol roared twice, shattering the lock and the door latch. Swinging open the trailer's doors, Bolan played the flashlight's beam over several stacks of wooden crates set at the back. A quick search turned up a crowbar and he took it with him as he climbed inside the big trailer.

Arm and shoulder muscles bunching against the fabric of his jacket, Bolan pried one of the crates open. A glint of metal and the smell of oil betrayed the contents even before Bolan illuminated the box's interior with his flashlight.

AK-47s and plenty of them. It was a deadly inventory that Bolan was about to liquidate in a blaze of hellfire. Working quickly, he packed wedges of C-4 explosives around the boxes and jabbed detonators into the material. Minutes later, he had rigged all three trucks to blow.

Back at the office, Rytova was exchanging words with one

of the prisoners. Bolan heard the anger in Rytova's voice as she spoke.

"For the last time, where is Ivanov?" she asked.

"Even if I knew, I would not tell you, woman," the man replied. He paused for a moment. "I recognize you. You're the crazy bitch who has hit our other operations. They've been warning us about you for months. One of your firebombs killed my brother along with several other men in Moscow. I had to return home to bury him."

When Rytova paused, Bolan thought he detected a hint of guilt in her voice. "I know of your brother, Victor, and if I killed him, he was a criminal. I have killed no innocent people. Perhaps now that you have lost a loved one you understand what drives me."

"You're just a crazy bitch. A fanatic. That's what drives you. You're just like your husband and look where it got him."

Rytova's voice hardened. "If I was a fanatic, you'd be dead already."

"Then why am I not?"

Bolan filled the doorway and pinned the hardman under his icy stare. Next to the Russian thug lay the other gunner, unconscious from blood loss or physical trauma.

"I'm not a fanatic," Bolan said evenly, "but I'll kill you and not think twice about it."

Apparently used to intimidating people, the mobster gave Bolan a hard look that broadcast that he wasn't afraid of the big American.

Bolan knew he'd fix that soon enough.

Rytova looked at the Executioner and spoke in a taut voice. "This is Victor Delyagin, a high-ranking member of Ivanov's organization. If he's like his brother, Mikhail, then he doesn't normally mix with the rank and file. We are very lucky to have caught him here."

Delyagin's sour look showed he didn't share Rytova's enthusiasm.

Bolan bracketed Delyagin's ruddy face in the Desert Eagle's sights. "I haven't got all night, Victor. We need to find Ivanov. You can help us. Maybe walk away intact. It's your play."

"You will not kill me. You're a policeman. Right? Go ahead and arrest me. I have lawyers. I will charge you with police brutality. With murder. I know your threats are empty."

Bolan gave him an icy smile. "Glad you're so confident of that."

The Desert Eagle roared once. A .44 Magnum boattail slug burned a path two inches from Delyagin's ear before punching through a desk at his back. The man drew in on himself and screwed his eyes shut. When his eyes reopened, Bolan stared at him without speaking. The warrior let thunderclap from the big pistol resonate around the room for a moment before he spoke again.

"I'm not a policeman or a federal agent," he growled. "So you'd better change your thinking real quick. Where's your boss?"

"I don't know where he is."

Bolan's gut told him the guy was playing it straight. "Why don't you know?"

Sweat beaded Delyagin's forehead and his left foot twitched, etching quick semicircles in the air like a windshield wiper cutting through raindrops. His eyes darted between Bolan and Rytova. The warrior guessed the Russian man was weighing whether to spill his guts before Bolan did it for him.

Her face taut with anger, Rytova moved to the injured man and began checking his wounds.

Finally, Delyagin spoke. "He calls us periodically, but I don't know where he is. We never see him. He has safehouses all over the city, the state. He could be anywhere right now."

"Give me an example of 'anywhere,'" Bolan demanded.

"I have none."

Bolan shot him a look of disbelief.

"It is true," Delyagin said. "The safehouses are meant to protect him from us as much as from police or rival gangs. He trusts no one except for his small cadre of guards and a handful of his closest lieutenants. He worries that one of us might try to kill him, take over."

Bolan weighed the Russian's words and decided they made sense. Experience told him that the savages he battled preyed upon one another as much as they did on innocents. They considered loyalty and honor things to be bought, sold or traded. Apparently Ivanov realized a bloody coup could take him down at any time, and he'd done what he could to shore up his power.

Bolan decided to go for broke. "Seems like Nikolai Kursk would frown on a bloody coup."

Delyagin's face went pale. "I know nothing of this Nikolai Kursk."

"You're an awful liar, Victor," Bolan said. "Truthfully, I'd expect a slug like you to be better at it. We know Ivanov works for Nikolai Kursk. That means you do too. Is Kursk in the United States?"

"I haven't seen Nikolai Kursk in years," Delyagin replied. "He very rarely comes to the United States. He has no need. Ivanov handles his business here."

"So why's Ivanov gone underground? And don't tell me it's because he's anticipating a coup."

"He would not tell us. He said to stand by and wait for orders. He calls me each day and checks on things."

"You talk to him today?" Bolan asked.

Delyagin shook his head.

Bolan walked over to the unconscious gunner and hefted him up in a fireman's carry. Rytova followed his lead and helped Delyagin to his feet. The man shook her away the moment he stood.

Minutes later, they'd exited the warehouse and returned to the Pontiac. Bolan palmed the detonator and flicked a couple of switches. The C-4 charges roared as flame and force pulverized windows and bowed or shredded sheet metal walls. Within minutes the hardsite glowed like a professional sports stadium on game night and choked the sky with thick, black columns of smoke.

Delyagin had his back turned when Bolan activated the explosives. He started at the initial roar and nearly fell over as he tried to turn to see what was happening.

"What the hell did you do to my warehouse?" he screamed.

"Tell Ivanov that justice just paid him a visit. And I'm going to keep paying him visits until I get some face time with the guy. Tell him that next time I won't go as easy on him. Understand?"

Delyagin turned back to Bolan, licked his lips and nodded. He seemed to regard Bolan with respect, or fear. The Executioner didn't care which as long as the guy did as he was told.

Bolan pulled a piece of paper from his pocket, crumpled it and tossed it at Delyagin's feet. "There's an address on that paper," Bolan said. "He's got two hours to make his decision."

His face illuminated by the orange glow of the fire, Delyagin gave Bolan another nod but remained silent. The soldier reached inside his jacket and withdrew one of the throwing knives hidden there. He tossed it about thirty feet to Delyagin's left. "Go cut yourself loose. By the time you're finished, we'll be gone."

Bolan spun and walked toward the car. Rytova kept pace with him. "Where are we going now?" she asked.

"I've made my point," he said. "Now I just need to reinforce it."

THE CHOP SHOP WENT down easy.

Aside from a couple of Ivanov's gunners, the place was populated mostly with gearheads and spray-gun DaVincis able to repaint, modify and detail a car until even the former owner wouldn't recognize it. These were blue-collar guys wanting to make a living, something a little better than honest labor at a repair shop might afford them. They were the kind of guys who taped their child's picture to the lid of their toolbox, but didn't sweat the source of their paychecks.

Not stand-up citizens, but hardly killers.

Mack Bolan knew this going in and planned accordingly.

He'd hit fast. He'd hit hard. But, as always, he'd be damn careful about who fell in his sights.

As bold as hell, he bulled his way into the building, navigated a sea of ravaged cars, trucks and sport utility vehicles and closed in on the guards. In unison, the Russians clawed for hardware while separating and trying to grab cover. Bolan sawed each with a blast from the 12-gauge. By the time the roar from the first shotgun round had died down, the spit of air compressors, the rattle of power wrenches and the murmur of voices had halted, replaced by an eerie, shocked quiet.

As the second gunner's corpse hit the concrete floor, a sea of frightened eyes rested on the black-clad killer in their midst. Eyes obscured by mirrored aviator shades, a grim look on his face, Bolan closed in on the workers. A few clutched big wrenches or small sledgehammers in front of them ready to make a desperate play for their lives if it came to that.

Bolan racked the slide once and shouldered the shotgun. He swept the barrel across the line of men.

"Go," he said. "And tell your boss I'll see him in an hour and a half."

The men went.

Bolan planted the C-4, then detonated it as the rented Firebird raced through the night. The building erupted in a hurricane of smoke, fire and debris as the warrior continued his short-lived blitz of Las Vegas.

As MACK BOLAN GUIDED the car to their final target, he noticed Natasha Rytova had fallen silent. She'd been that way since they'd left the weapons warehouse. When he'd announced his plans to hit the chop shop alone, she'd agreed quickly. The destruction of another arms warehouse had gone off without a hitch, but the woman seemed even more withdrawn as they sped toward the last stop of the night.

Something was nagging her, dividing her attention, and Bolan wanted to know what it was before they made the next hit. He couldn't afford a teammate whose head wasn't in the game.

He cut the wheel to the right, navigated the car into an alley and continued on. It was a shortcut he'd learned during previous strikes in Las Vegas.

He broke the silence. "Spit it out," he said.

The woman looked at him, as though shaken from sleep. She shot Bolan a confused look. "Spit what out?"

"I mean talk," he said. "Something's bothering you. What is it?"

She stared at her lap. "It's nothing."

"Natasha, I need you to watch my back and vice versa. We've got no room for secrets or distractions here. What's bothering you?"

She stayed silent for a moment, apparently organizing her thoughts.

"Delyagin called me a fanatic and the words hurt. That makes me wonder if what he said is true. I worry about what I'm becoming," she said.

"Which is?"

"A murderer."

Bolan slid into traffic behind a black Mercedes. A police cruiser appeared up ahead, causing the Mercedes' driver to stomp on the brakes and bathe Bolan and Rytova in a soft red glare. Bolan tapped his own brakes.

"You're not a murderer, Natasha," he said.

She stared straight ahead. Her voice sounded wooden. "You sound so sure. How?"

He shrugged. The Mercedes gained speed, and Bolan accelerated the rental. "You ever kill anyone who didn't draw down on you first?"

"No, of course not."

"Would you?"

She shook her head. "I'd only kill to save my life. Or to save someone else. I guess even with Nikolai Kursk I always figured I'd shoot him in self-defense. That when I found him, he'd try to kill me and I'd shoot him in self-defense."

"You can't always choose the circumstances," Bolan said.

"But that seems pretty realistic. He'd be happy as hell to murder you."

"Does it ever bother you?" Rytova asked. "All the killing, I mean?"

Bolan didn't hesitate. "Always. I take no joy in it."

He could tell from his peripheral vision that the woman was staring at him. Traffic rolled to a stop at a red light.

"You have seen a great deal of death in your time," she said. "I have sensed that about you, Matt. You have great compassion, but you also have seen terrible things. I knew that you were a good man when you disarmed the boy and ordered him to go home. You didn't want to hurt him, even to save your own life. Dmitri would have done the same thing. He was a strong, capable man, but he also had a good heart. It eludes me how you can keep your heart and do what you do."

Bolan nodded. The light turned green. They were another ten minutes from Las Vegas Boulevard, but already garish neon signs advertising towering hotels, casinos and nightclubs were lighting up the night sky. People milled along the streets, and he saw a couple of guys handing out papers advertising prostitutes and escort services.

Bolan finally spoke. "It's because I'm human that I do this. There are jackals out there, Natasha. People who hurt, terrorize and kill the innocent just because they can. I can't—I won't—sit back and let that happen. Even the ones who'd find my methods abhorrent need me to do what I do."

Rytova remained silent and stared out the passenger's side window. Her gaze seemed to stick on a young couple walking arm and arm along the sidewalk.

Bolan had made peace with his chosen path a long time ago; Rytova apparently hadn't. He let her stew for a moment before speaking.

"Look, Natasha, this path isn't for everybody," he said. "You're quick and good with weapons. You've got guts. You've proved that tenfold. No one—not your husband or your father—would fault you if you decided to walk away from all this."

Rytova nodded. "I just do not want to become an automaton. I killed Delyagin's brother, and I had completely forgotten about it until tonight. That bothers me."

"Delyagin got under your skin by appealing to your conscience. And, because you're a good person, it worked. Never justify your mission to the enemy. Never expect them to understand your motives. But always know what motivates them. It gives you the edge."

"I understand," Rytova said.

"Is your heart still in this, Natasha? Because if it's not—"

Rytova's head whipped in Bolan's direction. Anger flared hot in her eyes.

"Stop. Do not even say it, Matt. I will not step aside or sit by while you handle my business for me. I will not rest while Nikolai Kursk continues to run free. I was chasing him before you even knew he existed."

Bolan kept his eyes on the road.

The warrior was satisfied—for the moment, anyway. The woman retreated inside herself and Bolan used the silence to run the numbers on the next strike.

The way he figured it, he'd cost Ivanov thousands, perhaps millions of dollars in just an hour. Plus he'd drawn the kind of attention to Ivanov's organization that even the most corrupt law officer couldn't ignore.

So, he'd gotten Ivanov's attention.

Now that the bastard was looking it was time to hit him right between the eyes.

10

Mack Bolan rolled the rental into a parking lot several blocks from the Golden Creek Casino. Killing the lights and the engine, he pulled at the trunk release, exited the car and walked to the rear of the vehicle. Rytova met him there.

Silently, they prepared for battle. Bolan filled the satchel with more C-4 and detonators. The thermite grenades would also be within easy reach in the satchel. The M-16/M-203 combo was ready and waiting inside a carrying case that also contained 40 mm smoke, HE and stun grenades. Underneath his windbreaker, Bolan wore combat webbing with four extra clips for the assault rifle. Rytova took a shoulder bag that contained the Uzi submachine gun and a bandolier of clips.

They had arrived twenty minutes early for the meet. The mobster would probably have an advance team waiting for them as they walked into the kill zone. Bolan also was betting the guy would put in a personal appearance. Plain and simple, Ivanov would want to see the smoking corpse of the bastard who'd cost him so much money in so little time. It was too big a temptation for the man to resist.

Carrying their loads, Bolan and Rytova left the parking lot and trekked toward the casino's hulking shadow, which rose over blocks of restaurants, casinos and other tourist traps.

According to Brognola, the big casino–hotel complex had thrived for two decades until fire had raged through it and forced its closure a year ago. Ivanov had swooped in and purchased the grand structure from its owners at a fraction of its value cost and immediately sank millions of dollars into renovating it. Word was he expected it to become the crown jewel of his empire after it opened in the next couple of weeks.

The supernova of colored lights that turned night into day in Las Vegas did little to help Bolan's sense of security. The unending parade of strange faces filing by only compounded his uneasiness. If Ivanov's people were working the streets, Bolan or Rytova might be seen well before they reached the building.

Coming to a side street, they turned right and moved parallel to the casino for two blocks. Along the way, they passed a convenience store and a liquor store, and the smell of grease from fast-food restaurants hung heavily in the air. A group of bikers packed the liquor store parking lot, and Bolan felt their weighty gaze settle on him and Rytova as they passed. Involuntarily, his grip tightened on the handle of the M-16's carrying case and muscles tensed under his jacket.

The bikers went silent for a moment as Bolan and Rytova passed. With his short hair, conservative dress and telltale bulges of weapons, Bolan knew his looks screamed "Cop." But as he watched the bikers with his peripheral vision, he saw no threatening moves, and within moments they were again swearing at one another and breaking bottles against the asphalt.

"I didn't get even one whistle," Rytova said. "I feel hurt."

Surprised, Bolan looked at her. She grinned at him, and he couldn't help but return the smile. "There's no accounting for tastes," he said.

They walked past the hardsite and then another three blocks north before cutting back through a series of alleys and parking lots to get up close to the casino without being seen. Ivanov also owned the lot across from the casino and had razed the area to make room for new restaurants and stores that could leech more business off the hotel and casino patrons.

Bolan hunkered down next to a bundle of concrete reinforcing rods and set his weapons case on the ground next to him. Opening the case, he extracted the M-16/M-203 combo, loaded the rifle and rammed a 40 mm smoke grenade into the launcher. Setting the assault rifle on the ground, he hefted the launcher and prepared it for use. In the meantime, Rytova was arming herself with the Uzi.

The glare of headlights washed through the streets and announced the arrival of two black Lincoln crew wagons and a Mercedes. Experience told Bolan that his quarry most likely was in the middle vehicle—the Mercedes—while the Lincolns protected their boss's front and rear.

Bolan knew he had to hit fast and hard, avoid innocent casualties and encounters with the law. Of course Brognola would run interference for him if he got in trouble with the law. But the Executioner had no time to waste cooling his heels in a holding cell while the big Fed pulled rank with the local police. Not this night.

When he made his play, he had no margin for error.

Gates sprang open, and as the first vehicle rolled into the fenced area, Bolan shouldered the rocket and sighted in on the third vehicle. The weapon hissed out its deadly payload, burying it in the vehicle's back end. The projectile exploded, emitting an ear-shattering boom. The blast transformed the car into a mass of flame and twisted metal.

The force of the explosion heaved the wreckage several feet in the air before the carcass dropped back to earth, landing on the driver's side. Flames leaped out from every opening, crackling and licking up toward the skies.

Discarding the spent launch tube, Bolan grabbed the M-16/ M-203 combo and in quick succession launched a fragmentation round and then a smoke grenade into the fenced area. Outnumbered and outgunned, he wanted fear and confusion to reign when they blitzed the kill zone.

Bolan and Rytova crept across the road and through the gate. The soldier felt a wave of heat strike him as he passed the burning vehicle. Bullets lanced out of the smoke obscuring the strike zone while men shouted commands or cries for help in Russian.

Bolan dropped into a crouch and swept the M-16 left to right. The weapon chugged out a blazing line of 5.56 mm tumblers that ripped into shadowy figures, whipsawing them before leaving them to crash to the ground. Bolan kept the shooting tight so that stray rounds would slam into the massive casino or one of the other buildings looming before him, rather than buzzing into the streets and possibly injuring bystanders.

Rytova disappeared from view as a gunner stumbled from the smoke. A dark smear covered his left shoulder, and his arm hung limp at his side. Shouting obscenities, he raised a Glock clutched in his right hand and snapped off two shots at Bolan. The warrior dived off the firing line even as the man's arm came up. Bolan unleashed a second burst from the M-16. The volley of bullets burned at an upward angle, catching the man in his midsection.

A second gunner sprinted from the oily black smoke. He tried to insert himself between Bolan and the Mercedes, bolstering the soldier's theory that it was Ivanov's vehicle.

The guard triggered his stubby SMG and autofire blazed toward Bolan, landing just shy of him but ripping a jagged line through the asphalt that lay several feet ahead. The Executioner replied by tapping out a quick burst that cleaved the air just inches from the shooter's torso but didn't connect with flesh.

Both men raced to correct their aim, with Bolan winning by a microsecond. The M-16 rattled out a swarm of bullets that tunneled into the man's chest and shoulders and dropped him in his tracks.

The Mercedes growled as the driver gunned its power plant and made a bid to flee the carnage. Rubber screamed and smoked against the pavement as the car whipped backward in a long J-turn that left the vehicle's nose turned in Bolan's direction. The still-burning wreckage had blocked the gate and made escape that way impossible. But Bolan knew that with a good running start the Mercedes could make its own exit by smashing through the fence.

Before he could react to the Mercedes's moves, the doors of the remaining Lincoln flipped open and shooters disgorged from the vehicle. A withering hail of pistol and machine-gun fire burned its way toward the Executioner as the gunners spotted him and tried to take him out.

Emptying the M-16's clip as he moved, Bolan bolted to his left and thrust himself behind a stack of bricks.

The soldier cracked a new magazine into the assault rifle. Autofire sizzled overhead or pounded into the makeshift brick wall, and Bolan found himself pinned down. He heard what sounded like a separate gun battle and guessed that Rytova was also under fire. Glancing across the parking lot and to his right, he saw Rytova mow down two men with a sustained burst from her Uzi.

Footsteps sounded from behind. Whirling, Bolan peered around the barrier and caught a pair of hardmen approaching, weapons extended in front of them. The gunners had distanced themselves from each other and were converging on Bolan from separate directions.

The Executioner knew the chance of delivering a one-two punch and eliminating both men with the M-16 before taking a bullet himself was virtually nil.

At the same time the Mercedes' engine revved again, announcing to Bolan and everyone else that Ivanov planned to bow out early. If the mobster got his way, he'd split, disappear and leave Bolan back at square one.

Spotting the soldier, the first of the two approaching gunners squeezed off a round from his pistol. The guy was a damn good shot, and the bullet whistled just inches from Bolan's ear. The soldier's M-16 erupted, hurling out a quick blast of tumblers. Crimson spots blossomed on the white shirt of Bolan's opponent as the bullets pierced his ribs to the right of his sternum and knocked him to the ground as though bludgeoned by an invisible hammer.

Bolan began swiveling toward the next shooter, knowing he wouldn't make it in time. At the same time, the shooter aimed his Uzi at his adversary and prepared to fire. Suddenly, his body pitched forward in a burst of crimson and gray. Bolan looked toward the source of the shot and saw Rytova clutching a handgun. She turned and waded back into her own battle.

Bolan did likewise, looking for his next opponent while also moving closer to the Mercedes. A man built like an Olympic weight lifter, his lumpy head shaved clean and reflecting light like a waxed apple, rocketed up from behind the empty crew wagon. Resting massive arms across the trunk, the guy clutched a pistol in a two-handed grip and sighted down on Bolan.

Caught in the open, the Executioner hosed down the Lincoln and the muscle man with a firestorm from the M-16. The weapon went dry and Bolan reloaded it.

Bolan ran for the Lincoln, surveying the damage as he went. Bodies were strewed everywhere. Fire continued to ravage the remains of the crew wagon that Bolan had destroyed with the rocket. Terrified screams pierced the air outside the fence, and sirens wailed in the distance.

The Mercedes slowed and a gunner leaped from the rear driver's-side door of the still-rolling sedan. Bellowing a guttural war cry, the hardman triggered his subgun and sliced a fiery semicircle in the air meant to drive any opponents under cover. Bolan shouldered the assault rifle and dispatched the guy to hell with a single shot between the eyes.

The Mercedes' engine gained steam and roared across the parking lot. The driver plowed the vehicle over the remains of his fallen comrades as he navigated out of the hell zone.

Coming around the rear of the Lincoln, which still had its engine idling, Bolan tossed his weapon into the car, crawled into the driver's seat and slammed the door behind him. Strapping himself in, he gunned the engine and sped toward the Mercedes as it closed in the gate.

The warrior's mind ran through the scenario even as his

foot slammed against the accelerator. He knew he couldn't stop
the Mercedes with small-arms fire. A straight-on T-bone crash,
where his grille struck the Mercedes in the middle could be devastating, even between two armored cars, leaving all the occupants critically wounded or dead.

Bolan had accepted his mortality a long time ago and lived
with death at his right hand every minute. Still, he knew he'd
do no one any good if his ticket got punched too soon.

The Mercedes darted across Bolan's path like a shadow.
The driver was smart enough to know he couldn't plow past the
wreckage blocking the gate and was driving his vehicle straight
through the plywood-covered chain-link fence.

With the engine's whine filling his ears as the Lincoln gained
speed, Bolan steered the big vehicle toward the Mercedes. He
had to get the timing just right or forget it. There'd be no second chances.

Guiding the Lincoln, he smashed the vehicle's right tip hard
against the Mercedes' rear end. Metal ground into metal, setting off sparks and filling Bolan's car with an ear-piercing
screech. The impact knocked the Mercedes off course. Its back
end skidded out from behind it, and the front end swept side-
ways until it smacked into the Lincoln.

The force of the collision pressed Bolan against his seat, and
he gripped the steering wheel hard to keep the vehicle under
control. The car spun before he was able to bring it to a stop.

The Mercedes driver had also brought his vehicle under
control and was cutting a new path for the fence. Because of
the cramped quarters, Bolan estimated the other vehicle hadn't
broken the twenty miles per hour mark.

The Lincoln knifed across the parking lot, the right front corner striking against the Mercedes' tail. Gunning the engine, Bolan
continued to press his advantage and shoved the Mercedes up
against an overloaded trash bin. The big container shook under
the impact, and ragged sheets of drywall and floor timbers rained
down upon the Mercedes and bounced across the Lincoln's hood.

Freeing himself from the car, Bolan fisted his Beretta. Approaching the Mercedes with the pistol extended in a two-handed grip, he saw that two men occupied the vehicle. The Mercedes' driver had been knocked unconscious. The man seated in the back of the vehicle was scrambling for a lost gun.

Bolan whipped open the passenger's-side door and shoved the Beretta into the mobster's face.

Ivanov flashed Bolan a hard gaze, but instinct told Bolan his quarry wasn't about to take this one-on-one confrontation all the way.

"You and I need to talk," the warrior said.

"Kiss my ass," Sergei Ivanov said. "I know my rights and you have trampled them. I will sue the United States government for this atrocity. You have done a great deal of damage to my businesses and my reputation."

Seated behind a table and chain-smoking Marlboros, Ivanov gave Bolan a fierce look. The Russian Mob boss was slim, six feet two inches tall, and had a thick head of hair, as white as the Siberian snow. The combined cost of his tan summer-weight suit and the gold jewelry he wore probably equaled the gross domestic product of some developing nations.

He tapped manicured fingers against the tabletop. Even in captivity, his dark brown eyes regarded Bolan and Rytova with an arrogance that indicated he considered himself the master.

Getting Ivanov, Rytova and Bolan from the kill zone hadn't been a problem. A chopper had been on standby waiting to airlift them from the scene. A cleanup team from Stony Man Farm had been waiting in the wings to take care of Bolan's rental. Brognola, backed by the weight of presidential authority, was working hard to smooth ruffled feathers in Las Vegas.

That left Bolan and Rytova to interrogate Ivanov.

The trio was locked down in a suburban Las Vegas safehouse, one of several held nationwide by the Sensitive Operations Group. Blacksuits were positioned throughout the house, ready to take down Ivanov's men if they came to reclaim Bolan's prize. The room, a ten-foot-by-ten foot cube, was soundproofed. Bolan could keep in touch with the blacksuits waiting outside via a handheld radio.

Anger electrified Bolan as he rose up from his chair, letting it crash to the floor behind him. A challenge flickered in Ivanov's eyes and he smiled. He was at least two decades older than Bolan and didn't have the warrior's build. But, according to information supplied by Aaron Kurtzman and Hal Brognola, he was no pushover. Ivanov had handled wet work for the KGB for years before immigrating to America and adding the title Mafia boss to his résumé. No doubt Ivanov was tough. But Bolan was tougher.

Bolan fixed Ivanov with a steely glare. "So Sergei, enlighten me on what Nikolai Kursk is doing."

Ivanov stubbed out his cigarette. "Make me a deal," he said.

Bolan was ready to reply, but a hand on his shoulder caused him to stop cold. He jerked his head around, looked down and saw Rytova standing behind him. "Please," she said. "Let me handle this."

Bolan looked at her for a moment, nodded and stepped away.

Ivanov roared with derisive laughter. He slapped a palm against his knee with a loud crack and shook his head.

"Yes, please. Let the woman do your fighting for you. You are so obviously outclassed here, big man," he taunted.

Rytova drew the SIG-Sauer P-239 from her hip. Giving Ivanov a cold look, she screwed a sound suppressor into the pistol's barrel.

"Silence," she said in Russian.

Ivanov's face hardened. "I do not take orders from a woman," he said. "Especially not a crazy one."

Without a word, Rytova raised her shooting hand and the pistol sneezed twice. The 9 mm Parabellum rounds slapped into the seat of the wooden chair, pounding out a short line that led to his groin. His eyes burst from slits into wide circles.

In rapid fire, she squeezed off two more shots, each round traveling less than an inch as it passed by Ivanov's right, then left ears.

Rytova spoke in English. "You will take orders from me now."

"You will not kill me." His voice sounded smaller, less sure.

"I don't have to," Rytova said. "A well-placed round to the knees could leave you painfully crippled. Or I could shoot you in a more private spot. That would not kill you. You'd just wish you were dead. Or perhaps you will bleed to death. No real man would want to die so passively as that."

The mobster stared at her for a moment. Her gaze never wavered. The last vestiges of bravado cracked and his forehead pinched tight as he seemed to agonize for a moment, weighing his next best move. As far as Bolan was concerned, the guy had one option.

"What do you want to know?" Ivanov asked reluctantly.

"Nikolai Kursk. What does he plan to do in this country?" Rytova asked.

Ivanov started to protest but checked himself.

"You know of the plane?"

Rytova nodded.

"He plans to steal it. There are teams of men assembling right now to do so. The raid happens tonight."

Rytova continued to press. "How will he steal it? The base has tight security. How will he get the craft out of there?"

Ivanov shrugged. "It is simple. He has people inside who will help him breach security. Then he will fly the plane out of there. And Kursk himself will not even be there. He's not even in the country."

"There's maybe a half dozen people in the United States capable of flying that plane," Bolan interjected. "How in hell does he plan to fly the Nightwind out of the base?"

"As I said, he has inside help," Ivanov said.

He lit another cigarette, took a long deep drag. He stared at his shiny black loafers, bent and brushed away an imaginary speck of dust, before looking up again. Stripped of his arrogance, he looked smaller and older.

"He has one of the pilots in his custody even as we speak. A man named Jon Haley. He works for Sentinel Industries. Nikolai is exerting pressure on the man so he will fly the plane out of the base."

Bolan felt a burning in his gut as it twisted up with anger. But he held his tongue and let Rytova continue the interrogation.

"What kind of pressure?" she asked.

"We have his family. If Haley doesn't comply with our demands, we will kill them. He saw us take them, and he knows what we want of him."

"Where are they?"

"In Las Vegas." Ivanov gave her the address.

"What about the base?" Bolan interjected again.

"We have been planning this for months," Ivanov said. "Recruiting Dade was part of a much larger plan. We watched Haley for months and hacked into his military and his personnel files. We saw he was the best pilot to fly the craft under adverse conditions. We knew we couldn't buy the man off, so we grabbed the strongest leverage we could find."

"His family," Bolan said.

"Yes. As Ms. Rytova will tell you, families are fair game. For us, it's just business. Nothing personal."

The dig caused Rytova to stiffen. Otherwise, her gaze stayed stony. The woman was a real pro, Bolan thought.

"What makes Kursk think any country would buy the plane once it's stolen?" Bolan asked.

Ivanov dropped the cigarette to the carpet and crushed it into the fibers with a shoe.

"Everyone wants it," he said. "The Russians, the Chinese. Even Iran and North Korea want it. Those two have not forgotten that Axis of Evil comment that branded them. They worry that your government will try to topple their regimes, covertly if not overtly. And Iran has the resources to pay the price tag."

"Which is?"

"A cool one and a half billion. We have very low overhead on this deal, so it's pure profit. It is Nikolai's big score, so to speak. Plus the resulting tension is sure to create other ancillary conflicts, which is good for business."

"Tension? You mean from the plane theft?"

Ivanov nodded. "Yes. Of course. America will have to admit to the existence of the plane, something it created without the knowledge of its own people. Something it has denied was even scientifically feasible given the current technology. Your leaders don't have the political will to do that. So they'd probably wage a secret war or broker a deal behind closed doors to get the plane back. Or they will lie about the base's purpose, blame its destruction on terrorists and retaliate against someone, never explaining the real reason why. We have Soviet jet fighters, submarines, helicopters, even suitcase nukes ready to sell. We just want people to fight. When politicians talk, we make no money. You're obviously a soldier. I was a soldier. Surely we can agree that war is a state in which we're both happiest. It is a necessary evil."

"Real soldiers fight for peace. Not for the sake of fighting," Bolan replied.

"Real soldiers die. Sometimes they die for a cause, sometimes they die in vain. Tonight many will be killed on the battlefield, and they will never know what hit them. Consider it a friendly fire incident of sorts."

"What the hell does that mean?" Bolan asked.

Ivanov explained, and it turned the warrior's blood cold.

11

Jon Haley watched as the blacksuited men raced around the airfield, loading weapons onto the Black Hawk chopper with deadly efficiency. He had no clue as to his location. They'd blindfolded him and bound his hands before whisking him away from the house, his wife's screams still echoing in his ears.

He'd spent most of the two-hour car ride in silence. Nothing to do but listen for someone to drop a clue that might tell him what was going on. Or brood about the safety of his wife and children. The former never happened, and the latter train of thought roared through his mind nonstop.

The big pasty bastard sauntered toward him. The cool wind whipped the tails of the man's calf-length leather jacket about his legs as he moved, adding to his vampiric appearance.

After the car ride, they were deep in the desert and the night had quickly turned cool. Haley shivered under the pilot's suit he'd been given. *His* pilot suit. The one he'd left at the Haven for cleaning before heading home on vacation. If these guys had access to his uniform and flight gear—all of it stored on one of the nation's most secret bases—he knew he'd been sold out at levels he couldn't fathom.

In a word, he was fucked. Now he had to find a way to help himself and those he loved. For the moment, that meant playing along with Paleface, doing as he was told without argument.

The big man wore a combat harness underneath the leather duster, and extra magazines and hand grenades were easily visible. A second Uzi hung from a strap on his back. The man moved easily under the weight.

"You ready to destroy your country, boy?" the man asked, his mouth splitting open like a nasty gash into what barely passed as a smile. Even in the darkness, with only a few lights burning, the man wore his sunglasses. The black shades contrasted with his pallor and made him look like the big-headed aliens featured in television specials and books about abductions. He'd be almost comical if he wasn't so damn evil, Haley thought.

A switchblade opened in the man's hand and shimmered in the meager light. Haley felt his heart jump in his chest as the man stepped toward him. His muscles tensed, and the pilot shifted his weight to his back leg so he could bury a front snap kick into the man's gut. If he was going down, he'd damn well go down fighting.

Paleface grinned, but kept his distance. "Easy, boy," he said. "I'm just going to cut you free. I need you to carry your own gear."

Haley turned and the man cut him free. He brought his hands around front and began to massage at his wrists, rubbed raw from the plastic bindings. He started to turn, but a thundering blow hammered into his kidneys and propelled him forward. He fell to the ground, the cracked asphalt tearing open his palms as he put out his hands to cushion his fall.

Haley whirled, started to come up. He stopped short, the knife blade only inches from his face.

"That was your one warning," Paleface said.

"Kill me and who's going to fly your damn plane?" Haley replied.

"Kill you? Hell, I wasn't talking about killing you. That comes later. I'll kill your babies. Slay those little brats just like they were rodents. The lady comes next. You've landed in hell, son, a hell where I've got all the power. The sooner you bend your mind around that fact, the better off your family will be."

Haley sucked in a deep breath, tried to calm his stomach. His eyes burned with hatred, but he said nothing.

Paleface continued. "You work with us and your family lives." Another wicked smile twisted his face. "I can't vouch for their condition, of course. Your wife's a pretty lady and those Russians are the horniest bastards I ever saw. But she'll walk away." Paleface gave him a wink. "Hell, who knows? She might even enjoy it."

Rage pulsed through Haley's body and he nearly surged up at the guy, ready to literally rip the leering smile from the bigger man's face. Images of his family flashed across his mind, and he stayed still.

He'd behave. For now.

Paleface hadn't mentioned Haley's fate, and the pilot didn't bother to ask. He'd already resigned himself that this might be a death flight for him. They may keep him alive for a little bit. Force him to show them how to fly the Nightwind, but eventually he'd die. He also was pretty sure the same fate would befall his family, but he wasn't about to risk that.

The man continued speaking. "Now when you get into the plane, you disable all the tracking equipment and fly that thing out of here. We'll have a scramble team of fighters follow you in case you encounter any resistance or you get squirrelly on us. You go where we tell you, or we'll shoot you from the sky and scrap the mission. We'll scrap your family right after that. You just haul ass for the coordinates I gave you. We have a team that will disassemble as much of the plane as we can, put the pieces on a submarine and haul ass out of there."

"When does my family go free?"

"Once we've got what we want, we're done with them. How fast that happens is up to you."

"Just show me what to do," he said.

"Get your ass on that chopper, Cowboy, and I'll do just that."

Cowboy? A chill passed through Haley and he knew in an instant who'd sold him out.

HAROLD BANNER STEPPED inside the elevator and punched a button for the uppermost floor. As the cage silently slid up from the Haven's lower levels, the former military man tried to think of something other than the blood he was about to spill.

It was a wasted effort. A thousand thoughts swirled around in his mind, a fetid mix of doomsday scenarios and self-re-crimination. He popped another antacid and he occasionally had to remind himself to breathe. The Glock 17 holstered beneath his black leather bomber jacket irritated his conscience, a constant reminder of his treachery.

Maybe it wasn't too late. With the push of a button, he could return downstairs, retrieve the suitcase nuke and go home. He lived a lonely, Spartan existence. He had no family, and precious few friends or possessions. The gambling had stripped him of all of that. He could disappear without a trace in a matter of hours. Hell, he could even place an anonymous call to the police, let them know of the danger facing Haley and his family. Maybe point them to the suitcase nuke, help them take it out of circulation before it hurt someone.

Save the day instead of destroying it.

The elevator stopped, and Banner shook his head. He was in too deep now. Any fantasy of changing things, turning things around was just that. He stepped from the elevator and started down the long, sterile corridor that stretched before him. He unzipped the leather jacket to afford himself easier access to the Glock. A duffel bag swayed from his shoulder as he made his way down the hall.

He'd always loved to gamble and his postmilitary career with Sentinel Industries had seemed too good to be true. Double his military pay, all his expenses paid and living within driving distance of Las Vegas. Who in their right mind could turn their back on that?

With weekly pilgrimages to Las Vegas, it hadn't taken Banner long to get underwater in gambling debts, about eight hundred thousand at last count. But he hadn't worried about it. The Russians continued to extend him credit and had been discreet about his debt. Despite his losing streak Sergei Ivanov had treated him well, like royalty. The booze, the women and—most importantly—the credit had flowed like water from a burst dam. Sometimes he'd share a little secret information in exchange for a forgiven debt.

At last, Banner was a high roller. He'd gotten some damn respect and it had taken the Russians—the same people he'd spent a career training to fight—to give it to him.

Then that shifty bastard Ivanov had pulled the rug out from under him. All debts were due, immediately. Ivanov hadn't detailed the consequences of not paying. But the pair of thugs flanking him, a couple of ham-fisted assholes pumped up on steroids and cocaine, left little doubt as to Banner's possible fate.

He knew his life wasn't much, but it was still worth living. When Ivanov had offered him a deal—all debts forgiven plus a little cash to start over somewhere else with a new identity—it sounded too good to be true. That others in the government also were involved in the Russian's scheme had cinched the deal.

Banner had jumped at the prospect.

He didn't realize he was jumping feet first into hell.

He set the duffel bag down in a recessed doorway in the corridor—just like they'd told him to. Then he walked to blast doors sealing the security department's control room. Placing his eyes to the retinal security scanner, he waited for the apparatus to beep. The door hissed open and he stepped inside.

Because of his flawless military record and years of service to Sentinel Industries, Banner had access to all but the most classified sections of the Haven. This night he cursed the privilege.

The room was alive with the clicking of keyboards and multicolored displays. He counted three guards. Two sat at a large console, operating radar and communication equipment. The shift commander, a guy named Steve Cullen, sat at a bank of monitor screens, taking in views of the building's interior.

Cullen turned to Banner and smiled. "Burning the midnight oil, hotshot?" he asked.

Banner's body tingled with fear and anxiety, but he returned the smile. "You know it," he said. "No rest for the wicked."

"Amen." Cullen turned back to the bank of video monitors. "How can we help you tonight? You got some new hires you need us to background or what?"

Banner tried to keep it light. "Not quite," he said. "I need a cup of coffee."

Cullen turned. "Where's your cup?"

Banner felt his stomach lurch into his throat for a second. A former Las Vegas police captain, Cullen had led Clark County's organized crime division for years. The guy was hardwired with a suspicious nature, and he never missed a detail.

"Took it home last night," Banner said. "Thing had so much green in it, I didn't know whether to clean it out or cover it in salad dressing."

Cullen made a disgusted face, then grinned. "You gross bastard. Grab a foam cup, get your coffee and get out of here."

"Right." At the coffee maker, Banner poured himself a cup of the steaming liquid, made a show of cutting it with powdered creamer and sugar.

"Hey, Banner," Cullen called.

Banner froze. "Yeah Steve?"

"You can keep the cup."

The former cop laughed and Banner chimed in. He went back to preparing his coffee and checked his watch—12:30. Time was running out. He had to move.

He hesitated another moment. It still wasn't too late to walk away, a small voice cried out from deep within. Once he killed someone he'd have lost his last chance for redemption. He'd be one hundred percent committed. But at this moment he still had a chance. He could take the coffee, walk away.

And then what?

Trying to salvage his life now was like trying to find pristine wood on a centuries-old shipwreck. Forget it.

Cullen, staring intently at the monitors, spoke again. "So

what the hell you doing here this late, Banner? Your pilots not filling out their paperwork on time again?"

Fluidly, Banner slipped the Glock from under his jacket.

"Something like that, Steve." His voice sounded icy.

Cullen noticed the change and turned toward Banner. He never finished the move. From fifteen feet, Banner triggered the weapon once, twice. The handgun's crack reverberated throughout the room. Nausea passed through Banner for a moment as Cullen's head disappeared in a crimson spray. Banner shifted into autopilot and continued his slaughtering.

Swiveling at the hip, he sighted down the pistol and caught the other two security men thrusting themselves into action. The shock of being attacked by one of their own in their inner sanctum had bought Banner an extra moment or two. But he'd burned up most of that.

The men dived in separate directions, each grabbing for hardware. Banner panicked for a moment as he fired against two living, breathing targets and squeezed off two shots that went wild. A bullet sizzled past his ear and, more out of primal instinct than fear, he dropped to the ground. Handgun fire cracked like thunder about the room, and a pair of bullets whistled past Banner's ear as he went down.

He sought refuge behind a desk. Glock leading the way, he peered around the furniture and caught one of the guard's kneecaps protruding from behind cover. The Glock bucked once in his hands and a 9 mm round hurtled forward and bit into flesh. The wounded guard screamed in shock and pain. He pitched forward as he instinctively tried to gather up the wounded limb. The Glock barked twice more and Banner buried two rounds into the man's skull. Surrounded by his own blood, the man twitched briefly before releasing life.

Heart slamming in his chest like a jackhammer, breath escaping in panicked gasps, Banner listened for the third guard. It's either him or me, he thought. He realized the other guy was thinking the exact same thing.

A pair of pistols exploded, causing Banner to jerk. The guard had freed his backup piece and was firing both weapons. Slugs drilled through the desk, passing just inches from Banner's heaving torso.

The shots were hitting too close for comfort, Banner decided. He hauled himself up and sprinted for Cullen's console. He fired on the run, spraying bullets everywhere, trying to drive the guy under cover. The guard was better trained than Banner, and he held his ground. A bullet punched through Banner's jacket, but missed his torso. He dived forward, landing with a smack against the floor. Rolling into a ball, he tried to gather his breath and plan his next move. He felt something wet and realized he was sitting in the gore leaking from Cullen's shattered skull.

Banner heard only one weapon and assumed the guard's other pistol had run dry. Another bullet smacked into the console and then there was dead silence followed by a muttered curse. The guard's pistol had either run empty or jammed.

Banner brought himself up. A head of close-cut, bleached blond hair poked up from behind an overturned table. Banner raised his weapon and three shots later had murdered his third victim.

Moving to the monitor station, Banner rolled Cullen's body away with the tip of his foot and began studying the controls. Movement in one of the monitors caught his attention. Twelve men in navy blue jumpsuits, a security team, were hauling ass down the corridor and toward his position.

It turned Banner's stomach, but he knew what he needed to do.

Reaching inside his jacket, he pulled out a small detonator. He rested his thumb on the switch, then paused. He felt lightheaded and disconnected from his body, as though he were floating above it all watching someone else commit these atrocities unfolding around him.

He swallowed hard, flicked the switch.

An explosion resounded in the corridor, causing pieces of the ceiling to crumble down. For a moment, Banner wondered whether the Russians had packed the explosives incorrectly, whether he'd end up buried alive in this godforsaken desert tomb.

But the walls and the steel blast doors held. A quick look at the monitor told him that the security team had fared much worse. Severed arms and legs, battered torsos littered the passageway. Even though the image was a silent one, Banner knew there were no screams echoing in the corridor. He'd left no survivors.

The light feeling in his head grew worse. Sinking first to his knees, then to all fours, Banner felt his insides roiling, until finally he heaved out the contents of his stomach, his insides convulsing until he had nothing left.

Then he brought himself to his feet and with the press of a few buttons, laid open the Haven's defenses, leaving it ripe for invasion.

He pulled a digital phone from his pocket, hit a button activating a programmed number and waited for an answer.

When a voice answered, Banner said, "It's done."

"WHAT'S WRONG, Cowboy?" William Armstrong yelled over the helicopter's twin General Electric turboshaft engines. "You ain't getting sick are you? Not a big hot-shit pilot like you."

Jon Haley shot Armstrong a hard stare but said nothing. Armstrong returned the gaze with a cold one of his own and held Haley's stare until the pilot looked away. Just like two dogs trying to figure out who's boss, Armstrong thought. There was no doubt in his mind. He had Haley by the short hairs, and both men knew it.

Four men, all dressed in flight suits and body armor, sat on either side of Haley. A couple of them smiled or snickered as Armstrong needled the tense test pilot. Two others stared straight ahead, white-faced, wide-eyed and sweating. They were scared, and Armstrong knew why. Once inside the main hangar complex, they'd shed the body armor, board the jet fighters and escort Haley, Armstrong and the Nightwind out of the country. The pilots had a life expectancy of about twenty minutes, but the ones lucky enough to survive the escape would get a big payday.

Or so Kursk had told them. Armstrong knew better; the Russian didn't like to share his wealth with the rank and file. In Armstrong's case, though, the Russian knew better than to hold back even a dime of promised wages. Anyone stupid enough to be penny-wise and pound-foolish with Wild Bill Armstrong ended up dead. Pure and simple.

With practiced ease, Armstrong ran his hands over his gear, scrolling down a mental checklist and making sure he had everything he needed close at hand. He wanted to be ready to rock-and-roll once he hit the ground. When the communications blackout began, they had only minutes to get in and out of the Haven.

Granted, hitting the facility after Dade's kidnapping was risky. Word was that security had been cinched like a tourniquet after the incident. But, according to his sources, Sentinel Industries, the Pentagon and the CIA were expecting more kidnappings and concentrated their forces on a few scientists. Many of them had been moved underground.

No one expected an assault on the base itself. It was too audacious for anyone to conceive of.

Armstrong smiled.

That's why he was perfect for the job. Audacity was his stock-in-trade.

His former CIA handlers knew it. Nikolai Kursk knew it. Anyone else encountering him learned it in short order, usually to their peril.

Cole had been more soldier than killer, and it had cost him his life. He'd taken a bullet for a man he hated because the guy promised him some money. He'd fought alongside his men like a commander. His mistake.

Given the chance, Armstrong would have dropped napalm by the ton over every square inch of Kursk's precious little island, burned every last blade of grass and sacrificed every man there if it meant killing that bastard from the Justice Department. Scorched earth suited him fine as long as it produced results.

He considered his men the chess pieces and himself the chess master. He'd gladly sacrifice dozens of his own people to get in one good lick on the enemy, to win the game.

His headset crackled to life and he heard the pilot's voice. The guy sounded cool and calm, like a commercial airliner pilot urging passengers to put their trays in the upright position before he landed the plane.

"Thirty seconds to target, sir."

"Right," Armstrong said. "Any resistance?"

"Token. Our ground crew took out the patrol choppers with surface-to-air weapons. Our insider killed a large part of the security team with the bomb. But we still have pockets of resistance popping up."

"That's why you've got machine guns on this bird," Armstrong said. "Lay down some cover fire and then put us on the ground."

A pause. "Clear."

The helicopter began its descent. Armstrong hauled himself to his feet and braced himself. The other men stayed seated, waiting for his orders. He stared through the cockpit window as they went down and saw a vision of hell. Flames ravaged the wreckage of helicopters shot down by his fighters and raged through overturned vehicles. Dark shadows ran along the ground. Muzzle-flashes flared against the black backdrop, and red tracer rounds wound their way through the air. The din of gunfire could be heard even over the beating propellers and throbbing engines.

The craft jerked for a moment as the wheels touched the ground. A crew member opened the door, and fighters poured from the Black Hawk's belly. Armstrong crossed the chopper's interior, grabbed Haley by the shirt and hauled him to his feet. As Haley got his footing, Armstrong grabbed a Kevlar helmet and shoved into the pilot's hands.

"Put it on," he growled.

The orders had been explicit: Haley was to be protected at all costs. Everyone else could go to hell.

That was fine with Armstrong. He'd see that they did just that.

A CHILD'S WAILING snagged Rytova's attention immediately.

Hidden behind a fire-engine red PT Cruiser parked curbside, she listened to the sounds emanating from the Haley's two-story house. The crying came and went quickly and had sounded like the normal noises of a hungry baby. The Russian woman thought briefly of her lost child, her lost family, and anger coursed through her.

These bastards wouldn't cost another person their family. She'd damn well see to that.

She listened again and the house returned to silence.

Still dressed in black street clothing, she had smeared her face with black camou cosmetics. She crouched lower, hoping the vehicle's bulk would shield her from view. As she hunkered down, she felt the micro-Uzi riding in a shoulder holster dig into her ribs. Her jacket slipped up a bit, revealing the muzzle of the SIG-Sauer P-239 holstered on her right hip. She also carried magazines for both weapons. She wore a Kevlar vest underneath the oversized jacket.

A car with a bad muffler rumbled a few streets away. Three houses north of her, a big dog sensing something amiss barked incessantly. Occasionally, the owner shouted the dog's name, silencing it for a moment before it resumed making noise. Rytova cursed under her breath. At this hour, the disturbance might prompt one of the Haleys' captors to peer through the windows or step outside and compromise her approach.

She listened through her headset as her backup team positioned themselves, ticking off their names as they did. Cooper's men—he'd simply referred to them as blacksuits—had cordoned off a three-block perimeter around the street to prevent innocent motorists or Ivanov's men from happening upon the rescue attempt. With a couple of phone calls, the blacksuits had secured vans and uniforms from the local utility company and were warning people away with stories of a major gas leak.

Rytova checked her watch and realized that in another two minutes the action would begin. Crews would shut off power to the house, the team would storm inside and save the Haleys.

Maybe.

The notion of negotiations had been scratched. They needed to rescue the family even as Cooper pulled off his own mission. The gunners at the Haven needed to believe everything was going to plan to preserve as many lives as possible. It was a high-wire act in which a misstep could have lethal results.

She checked her watch again, realized only thirty seconds had passed. She felt impatience begin to overtake her.

Where the hell were the others? When would they give the signal?

Shelving the questions, the Russian tried to focus on the moment at hand. She needed to keep her senses about her. Lives depended on it.

She looked at the house, saw light shining through two of the second-story windows. The bluish glow of a television screen danced behind the white lace curtains obscuring a first-floor picture window. An occasional shadow passed by a window, but otherwise nothing seemed amiss.

Then a scream pierced the silence and things began to move quickly.

"YOU SURE YOU DON'T want me to go in with you, Sarge?" Jack Grimaldi asked. He patted a Beretta 92-F holstered on his right hip. An Uzi submachine gun rested just inches out of the Stony Man pilot's reach. "You say the word, I'm ready to rock-and-roll."

Bolan gave his friend a grim smile.

The two men had hooked up at Nellis Air Force base and Grimaldi was flying Bolan to the hardsite in an Apache helicopter. A second chopper followed behind them. They'd left

Route 93 behind several minutes earlier and were traveling over open desert toward the Haven.

"I need you in the air on this one, Jack. If they produce more air hardware, I'm going to need someone to cover my ass. Don't worry. You'll get your time on the ground, too."

"Right. I saw a team of pilots warming up at Nellis. Does that mean what I think it does?" Grimaldi asked.

Bolan nodded. "If the Nightwind leaves the ground, they move. Word's come down from the Man. That plane doesn't get past our southern border. If it gets to that point, Jon Haley's a dead man and the aircraft goes with him. But those could be the least of our worries if Kursk sets off a one kiloton nuke on American soil."

Grimaldi forced a grin. "At least the stakes are high on this one, huh?"

Bolan couldn't even muster another smile. When he spoke, the weariness in his voice surprised him. "They always are."

Grimaldi said nothing but punched his old friend on the shoulder. "Time to go dark, Sarge."

Both men slipped their night-vision goggles into place and Grimaldi relayed the same command to the chopper tailing them. During the next few minutes, they passed over the desert in silence, flying at low altitudes and without lights.

"There's the access road, Sarge," Grimaldi said.

"Put her down here, Jack," Bolan replied.

Within minutes, Bolan was grabbing his gear and disembarking from the combat chopper. He removed his night-vision goggles and relied on the moon's glare to illuminate the scene.

The second chopper touched down behind the first. A pair of soldiers had jumped out and stood, assault rifles at the ready, on the access road. Another soldier rolled a motorcycle down a ramp and brought it to Bolan. The guy was about Bolan's height with a medium build and intense brown eyes. He stopped five feet from Bolan, secured the bike on its kickstand and gave Bolan a hard stare.

"It's not too late, Striker," the man said. "We can all go in, hit them from all sides. I don't have to tell you there's strength in numbers. There's no need for you to play lone wolf here."

Bolan shook his head. "Forget it. You people are here to do a mission, and it doesn't involve being commandos. If I lose you, the whole thing's scrubbed. I can't deactivate the suitcase nuke."

The soldier, a U.S. Air Force captain, nodded. "That's fine— for now. But if something happens to you, I'm not wasting my time waiting on Washington to clear us for action. I'm going in. I've got a wife, two kids and a lot of friends sitting a couple of hours downwind from this place. I'll risk a court-martial to keep them safe."

Bolan took the bike from the captain's hands, straddled it and looked back at him. "I hope we don't have to go there."

The warrior fitted the night-vision goggles in place and the world went green. He fired the bike to life and roared off down the access road. As the bike gained speed, Bolan felt the cool desert air whipping against his black leather jacket and the exposed parts of his face. On any other night he'd have enjoyed a ride through untamed country. This night he only could think of the mission at hand.

Ear-shattering explosions tore through the night, illuminating the sky ahead of Bolan as passed between a pair of towering rock formations bordering both sides of the access road. Taking the bike to the side of the road, he killed the engine, laid the vehicle down and sprinted up the nearest incline.

Cresting the hill, he scrambled to a ridge, hoping to gain a bird's-eye view of the source of the explosions. Along the way, he found the slumped-over forms of two Sentinel Industries guards, both dead from gunshot wounds.

He slipped the NVGs from his face and stared down at the hell zone. Flames engulfed wrecked choppers, belching thick plumes of smoke into the air. A team of commandos dressed in camou fatigues exchanged fire with what Bolan assumed were Sentinel's security forces. Panicked civilian workers bolted across open areas, seeking refuge, but finding death as crisscrossing hails of autofire cut them down. Bolan guessed that at least a dozen bodies were strewed about the grounds. Even from his position, he could see the faces of the wounded contorted in agony, smell the oily black smoke and cordite odors rising from the besieged camp.

He'd seen enough. Kursk's people obviously had overwhelmed the security team.

The Russian's greed and his pursuit of the high-tech jet fighter had already shattered too many lives.

It was time for the Executioner to tip the scales in favor of justice. He slipped out of the bomber jacket and let it fall to the ground. He wore his black combat suit, combat webbing and carried the Beretta, the Desert Eagle and the Colt Python. Returning to the motorcycle, he retrieved the M-16/M-203 combo and an Uzi. He checked both weapons, wanting to make sure they were ready to deal out death.

Without a doubt, *he* was.

12

Natasha Rytova pushed aside the six-foot wooden gate and stepped into the backyard. She held her breath, worried the gate would squeak on its rusted hinges. It didn't, and she vowed not to squander her good fortune. Shutting it behind her, she continued moving along the driveway that led through the gate, her SIG-Sauer ready.

Her first impressions were of the smells of cigarette smoke and cheap aftershave. Wrapping herself in a blanket of shadows, she knelt and scanned her surroundings.

The driveway led to a detached two-car garage clad in the same sunbaked, warped cedar siding that covered the house. The garage door was rolled up, and Rytova saw a big sedan and a small yellow sports car sitting inside. A bulky man stood between the two cars, smoothing his hair as he stared into the sedan's side mirror.

White light suddenly cut through the backyard, causing Rytova to scramble to the side of the house. Someone had turned on a patio light, and Rytova heard a glass door sliding along its track as it came open.

"You look like shit," the man said in heavily accented English. He released a big belly laugh. The sudden infusions of light and noise startled the other man, and he whirled toward the house. He glared at the other man.

"I look like shit? Me? Your wife, she looks like shit," he said.

"I know," the other man replied. "That's why I keep two girlfriends."

Another rumble of laughter. "Get inside. We cannot reach the others and Joseph is worried something happened. Plus our guests are getting restless."

The sentry scowled but made a beeline for the house. As he moved inside, he glided his fingertips over perfectly coiffed hair and tugged at his suit jacket to straighten the fabric. Just like Sergei Ivanov in miniature, Rytova thought.

A voice sounded in her headset. She recognized it as belonging to Dale Gilmore, the team leader.

"Ripper team in place, Natasha. Can't get a visual on you. Where the hell are you?"

"I'm in the backyard," she replied. "I heard a scream. I went to investigate."

"Negative. That's not the plan, Natasha, and you know it," Gilmore said.

"Stand fast," Rytova said, stressing each syllable.

Perspiration slid down from her hairline and stung her still-healing head wound, causing her to wince. She heard the glass door slide open again and heard footsteps as one, then a second man stepped outside. Gilmore's voice filled the headset as he began to argue. Rytova expelled a quick "shh" from between clenched teeth and the radio went silent.

The dapper man from the garage and a second person she didn't recognize both stepped into view. The second man—tall, slim with a hawkish face—dug a pack of cigarettes from the breast pocket of his shirt and tapped out two smokes. Taking one, he offered the second to the pretty boy, who snatched it away and jabbed it between his lips.

"I thought you said Joseph was worried," the smaller man said.

The hawk-faced one shrugged. "How was I to know Sergei called? I was here with you."

"So he is okay?"

"He says he got held up somewhere. He will be here soon enough. He said to sit tight."

Rytova knew that much was true. She'd arranged for the Russian mobster to call his people, assure them of his safety so they wouldn't panic and flee from the house, either taking the Haleys with them or killing them on the spot. A cleanup team sent from Washington had taken control of the casino shooting scene and was trying to clamp down on media coverage for as long as possible. Cooper's people were leaning on Ivanov, forcing him to pump his people full of lies so they'd stay put and let the Haleys live.

"I heard the woman scream," Pretty Boy said. "What happened?"

"She sneaked into a bedroom, picked up a phone," the other thug said. "Do not look worried. We caught her before she could dial a number. But we decided to take some of the fire out of her. Joseph hit her in the face, broke her nose. She screamed."

"He let her off easy."

"Not so. Last I saw he had filled the bathtub with steaming hot water and held her head under it. Joseph is feeling nasty tonight."

The smaller man snorted. "Joseph is nasty every night. I just hope we get to have time with her before tonight ends. She's got fire. I will put it out."

"But my friend, you have such a small hose." The bigger man again erupted into laughter and slapped Pretty Boy on the back. The smaller man took the blow between the shoulder blades and stumbled forward under the impact. He caught his footing but dropped his cigarette.

Rytova felt nauseous as she listened to their callous banter. Then white-hot rage overtook her. She'd heard enough. Earlier tonight, she had started to go soft on these killers, to doubt her mission. There was no room for that, she decided with certainty.

She raised the SIG-Sauer, triggered it twice. The first round burned past Pretty Boy's face. The second crashed into his skull, just above his ear before the hollowpoint round tunneled out the other side of his head. Blood and brain matter splattered over the hawk-faced man's shoulder. He grabbed for a hidden handgun, began to whip around and open his mouth to shout a warning. A 9 mm round whacked into his open mouth, whipping his head back hard before ripping away the back of it. He crumpled to the ground, falling on top of the other man.

Pulling the two men out of the yard, she hid them in the shadows. No one had looked out the windows during the precious seconds it took to move the bodies. "I've got two of Ivanov's men down. We need to go in now before the others find them."

"Right," Gilmore said. He sounded exasperated with Natasha. "Stay put. We're coming in."

Another scream sounded from within, and Rytova decided she could no longer wait.

Sliding the patio door, she peered inside, saw the room was empty and slipped inside. The mobsters had furnished the room with a threadbare chocolate brown couch, six empty pizza boxes, overstuffed ashtrays and empty beer cans. They'd turned the air conditioner down to what seemed like meat-locker temperatures, and Rytova shivered involuntarily as she crossed the room.

She cleared the kitchen and the dining room. The muscles of her rib cage tightened, constricting her breathing as she heard the sloshing of water and a woman's pleadings from upstairs. She stepped into the entryway, peered into the living room, alive with the television screen's dancing glow. Her heart told her to rush up the stairs, but her head told her to clear the final first-floor room.

Her head won. Pressing against the wall, she snatched a peek inside the living room and saw one man sitting on the couch. Despite the ruckus upstairs, the man's head lolled to one side and rattled out long snores. The room stank of alcohol, and Rytova assumed the man had drunk himself into oblivion. How else could anyone sleep through the horrible cries? With a closer look, she saw more than a half dozen beer bottles, all empty, standing on a small coffee table in front of the man. She guessed her hunch was right.

Switching the SIG-Sauer to her left hand, she filled her right with the micro-Uzi, setting it for single-shot mode as she did. She wasn't going to risk spraying down the hallways with 9 mm bursts with at least four innocent people crammed in a confined space. Steel struck bone as she smacked the drunk in the back of the head with the Uzi, shoving him deeper into unconsciousness.

Where the hell was her backup? She turned and started out of the room. Along the way, she heard the blacksuits talking to one another through the headset as they closed in on the house. She wanted to wait for the help, but another scream all but dragged her to the stairs.

She felt more than saw someone sneak up behind her. She came about, both weapons tracking in on a shadow.

She stopped.

It was a small child, a little girl. Her eyes were wide and she looked too frightened to cry. The poor thing, Rytova thought. Holstering the pistol, she gathered the girl into her arms and took her into a nearby room. The girl didn't resist.

As she clutched the girl to her, the child seemed to thaw and started to sob.

Putting herself between the girl and the door, Rytova set the child down and began stripping off her Kevlar vest. She felt a sudden coolness surrounded her torso as she unsheathed herself and began wrapping the child in a protective cocoon of Kevlar.

"I want my mommy," the child said.

"I'm sorry, sweetie," Rytova whispered, "but I need you to stay here for a moment. I'll go get your mommy for you."

The girl spoke in a low voice. Rytova guessed that shock kept her from becoming completely hysterical. "Mommy's crying. They're yelling at her. Did she do something bad?"

"No, sweetie." She ushered the girl into a closet. She knew

time was burning down fast and she had to move. "Please stay in here for just a minute, and I'll get your mother for you. You must stay until someone comes for you. Can you do that?"

The girl hesitated, nodded.

"Good girl." Rytova shut the door and went back on the move.

Another scream from upstairs, this time followed by a male voice.

She assumed it was the one Hawkface had called Joseph.

"You stupid bitch! Perhaps I should cut open your face. See how you like that. I will make this a very long night for you. And I will make your children watch it all."

Like hell, Rytova thought as she slipped up the narrow stairwell. She refilled her left hand with the sound-suppressed SIG-Sauer as she went.

"Please let us go," a woman pleaded. "I want my husband back. I want my children safe. Can't you see that?"

Gilmore's voice, hushed but edgy, sounded in Rytova's earpiece. "We're in the house. Just another few seconds."

Before she could stop herself, Rytova had burst upstairs into the hallway. Everything slowed to one-quarter speed. She could hear blood pounding in her ears but could no longer feel herself breathing. She'd lost all sense of time. A big shape registered in her peripheral vision. She turned. Her brain analyzed the shape, synapses fired and the micro-Uzi rumbled in her hand as she pumped bullets into a big man with a pump shotgun closing in on her position. He backpedaled, fell and she jerked her head to the left. A man in a white dress shirt, the tails pulled out from his pants, was dragging Monica Haley through the bathroom door. The woman's face had been burned red by exposure to the hot water. Her soaked hair hung limp around her face.

The man brought up a straight razor, ready to fling it overhand at Rytova. The SIG-Sauer whispered, bucking against Rytova's palm as she fired the weapon. The first round pounded into the man's chest and he jerked to a stop as though colliding with a wall. The second bullet buried itself just under his collarbone, coring its way through his body before ripping out his shoulder muscles. When he refused to fall, Rytova pumped a third shot into his forehead. He teetered back and fell head-first through the bathroom door.

Rytova made eye contact with Monica Haley. The woman's face was alive with terror, and Rytova at first thought Haley was scared of her. It was too late when she realized the woman was looking over her shoulder at someone else.

A gun barked. A bullet plowed into Rytova's back. It hurt too bad for her to determine the exact point of impact. Her mind reeled. She sank first to her knees, her weapons slipping from her grip as she went down. She went facedown on the floor, her body consumed in fire, her mind still registering the melee erupting around her.

A man was curled around a door frame, a gun homed in on Rytova. She realized the killing blow was imminent. Steeled herself for it.

A black blur erupted from the stairwell. A submachine gun spit fire and flame. A sustained burst pounded into the hard-man, spun him and heaved him down the hallway.

More black shapes poured onto the second floor, securing Monica Haley, and the remaining two children, ministering to Rytova's wounds. A dark shape loomed over her, and she saw Gilmore's face.

"Closet. First floor," she whispered.

With the worst over, she slipped into a welcome blackness and wondered whether it was time to reunite with Dmitri.

FUELED BY ADRENALINE, Bolan raced the motorcycle down the hill, took it into a tight turn and aimed it toward the Haven. Gunning the engine, he closed in on the front gate, which had been knocked from its moorings by a charging vehicle and hung in two pieces.

The facility had been turned into a war zone: a sea of overturned vehicles engulfed in flames, corpses everywhere, muzzle-flashes splitting the darkness like lightning bolts.

The warrior brought the bike to a halt and caught a ragged line of gunners initiating a death march toward him. They were moving fast and aiming weapons at him. Holding the M-16's butt in close to his hip, Bolan fired the weapon with one hand, dousing the killers with a sustained fusillade of 5.56 mm tumblers. Two of the men crumpled to the ground. A third fired off a burst of autofire at Bolan. The slugs passed to his right and punched through the windows of a nearby building, showering the surrounding terrain with glass. The Executioner triggered another burst at nearly the same time as his opponent. The M-16 chugged, the shots ripping into the man's head and throat.

The beat of chopper blades sounded to the north of Bolan and he saw one of the Black Hawks coming to life, preparing for a takeoff. At the same time, a gunner poised in the chopper's side door fired upon a pair of blue-suited Sentinel security guards. Bolan knew he couldn't let the chopper get into the air, or they could pulverize him and everyone he'd come to help.

Pulling the M-16/M-203 combo to his shoulder, the warrior squeezed off a high-explosive round, planting it squarely in the side door. A moment later, the HE round blew, ripping apart the helicopter's interior and eventually igniting the fuel tanks. The chopper—a roiling orange fireball—heaved up and spun away before falling to earth and smashing into what appeared to be a motor pool building with large bay doors. A storm of glass and shrapnel sliced through the air, forcing Bolan to tip the bike, hug the ground and wait out the explosion.

With his leg pinned under the motorcycle, Bolan spotted two more hardmen bolting from a nearby building and closing in on him. He figured he'd expended two-thirds of the M-16's 30-round clip and decided to go for broke. The assault rifle blazed to life, hurling a punishing fusillade of tumblers toward the approaching gunners. The closer of the pair bore the brunt of Bolan's skilled marksmanship, absorbing most of the burst in his chest. Another slug grazed the second man's shoulder, but barely slowed him as he whipped up a machine pistol and sprayed Bolan's position. The warrior freed the Desert Eagle from his right armpit and unloaded three of the 240-grain man-stoppers in the guy's direction. The man corkscrewed toward the ground.

Pushing the motorcycle off his leg, Bolan rolled to his feet, ejecting the M-16's clip as he rose. Stuffing the Israeli-made pistol between his ribs and his biceps, he reloaded the assault rifle and moments later was on the run, both weapons held at the ready.

A shrill scream to his right caught the warrior's attention. Jerking his gaze toward the sound, he saw a woman—a civilian worker—who'd fallen to the ground as she tried to elude a pursuer. Face twisted in panic, she crawled along the ground and tried to distance herself from a gunner who stepped from the shadows. Raising an Uzi, the man drew down on his victim, prepared to deal a killing strike.

Bolan struck first. The assault rifle barked out two quick bursts that ripped the killer apart before he could squeeze off shots of his own. Slinging his rifle over his shoulder, the Executioner moved in on the woman, scooped her up and carried her to one of the nearby buildings. It was locked.

"You have clearance to this place?" he asked.

The woman nodded. Reaching inside her lab coat, she withdrew a security card and swiped it through the reader. The door hissed open. Dim fluorescent lights illuminated the main corridor, but the rooms to each side sat dark.

Moving inside, Bolan carried the injured woman down the hall and into a windowless office. Setting her on the floor, he turned and started back out the room. The woman grabbed his pants leg and he halted.

"What if they come for me?"

Reaching behind his back, Bolan drew the Colt Python. "You know how to use one of these?"

The woman nodded. "I grew up around guns."

Bolan handed her the pistol, two speed loaders and a flashlight. "Pull yourself into a corner and wait. I'll send someone for you as soon as possible. Make sure you ID your target before you shoot."

The woman nodded and Bolan was again on the run. Using her security card, he passed through the door and back into the battle zone. Taking the woman to safety had cost him precious seconds, but he had no choice. If he had to sacrifice even a single innocent life, reaching his ultimate goal was meaningless.

Firing from the dark, he mowed down two more rogue fighters as they ran by.

Bolan remained in the shadows and glided along the buildings. Looking around, he identified what he thought was the primary hangar. The curved roof rose above the other two- and three-story buildings surrounding him. He estimated the distance at about three hundred yards. An easy run under any other circumstances.

This night it was a race through hell.

13

William Armstrong saw the blacksuited man mowing down his people, uttered an expletive and kept on moving. His first instinct was to turn, help his men fight. Not because he felt a kinship or camaraderie with them. Hell, no. They were hired hands.

He just hated to turn tail and run from a fight, especially from someone able to do battle like that big bastard cutting a swath through a team of elite soldiers.

Jon Haley also saw the stranger running interference, and his face hardened. Armstrong could practically see the wheels turning. Haley was no longer alone, and his soldierly instincts were kicking in. Maybe the odds were moving in his favor.

Armstrong cracked him across the jaw. The sucker punch sent the pilot reeling to the dirt.

"Don't even think it, Cowboy," Armstrong said. "Any of my crew sees you trying to rebel, they have orders to call back to Vegas and have your family wiped out. You got it?"

Haley pulled himself to his feet and wiped blood from his lips. He said nothing, but his expression told Armstrong he still was willing to play along. Armstrong grabbed the guy by the back of his flight suit and shoved him forward. "C'mon, Cowboy, you got the clearance."

At the hangar door, Haley went through the ritual: first the retinal scan, followed by a thumbprint check, followed by a voice-recognition check. The heavy steel doors slid open and Haley went inside, followed by Armstrong.

"Halt."

Armstrong saw a pair of security guards down the corridor. One had sought cover inside a door frame while the other was hidden behind a steel locker. Both men had weapons trained on Haley and Armstrong. Armstrong grabbed the pilot by the neck and held him at arm's length from himself.

"Sir," the guard in the doorway shouted, "you need to drop that weapon."

Armstrong stood fast.

"Drop the fucking weapon," the other guard yelled.

Armstrong shoved Haley aside, dropped into a crouch and triggered his weapon. The Uzi etched out a blistering figure eight that flayed open the guards' thighs, pounded at their body armor and ripped into their faces before either man could squeeze off a shot.

Still in a crouch, Armstrong ejected the Uzi's clip and reached for a fresh one. A shadow stirred behind him, causing him to turn. Fisting his Glock as he whirled, he extended his arm and planted the Glock's barrel in Haley's belly. The pilot was less than a foot away, caught dead to rights in his sneak attack.

"Bang," Armstrong said through clenched teeth. He laughed and pushed Haley ahead of him. Armstrong reloaded the Uzi and holstered the Glock as they neared a stairwell.

"You're a psychotic piece of shit," Haley said over his shoulder.

Armstrong grinned. "Ain't it the truth? And guess who's next on my hit list if he doesn't shut his damn mouth?"

Haley gave him a defiant look. "I'm not afraid to die."

"Doesn't matter, Cowboy. You're afraid for your family, which gives me the same results. Now get down those stairs."

Minutes later, they'd passed through two more steel doorways and a labyrinth of reinforced concrete tunnels. Each step of the way, Haley reluctantly used his all-points security clearance to get them through the next security hurdle. They stepped inside a cavernous underground chamber about the size of a football field.

The Nightwind prototype sat on a platform, the plane's black skin gleaming under rows of recessed fluorescent lights. The cockpit hatch rested open.

"Cold in here," Armstrong said.

"That's to keep the diagnostic computers cool," Haley said. "We run the plane through an extensive series of tests before we stick it in the air. Usually takes a dozen technicians working constantly for three or four hours to get this thing in the air."

"Tonight you got three minutes. The escort pilots should be along any minute. Once they're here, we take this thing topside and fly it the hell out of here."

Footsteps sounded behind the two men. Armstrong wheeled, raising his weapon as he did. He saw Banner approaching, and the guy held up his hands. Armstrong lowered his weapon and looked at Haley who had also turned in Banner's direction. The pilot's face reddened, and he clenched and unclenched his fists.

"You son of a bitch," Haley said. "You set me up. You put my family in harm's way."

Dressed in a flight suit, Banner crossed the room but avoided Haley's fiery stare. Blood crusted his clothes, and he had a deep gash on his forehead. He carried a mesh bag filled with two flight helmets and other gear in one hand and a pistol in the other.

"I didn't want it to work out this way, Cowboy," Banner said. "But I had no choice. You have to believe that's the case."

"I'll show you what I believe," Haley said.

The pilot stepped forward but stopped when Armstrong threatened him with the Uzi.

"Forget it, Cowboy," Armstrong said. "Much as I'd love to watch you two pukes have a slap fest, I'm working on a tight timetable. Now take the helmet like a good boy and get your ass on that airplane. Give him his fucking helmet, Banner."

The older man leathered his pistol, reached inside the mesh bag and pulled out the headgear. Keeping his distance, he tossed the helmet to Haley. The test pilot gave the older man an icy look but took what was offered to him.

Armstrong had expected the conflict to explode and felt almost disappointed when it hadn't. He knew he'd enjoy watching these two mix it up, but he also knew he didn't have the time.

Still, he couldn't resist one more dig.

"Hey, Haley, forget about the Beretta and the flare guns stowed in the survival gear. Banner removed that from the craft earlier tonight. Right, Banner?"

Banner's voice was quiet. "You know I did, Armstrong."

"Yeah, but I want the kid to know."

Haley stopped and turned back toward Banner, pinning the older man under his gaze. "Why did you do it, Banner?"

"It's complicated, kid."

"We're burning time," Armstrong said. "Get on that plane before I shoot your legs off and leave you to bleed to death down here."

Haley frowned but continued to walk toward the jet fighter.

Armstrong jabbed his index finger in Banner's direction. "You. Start the hydraulic lifts. I want that hunk of steel topside in two minutes." He barked into his headset. "Where the hell are you people? I need my pilots front and center five minutes ago."

"We're one minute from your position, sir," came the response.

"Let's go. I want us out of here and this place glowing in another couple of minutes."

Haley stopped in midstride and turned. "What the hell did you say?"

A cold feeling passed through Armstrong, and he realized he'd almost said too much.

He checked his chronometer, realized more than a minute had passed. Where the hell where the pilots? Before he could shout the question into the headset, a blast thundered from somewhere inside the building. Gunshots followed close behind.

"Get your ass in that plane now," he bellowed.

As his blitz continued, Mack Bolan came upon a pair of Sentinel security guards caught on the losing end of a gun battle against a group of killers. Hidden behind an overturned Chrysler, one of the guards held his abdomen with bloodied hands while a female guard wielding a handgun fought back against three-to-one odds. Two other civilian workers were huddled together behind the vehicle, trying to make themselves as small targets as possible.

Bolan hid behind another car and scanned the area. A half dozen of Kursk's soldiers were spread out on the opposite side of the street, hiding behind cars and buildings. Orange ribbons of fire streaked from their weapons as they battered the innocents with gunfire. Bolan saw three more shadows moving along the rooftops.

"Striker to Ace," Bolan called into his headset.

"Go, Striker," Jack Grimaldi said.

"I think Kursk has people up on the roof. I need air support."

"I'm on it, Striker. Been waiting for your call. You seen any signs of Haley yet?"

"Negative."

"That's no good. Once that plane leaves the ground, they're going to unleash the big boom. We're all screwed then."

"Right. Tell the disposal team to get ready to move. We need them on the ground ASAP."

"Roger that."

Coming around from behind his protective shield, Bolan bracketed one of the invaders in the M-16's sights and tapped out a quick burst that pulverized the man's head and pitched him to the side. Other shooters turned in Bolan's direction and began firing upon him, pinning him down.

He picked off another hardman before the gunfire intensified, forcing him under cover. A quick glance told him he'd bought the embattled Sentinel workers enough time to disappear from harm's way. Bullets pounded through the car, showering Bolan with bits of window glass. Gunfire from above pierced the car's steel skin.

The distant beat of helicopter blades registered in his mind. Friend or foe? He'd know in a minute.

Cracking a frag round into the grenade launcher, Bolan fired the weapon. Landing in the middle of the knot of shooters, the weapon exploded, hurling streams of unforgiving shrapnel and plunging the gunners into a microsecond of hellish terror and pain before granting them death's sweet relief.

The thrumming of helicopter blades grew closer. A thunderclap followed by a brilliant burst of daylight rent the air east of Bolan. The warrior heard a massive object strike against the ground accompanied by smaller bits of debris showering the area just out of his line of sight. A piece of propeller whizzed about three feet overhead and crashed through a nearby window. For a moment, it seemed, Bolan's heart stopped beating and leaped into his throat.

"Jack! Jack! Report."

Grimaldi's voice was calm. "Right, Striker. I'm okay. I caught the other bird swooping in on your position. You'll get a visual of me in a few more seconds."

More gunfire erupted from above, reminding Bolan of his own predicament.

"Jack…"

The whirring of helicopter blades almost drowned out Grimaldi's reply as he moved in. A gale force wind rushed through the area as Grimaldi came into view.

"Already on it, Striker."

Grimaldi's chopper hovered and he loosed the machine guns, raining death upon the rooftop shooters. Muzzle-flashes illuminated the scene in fits and starts and Bolan caught glimpses of several hardmen being jerked around under the withering hail of lead.

"Nice job, Jack. Now get that thing out of here before someone shoots a rocket-propelled grenade up your tailpipe."

"Roger that, Striker. I'll land and escort the disposal team into the area."

Bolan hauled himself to his feet, reloaded the grenade launcher with another frag round and moved in a run. Disappearing into the shadows, he scanned the streets for his next opponent. Rounding a corner, Bolan found three of Kursk's gunners standing over a tangle of corpses. He could tell from their uniforms that the dead had been members of Sentinel's staff. Firing from the hip, the Executioner swept his weapon over the group and caught the first two men with a blast of autofire.

The third guy had better reflexes and an admirable hunger for survival. Hurling himself forward, the intruder rolled and came up in a prone position with a stutter gun clasped in both hands. The shooter tried to lock the muzzle on Bolan, but the warrior stopped him cold with a burst from the M-16.

Bolan spun and caught a pair of gunners about ten feet apart from each other approaching from behind. Even as he turned, a round ripped through his leather jacket and plowed into his Kevlar vest. The force knocked him off balance, and he suddenly found himself gasping for air.

As his body tried to process the trauma, the warrior fired the grenade launcher and planted a frag round into the ground about five feet in front of the men. The weapon detonated, taking out both gunners. Grimacing as he hauled himself to his feet, Bolan gingerly touched the point of impact. He'd have a hell of a bruise on his ribs, he knew, but it beat the alternative.

With most of Kursk's soldiers dead, Bolan covered the remaining distance to the hangar without incident. When he arrived, he caught a man in what looked like a black flight suit moving through a windowless, steel door that had been left ajar. Bolan waited fifteen seconds and followed the man inside.

The M-16 clutched at hip level, he came upon a set of stairs that he descended in a sidestepping motion. Eyes and ears probed the dust- and smoke-choked surroundings for signs of life.

"Ace to Striker."

"Go," he whispered.

"I've brought in the disposal team. We're on the ground and breaching the main building. We've got a lock on our errant bomb."

Finally some good news. "Roger that."

"You get our plane yet?"

"Negative. Working on it."

"Roger that, Striker. Ace out."

Stepping onto the next landing, Bolan knelt and, using the preceding staircase for cover, looked into the dimly lit corridor that yawned open one flight below him. A bulky, square shadow—presumably a locker or cabinet—suddenly sprouted a head and arm before morphing back into its previous shape. Something shifted in the darkness, and Bolan heard the rattle of something metallic.

Snatching a flash-stun grenade from his gear, Bolan activated the device and heaved it into the target area. A whump and a white glare filled the corridor below. He surged down the final flight of stairs, the M-16's barrel fanning the area in front of him as he tried to acquire a target.

One of Kursk's troopers—dressed in a black flightsuit—stumbled across Bolan's line of sight. The man had covered his eyes with a forearm and was indiscriminately firing his SMG ahead of him. Parabellum rounds flew high and to Bolan's left, chewing into concrete or clanging off steel.

Robbed of his senses, the man's aim was bad. But in such a confined space, even a marginal improvement could have lethal results for the Executioner.

Bolan didn't give his opponent room for improvement. Instead he hosed down the hallway with sweeping swaths of auofire. Lead cleaved into the man's head and throat, and twisted him in a violent pirouette. With the same blast, Bolan burned down a second gunner who strayed from cover.

A blur farther down the corridor caught Bolan's attention. Another fighter bolted from cover, his SMG cracking out a deadly challenge. The Executioner threw himself into a prone position and caressed the assault rifle's trigger. The resulting burst of tumblers ripped into the running man's left shoulder at an upward angle before exploding out his lower back near the kidneys.

Ninety seconds later, Bolan had moved deeper into the facility and found himself faced with another steel door. Running through a mental image of the building's layout, he realized he was just outside a chamber that sat below the Nightwind's hangar. He tried swiping the access card the woman had given him, but a small red light on the reader never blinked.

"Access denied," a programmed voice said.

"Striker to Ace."

"Go Striker."

"Any word from Vegas?"

"Yeah. Team pulled it off. You get to Haley, you can tell him his family is safe."

"Rytova?"

A pause. "She got hit, Striker. She'll live, but at least one of her kidneys took a nasty wound. Sorry."

Though he was alone, Bolan nodded at Grimaldi's words. "Has Bear been able to patch into the computer systems here?"

"Right. Wasn't easy. Some asshole initiated a system shutdown. Bear had to jump-start the damn thing from Virginia."

"He download my biometric information into the security system?"

"Retinal. No fingerprints, just like you requested. You have an all-points clearance with just an eye scan. He'll purge your information from the system when you give the word."

"Roger that. Maintain radio silence until I say otherwise. Striker out."

"Ace out."

Slinging the M-16, Bolan fisted the Desert Eagle. He stepped to the retinal scanner, pressed his forehead against the contoured face piece and waited. For a heart-stopping second the warrior wondered whether he'd get inside in time. He didn't have the minutes necessary to find an alternate entrance, if such a thing existed.

This was his best shot.

"Identity confirmed," the voice said. The portal slid open and

Bolan scrambled inside, the Desert Eagle in a two-handed grip as he glanced around the room for the next threat.

Empty.

The thick columns of the aircraft lift were fully extended, indicating the plane had been moved into the main hangar. Apparently someone had heard the gunshots outside and accelerated their timetable.

Bolan saw a steel ladder bolted into a wall in the room's northeast corner. Moving to the ladder, he stared up its length and saw that it led to a portal that measured about three feet in diameter. Ascending the ladder, he reached the top and found the steel portal sealed shut. He again used a retinal scanner and the door hissed open.

Pushing himself up through the hole, the warrior found himself inside a hangar that measured the length of four football fields laid end to end and stretched another hundred yards across. Four unmanned fighter jets stood by. The Nightwind sat between them, two fighters on each flank. A bay door yawned open at the end of the structure.

Bolan saw Jon Haley, whom he recognized from a photograph, climbing a portable ladder that led into the aircraft while a pasty-faced giant and another man aimed their weapons at him.

Stepping out of the hole and coming to his full height, Bolan raised the Desert Eagle and caught the two gunners in his sights. The older man's hand shot up, and he tried to sight in on Bolan with his handgun. The Desert Eagle roared once and sent a .44-caliber crashing into the man's sternum. His handgun slipped from his grip and skittered across the floor.

Bolan shifted and locked the Desert Eagle's muzzle on the second man. He assumed from his briefing the man was William Armstrong. The features had changed since the man's days in Afghanistan but not his skin pallor or his enormous size.

Armstrong trained his Uzi on Haley and stared at Bolan.

"You'd better let us go, hero. My boy and I have an appointment to make. If I don't make it, his family dies. You don't want that on your head do you? Not a big hero like you."

Bolan's gaze stayed locked on Armstrong. But from his peripheral vision he saw Haley, his features contorted with concern, also staring at him. Confused and scared for his family, Bolan knew Haley was the wild card in this play.

Keeping his gun hand steady, Bolan shook his head.

"No go, Armstrong. We've got his family. They're all safe. You're done."

Doubt flickered briefly in Armstrong's eyes but was quickly replaced with steel. "You're full of shit, hero. You're trying to screw with my head."

"It's the truth," Bolan said. "And a good friend of mine took a bullet in the op. That makes things between you and me personal."

A small grin played on Armstrong's lips.

Haley had grabbed some distance, but still was too close for Bolan's comfort. A stray shot could result in the young man going home in a body bag.

Almost against his will, Bolan's thoughts shifted to Grimaldi and company, wondering whether they'd taken the suitcase nuke out of commission.

"It doesn't have to go bad, Armstrong," Bolan said. "You fought for your country. What the hell happened to you?"

"I got a better offer. Obviously you didn't," he said, laughing.

Haley erupted in a sudden flurry of movement. He drove his booted right foot into Armstrong's ribs, knocking the big man off balance. Before Armstrong could react, Haley heaved himself backward, hitting the floor hard but falling out of Armstrong's immediate reach.

Armstrong's Uzi chugged out an upward line of fire that ripped through empty space. But the big guy was a pro, and within a moment was already regaining his balance. He swung the Uzi around and tried to bring Bolan into his sights.

The Executioner dropped into a crouch and squeezed off two shots from the Desert Eagle. The bullets thudded into Armstrong's chest, smashing through bone and flesh as the force tossed the big man around. The Uzi clattered to the floor, well out of the reach of Armstrong's dead fingers.

His face twisted with rage, Haley rose, closed in on the body and repeatedly drove his foot into the bigger man's bloodied torso.

"Son of a bitch. Son of a bitch."

Bolan knew the anger and frustration of several hours of terror were flooding out of the man. He figured he had a release coming. Besides, Bolan had more important things to worry about.

"Jack, give me a status report."

"We disarmed it. Just finished. It was touch and go for a little bit though."

"It's still touch and go," the Executioner said. "I have a final score to settle."

14

"They're here, sir," the young woman said.

Seated at the edge of the exercise bench, Nikolai Kursk turned his bull neck around and regarded the servant standing in the doorway of his personal gymnasium. She was a slender woman clad in a simple white dress, and her thick, black hair was tied back in a ponytail. She cast dark eyes to the ground as Kursk ran his gaze over her. She shifted from foot to foot, waiting for his reply. From the moment he'd arrived, the Russian had taken an instant interest in the woman, and his attention seemed to make her squirm.

He liked that.

"Make them comfortable," Kursk said. "Get them drinks. Tell them I'll meet them in fifteen minutes."

"Yes, sir." She turned and left.

Standing, he toweled the sweat from his forehead, shoulders and biceps. Power coursed through his blood-charged muscles, and he reveled in the feeling. He smiled, knowing things were getting back on track.

He'd lost the battle, but not the war. Matt Cooper and Natasha Rytova had cost him dearly both in money and pride. They'd hobbled his organization, made him look like a fool, left him on the run with only a handful of men.

But he knew that they'd also made a fatal mistake. They'd let him escape, let him live. Their failed attempt to capture him would prove their undoing. Before the week was out, he'd dispatch death squads to hunt down and kill them both. Then he'd move on to his next venture.

But first he needed some money.

Kursk dropped the soiled towel on the floor, left it for one of the servants to pick up. Moving to the locker room, he shaved, showered and changed into khakis, a white polo shirt and loafers. He slipped the holstered Tokarev into the small of his back, clipping it onto the waistband of his pants, and exited the locker room.

After a quick trip to his study to grab a small leather case, he made his way through the house and arrived for his meeting thirty seconds earlier than promised. Satisfied with himself, he stepped out of his home and into the afternoon sun.

Spurred by habit and prudence, Kursk scrutinized his security arrangements. A pair of Uzi-toting guards walked the perimeter, staring at the lush mountains caps that surrounded the villa and seemed to extend forever. Another pair of hardmen stood closer to the patio.

After all that had occurred, Kursk was glad to be in Colombia. He'd done business with drug lords and rebels for years and they left him alone, as did the government officials whose loyalty he commanded either through intimidation or bribery. He felt safe here.

A dark man sat at the table, drinking spring water from a plastic bottle. When he saw Kursk, he stood.

"Azid," Kursk thundered. "So good to see you."

Kursk offered his hand and Azid Khordadian, a high-ranking Iranian intelligence official, took it.

Khordadian responded to Kursk's enthusiasm with a reserved look of his own and said, "It also is good to see you my friend."

Kursk sensed something amiss almost immediately. He gestured toward the chairs. "Please, have a seat."

Khordadian settled his round body into a wrought-iron chair. Kursk also sat. Clasping his hands together, the Iranian rested them in his lap and leaned forward. A pair of Khordadian's security men sat within easy reach of their boss.

"We must dispense with the pleasantries, my friend," the Iranian said. "I do not have long and we must talk of the plans."

"Of course," Kursk said. He snapped his fingers and a nearby servant brought him a cup of coffee, black. "I do have them. I had a copy burned to compact disk shortly after I met with the scientist. It's a good thing, too. All things considered."

Khordadian nodded. "Yes, all things considered. Actually I need to talk to you about that. I have bad news. The plans, my country cannot take them. Your actions have created an uproar in the intelligence and diplomatic communities. You are perhaps the most sought after man in the world right now. Not publicly, of course. But you now are notorious in important circles."

Kursk's features creased with concern. "We cannot negotiate this?"

"I'm afraid not. My superiors have asked me to sever all relations with you. I am afraid I must do precisely that."

"How unfortunate. I hope the North Koreans and the Chinese have more spine than your superiors. I am slated to meet with them later this week. Their money spends as well as yours," Kursk said.

Khordadian stiffened visibly, and his eyes narrowed. "You insult me and my country. No one will buy the plans right now. You should wait."

"I need capital, Azid, not advice."

The Iranian shot up from his chair, his eyes fiery. "Then I will leave. My superiors didn't even want me to come here. I journeyed here out of loyalty for an old friend. This is how you repay me? It's an insult."

Kursk shrugged. "Azid," he said, "I have no friends."

Before Khordadian or his guards could react, Kursk's gunners unloaded their Uzis into the visitors. A moment later, the three Iranians lay on the patio in a twisted heap of flesh and spilled blood.

"Clean this up," Kursk said. He noticed a couple of his men looked pale, shaky. That struck him as odd; these were professional killers not given to squeamishness. Two others had fallen ill earlier in the day.

"What the hell's the matter with you two?" Kursk snapped.

"Nothing sir," one of them said.

"Then do your damn job."

"Of course."

Kursk rose from his chair and stepped inside. He furrowed his brow in worry as he journeyed up the stairs and into his study. What if Khordadian was right? What if no other countries would deal with him? Locking the door behind him, Kursk walked to a mahogany bookcase, pressed a button and slid the fixture back, revealing a safe set into the wall.

As he opened the safe, the hair along the back of his neck prickled, and a cold sensation passed down his back. He dropped the case and reached for his Tokarev.

"Don't," a graveyard voice said.

Kursk turned and saw a big man dressed in black. Black combat cosmetics streaked his face. Ice blue eyes regarded Kursk over the barrel of a Beretta handgun tipped with a sound suppressor.

The Russian let his hands hang at his sides. He'd be damned if he'd raise them without being told.

"You are Cooper?" he asked.

Bolan nodded. "Put up your hands."

Kursk did as he was told. "Even if you kill me, you'll never leave here alive. I have gunmen positioned all over."

The Executioner shook his head. Kursk felt sweat bead on the back of his neck and dribble down the length of his spine.

Bolan continued. "Your gunners are as good as dead. The young woman you're so fond of is a DEA informant. She's been pumping bacteria into the food and making your men ill. I have a team of snipers poised around the building to handle the ones who don't get sick. If necessary, I'll be stepping over corpses when I leave."

"It seems," Kursk said, "that you've thought of everything. You're as bullheaded as the woman."

"You'll be glad to know she's healing nicely. She sends her regards."

Kursk made a sudden move for his gun.

The Beretta whispered once. A 9 mm Parabellum hurtled into Kursk's nose. The impact caused the Russian to smack against the wall and sent his arms flailing. When he collapsed to the floor, his shattered head landed on the leather case and soaked it with blood.

A moment later, Mack Bolan heard sniper rifles crack outside, followed by a brief reply of autofire, then more rifle shots. Then silence. Grabbing the plans, he started out the door knowing that the bloodshed of the past few days had finally come to an end.

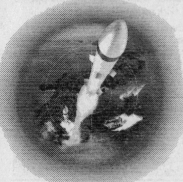

James Axler
Outlanders®

ULURU DESTINY

Ominous rumblings in the South Pacific lead Kane and his compatriots into the heart of a secret barony ruled by a ruthless god-king planning an invasion of the sacred territory at Uluru and its aboriginals who are seemingly possessed of a power beyond all earthly origin. With total victory of hybrid over human hanging in the balance, slim hope lies with the people known as the Crew, preparing to reclaim a power so vast that in the wrong hands it could plunge humanity into an abyss of evil with no hope of redemption.

Available November 2004 at your favorite retail outlet.

TAKE 'EM FREE
2 action-packed novels plus a mystery bonus

NO RISK
NO OBLIGATION TO BUY